PENGUIN BOOKS
A Guide to the Beasts of East Africa

Nicholas Drayson was born in England and moved to Australia in 1982, where he studied zoology and gained a PhD in nineteenth-century Australian natural history writing and two daughters. He has worked as a journalist in the UK, Kenya and Australia, writing for publications such as the *Daily Telegraph* and *Australian Geographic*. He is the author of three previous novels, *Confessing a Murder*, *Love and the Platypus* and *A Guide to the Birds of East Africa* (Penguin, 2008). He is now wandering through England aboard his boat, the *Summer Breeze*.

D1580542

70004100620

A Guide to the Beasts of
East Africa

NICHOLAS DRAYSON

PENGUIN BOOKS

PENGUIN BOOKS

Published by the Penguin Group
Penguin Books Ltd, 80 Strand, London WC2R ORL, England
Penguin Group (USA) Inc., 375 Hudson Street, New York, New York 10014, USA
Penguin Group (Canada), 90 Eglinton Avenue East, Suite 700, Toronto, Ontario, Canada M4P 2Y3
(a division of Pearson Penguin Canada Inc.)
Penguin Ireland, 25 St Stephen's Green, Dublin 2, Ireland
(a division of Penguin Books Ltd)
Penguin Group (Australia), 250 Camberwell Road, Camberwell, Victoria 3124, Australia
(a division of Pearson Australia Group Pty Ltd)
Penguin Books India Pvt Ltd, 11 Community Centre, Panchsheel Park, New Delhi – 110 017, India
Penguin Group (NZ), 67 Apollo Drive, Rosedale, Auckland 0632, New Zealand
(a division of Pearson New Zealand Ltd)
Penguin Books (South Africa) (Pty) Ltd, Block D, Rosebank Office Park, 181 Jan Smuts Avenue,
Parktown North, Gauteng 2193, South Africa

Penguin Books Ltd, Registered Offices: 80 Strand, London WC2R ORL, England

www.penguin.com

First published 2012
Reissued 2013
001

Grateful acknowledgement is made for permission to reprint lyrics from 'Is That All There Is'.
Words and music by Jerry Leiber and Mike Stoller. Copyright © 1966 Sony/ATV Music Publishing LLC;
copyright renewed. All rights administered by Sony/ATV Music Publishing LLC, 8 Music Square
West, Nashville, Tennessee, TN 37203. International copyright secured. All rights reserved.
Reprinted by permission of Hal Leonard Corporation.

Typeset in 12.5/14.75 pt Garamond MT by Palimpsest Book Production Ltd, Falkirk, Stirlingshire
Printed in Great Britain by Clays Ltd, St Ives plc

ISBN: 978-0-241-96917-5

www.greenpenguin.co.uk

MIX
Paper from
responsible sources
FSC
www.fsc.org   FSC® C018179

Penguin Books is committed to a sustainable
future for our business, our readers and our planet.
This book is made from Forest Stewardship
Council™ certified paper.

I

The wings of a butterfly do not give the power of
an eagle

'I tell you she didn't do it.'

'And I tell you she jolly well did.'

'Listen, A.B.' Mr Patel leaned forward over the table. '*He* admitted it – why won't *you*?'

'Patel, my dear chap.' Mr A. B. Gopez put down his glass of Tusker beer and forced a smile. 'I, too, have read the accounts. I accept that some people have *claimed* that he admitted it, but it's pure hearsay, all of it.'

'Here-say-there-say, it's on the record. Three times he admitted it, to three separate people. Then he topped himself – and if that wasn't an admission of guilt then what, I ask you, is?'

'Hearsay, and circumstantial evidence,' said Mr Gopez. 'It would never stand up in court. Look, here's the Tiger. There's nothing he doesn't know about the law. If you don't believe me, ask him.'

To say that H. H. 'Tiger' Singh, LLB, MA (Oxon.) was a good lawyer would be like saying that Walter Lindrum – World Professional Billiards Champion from 1933 until the day he retired from the game in 1950, the man who once while touring South Africa scored 1,000 points in

28 minutes, and whose single break of 4,137 against the great Joe Davis on the 19th of January 1932 at the Victoria Club in London still stands as an unbroken record – was a handy chap with a cue. In matters of law the Tiger was both craftsman and artist. Not only was his knowledge of the law unmatched in the courtrooms and chambers of Nairobi, but his ability to read the court, to understand the hopes and passions that drove plaintiff, defendant, judge and jury, was wondrous – some said uncanny.

Tiger Singh put his own glass down on the table and eased himself into his usual chair in the barroom of the Asadi Club beside his two friends.

'Good evening, gentlemen – please, don't let me interrupt your conversation.'

'Ah, Tiger. You're just in time to tell Patel here that he's talking tosh. Please explain to him, using if you will the very simplest of words, that hearsay evidence is no damned good.'

'You are quite right, A.B. The type of evidence to which I think you are referring cannot be used against an accused in a criminal case.'

'There,' said Mr Gopez. 'What did I tell you?'

'I should emphasize that I'm only referring to criminal cases here, of course,' said the Tiger, settling back. 'In civil proceedings the rules are somewhat different – *onus probandi* and all that.'

'Civil, criminal, what does it matter? We're not talking about a trial, we're talking about what he said *after* the trial. He admitted it to three separate people.'

'Ah,' said Tiger Singh. 'May I assume, gentlemen, that you are discussing the case of Lord Erroll's murder?'

*

Do you get a kick from champagne?

Do cocaine and heroin give you a thrill?

And tell me if it's ever true that unconstrained sex is for you?

If you have answered yes to one or more of the above questions you may well have felt at ease with the small band of settlers who between the two world wars made their homes in Nairobi and the rich farming land to the north. At 'Happy Valley' such fun was to be had by all – providing, that is, that you were young, wealthy and white. But early one rainy morning in January 1941, everything changed. The 22nd Earl of Erroll, known to his friends as Joss and one of the most active members of the Happy Valley set, was found dead in his car, shot in the head with a revolver.

Josslyn Hay had eloped from Britain to Kenya in 1924 with a rich English widow. Four years later he assumed the Earldom of Erroll on the death of his father and twelve years later was already divorced from his first wife and separated from his second. He was by all accounts a singularly good-looking man and his conquests were legion – he sometimes had two or three affairs going at the same time. No one was surprised when in the December of 1940 the beautiful Diana Broughton, then aged twenty-seven and recently arrived in Kenya with her new husband, the 57-year-old Sir Jock Delves Broughton, fell for him. Broughton soon found out. On the 10th of March, having just returned from a two-week hunting safari with his wife, Sir Jock Delves Broughton was arrested by police for the murder of Lord Erroll.

The trial made headlines not only in Kenya but around the world. The police produced evidence that on the night of the murder Broughton, Diana, Erroll and their friend June Carberry dined at the Muthaiga Club. Several witnesses saw them, and heard Erroll ask Diana to go dancing with him after dinner at the late-night Claremont Club. Broughton did not want to go dancing, but asked Erroll to bring Diana home by 3 a.m. Broughton and June Carberry went back to the house he had been renting in the Nairobi suburb of Karen. The prosecution alleged that when Broughton heard Erroll return with Diana at about 2.20 a.m., he put on a pair of white gym shoes, climbed out of his bedroom window and down the drainpipe without being seen. Armed with a revolver that he had previously reported stolen, he hid in the back seat of Erroll's car. When Erroll slowed down at the first road junction, he shot him. He then ran back to the house and climbed back into his room, again without being seen.

Broughton maintained his innocence and paid £5,000 plus a bottle of whisky a day to the best barrister in Africa to defend him. On the 26th of May the trial began. Late in the evening of the 1st of July the foreman of the jury stood to deliver their verdict.

Not guilty.

But if not Broughton, then who?

For more than sixty years this question has been the subject of many a heated conversation in every hotel bar and club in Kenya – and in this respect, at least, the Asadi Club is no different.

'Damned right we're talking about the Erroll case,' said Mr Patel. 'But as I say, it's not the trial I'm talking about, it's what happened after the trial.'

'And as I keep trying to explain, my dear Patel, second-hand reports of what Sir Jock Delves Broughton might or might not have said are of no more use outside a court of law than they are inside. Next thing you'll be asking us to believe all that stuff about the British Secret Service – SOD or whatever-they-were-called – being in on the job.'

'SOE is the correct acronym, I believe, A.B. – Special Operations Executive. You've read that book too, have you? But never mind your conspiracy theories. It was Broughton.'

'It was Diana, I tell you. She and Erroll had a row – the maid heard it. He was probably going to dump her. It stands to reason – the woman scorned, and all that. She'd probably stolen that gun herself – the one Broughton reported missing. Ah, forgot about that, did you?'

'What *you* seem to have forgotten, A.B., is that Diana had an alibi.'

'Oh, they all had alibis. In those days you got a free alibi in every jolly box of cornflakes.'

'Well, why didn't the police chappy arrest her then?'

'Because, my dear Patel,' said Mr Gopez, turning again to the third person at the table, 'and I'm sure the Tiger would agree with me here – the "police chappy", as you call him, was an incompetent twit who couldn't see where the evidence pointed if it was tattooed on his *tululu*.'

'Quite,' said the Tiger. He drained his glass and rose from his chair. 'Now, if you'll excuse me, gentlemen, I promised Bobby Bashu a quick game of billiards before Malik arrives. Let me know when he's here, would you? I need to talk to him about the club safari.'

2

The eagle on an anthill sees as far as the ant

The annual Asadi Club safari is now something of an institution. The first one had been a pretty relaxed affair, though not without adventure. One Friday afternoon in the November of 1958 five members of the club had packed their families into their cars and driven a couple of hours south of Nairobi to the Athi Plains. They chose a campsite near the river, where the men set up the three heavy old ex-army tents and camp stretchers, kindly supplied by Amin and Sons General Emporium – then, as is still true today, an Aladdin's cave of objects from the mundane to the arcane. The women made the beds, the children gathered firewood. Under the stars they all dined on rice and the various curries they'd brought with them ready cooked. They went to bed early – the men in one tent, the women in another and the children in the third.

Used as they were to the hum of the city, no one slept a wink. That rustling in the bushes, was it a mouse or the soft tread of a hungry leopard? That distant coughing sound, was it some kind of harmless night bird or the call of a frenzied hyena? That nearby rumble, was it a lion or was it Sonny Bashu snoring? But when the following day dawned clear and bright all terrors of the night were forgotten. The families breakfasted on chapattis and leftover curry and drank cups of tea, sweet and milky. While the women went about the business of cleaning up, the men undertook the far more onerous task of planning the day ahead. The children played.

But when it came time to get ready for the first game drive no one could find young Bindu Ghosh. He had been playing Cowboys and Indians (oh, those innocent days) down by the river with four of the other boys, but they didn't know where he was now and he failed to respond to his mother's call. When he also failed to answer his father's increasingly authoritative summons a small search party was organized which, while finding no small boys, did locate a large python curled up under a bush beside a waterhole. About a third of the way down from its head towards its tail Mr Ghosh saw a suspicious swelling.

My friend Kennedy told me he was once driving out of Nairobi on the back road towards Limuru when he noticed a log completely blocking the road ahead. His first thought was that it must have fallen from a truck, perhaps engaged in some unauthorized firewood removal from the nearby state forest. Then he saw it move. It was not a log, it was a rock python, as thick as his thigh. As for its length, he waited until it had moved well off the road before pacing the measurement. Eight metres. Twenty-six feet. Having found a python of similar size down by the river, Mr Ghosh was now in something of a quandary. As a follower of the Jain religion – the more zealous among whom will sweep the path before them as they walk to clear away any small creatures that might be crushed beneath a careless sandal – he was naturally reluctant to kill the snake that lay somnolent but clearly sentient before him. But if there was the smallest possibility of saving his little Bindusar from being slowly digested within said sentient being then there seemed no alternative. He remembered seeing a couple of bush knives back at the camp and it was towards the camp that he smartly hove, oblivious of any ant, bug or beetle beneath his flying feet.

His arrival was greeted by a smiling wife, who informed him that his son and heir was safe and well. It turned out that young Bindu had got tired of Cowboys and Indians and, returning to the camp unnoticed, had fallen asleep under his blanket. His father reacted to this joyful news in the time-honoured fashion. He hugged Bindu to his bosom, cuffed him round the ears, gave him a thorough dressing-down and sent him back to bed. The python was left to digest the small dik-dik it had swallowed earlier that morning in peace (though the dik-dik was in fact considerably smaller than Bindu Ghosh, who was a well-fed child).

The choice of this year's venue for the Asadi Club safari had not been an easy one. Some members were in favour of going down to the coast, others said that wasn't a safari it was a beach holiday and that the Maasai Mara was the place to go. Krish Advani said he'd heard that Lake Magadi was very good for flamingoes this year, to which Abby Antul retorted that a weekend watching pink feather dusters with their heads upside down in three inches of water that smelled like rotten eggs was not his idea of a weekend well spent. The impasse had been resolved by Mr Malik who, chatting to Hilary Fotherington-Thomas on one of the East African Ornithological Society's regular Tuesday bird walks, had discovered that a friend of hers had a place near Meru.

'The old Johnson place on the Thanandu – the river, you know. Hippos, elephants, waterbuck – all that sort of thing. There's a perfectly lovely spot for camping down by the river, and an old homestead that's been taken over by a troop of baboons – great fun. I'm sure Dickie would be happy to have you and your pals up for a few days. Would you like me to find out?'

'Are there lions?' (No Asadi Club safari is complete without at least the chance of seeing a lion.)

'Lions? Oodles, I should think. Anyway, I'll ask him. When it comes to wildlife, Dickie Johnson knows *everything.*'

'Then thank you, Mrs Fotherington-Thomas,' said Mr Malik. 'I would.'

Dickie Johnson told her that yes he'd be delighted. She told Mr Malik. Mr Malik told the committee, who agreed that it sounded perfect. Now all Mr Malik had to do was find out which members, wives and children wanted to come, book a coach and the appropriate number of open-top safari buses and drivers, liaise with Ally Dass about the catering arrangements, make sure the camp was set up and get everything and everyone there and safely home again.

So times have changed, numbers have increased and the choice of venue has become a little more adventurous, but the spirit of that first Asadi Club safari lives on. As usual this year there will be one tent for gentlemen, another for ladies and a third for children under twelve.

There will also be a tent for cooking and a tent for eating and another for the staff. This year, though, there will be an extra tent – a seventh tent. For this year Mr Malik has arranged a surprise.

'Ah, here he is.' Mr Patel looked up from his still heated conversation with A.B. towards a short round man of careful coiffure making his way towards them across the Asadi Club Bar. 'The Tiger's been looking for you, Malik old chap.'

'Oh really, do you know what he wants?'

'Something about arrangements for the safari, apparently. And talking of arrangements, I forgot to ask you on Friday – any news on the wedding reception?'

Mr Malik nodded. 'I spoke to her this morning and everything's settled. We've decided on a marquee in the garden – as you suggested, A.B. And as you suggested, Patel, I'm going to ask Ally Dass here at the club if he can do the catering.'

'He did Shobah's bash – my brother's eldest daughter, you know,' said Mr Patel, reaching for the chilli popcorn. 'Made a jolly good biriani, I remember – silver leaf and all that – though I remember thinking the prawn curry was lacking a certain oomph.'

'Tricky thing, curry,' said Mr Gopez, 'especially if you've got any *wazungu* on the guest list. Your average white man, I have observed, can seldom handle the heat.'

'Oh, I don't know,' said Mr Malik. 'I read recently that chicken tikka masala is now the most popular dish in the UK.'

'Yes, but have you ever tried it?' Mr Patel rolled his eyes.

'I read a recipe for chicken tikka masala in one of those women's magazines – ready-roast chicken, curry powder, evaporated milk and tinned tomato soup.'

'That's not a curry, that's a criminal offence,' said Mr Gopez. 'Anyway, rest assured, my dear Malik, that Ally Dass would not allow a jar labelled "curry powder" within a hundred yards of his kitchen. And no peas in his samosas. I really can't stand peas in samosas.' He helped himself to the popcorn. 'So, make a habit of it, do you, Patel?'

'What?'

'Reading women's magazines.'

Mr Patel turned towards Mr Malik.

'By the way,' he said, 'who do you think I saw in town this morning?'

'Your therapist?' muttered Mr Gopez. 'Ah well, best keep trying, I suppose.'

'Ha ha, A.B. No, Malik's old school chum.'

Oh no, thought Mr Malik, not . . .

'Yes, Harry. Harry Khan.'

While it is true that Mr Malik and Harry Khan had indeed attended Eastlands High School together – they had in fact arrived as boarders on the same day in September of 1955 – it would be stretching the meaning of the word to call them 'chums'. Then, as now, Mr Malik was of quiet disposition, more eager to turn the pages of a book than turn the dial of a contraband wireless after lights-out, happier sitting on the pavilion steps with pencil in hand and scorebook on his knees than swinging the willow out on the cricket pitch. Harry Khan was of a different stripe. In the classroom and on the sports field it was he who stood out. It was he who knew everybody and was known by everybody, he who led the gang, he who gave clever nicknames to boys and masters alike. Whether flashing his bat at the wicket or flashing his smile on the stage in the end-of-term play, Harry loved showing off – his Punjabi Shylock in the 1959 Eastlands High School Production of *The Merchant of Venice* had brought the house down, and his score of thirty-four in a single over still stood as a school record. And while Mr Malik – or 'Jack' as he had, for reasons which we need not go into here, been nicknamed – was not the only butt of Harry Khan's jokes both verbal and practical, there is no doubt that he came in for more than his fair share.

Why? Why does the sun rise in the east? Why does a cat play with a mouse? Harry Khan could no more refrain from teasing Mr Malik than could Brahma not create or Shiva not destroy. Though the events of those distant days have now become more school myth than memory, the story of the python and pyjamas can even today be relied upon to bring a smile to the lips of the most surly fourth former, while the petroleum-jelly sandwich still makes the occasional appearance at Eastlands High more than half a century since its first inspired use by Harry Khan at Mr Malik's thirteenth birthday bash. When the Khan family left Nairobi for Canada in 1962 taking Harry with them, Mr Malik could not pretend he was sad to see them go.

'Harry Khan, eh?' said Mr Gopez.

'Yes. He said he's over here on business. I said he should try and drop by the club.'

'This club?' said Mr Malik.

The last time he had seen Harry Khan was four years

ago when Harry, visiting Kenya with his ancient mother, actually started making a play for the lovely Rose Mbikwa, who used to lead the Tuesday bird walks and on whom Mr Malik, widowed these several years, had long had a serious crush.

'Yes. He's still a member, you know – kept up the subs and all that.'

'I wonder,' said Mr Gopez, 'if he'll bring that niece of his again. What was her name – Emily, Ermintrude?'

'Elvira,' said Mr Malik.

Harry Khan's niece – or, to be more exact, his cousin's wife's sister's youngest daughter – had made quite an impression on the members of the Asadi Club.

'That's it. Pretty girl . . . damned fine –'

'Dancer?'

'Now you come to mention it, Malik old chap, I suppose she was.'

Few present that night at the Nairobi Hunt Club Ball would forget the sight of Elvira in her short red dress dancing rock and roll with her uncle Harry to the music of Milton Kapriadis and his Safari Swingers. But to the surprise of many it had been Mr Malik with whom Rose Mbikwa had danced that evening, and Harry Khan disappeared back to the US soon afterwards.

What exactly, Mr Malik now wondered, was Harry Khan doing in Nairobi this time?

'*She* was a good dancer too,' said Mr Gopez. 'They went dancing – at the Claremont Club, you know – the very night she shot him.'

Mr Patel was spared further discussion of the Erroll case by the reappearance of Tiger Singh, fresh from victory at the billiard table (when the Tiger had last lost a court case or a game of billiards, no one could remember).

'Ah, there you are, Malik – I was hoping to see you. What news on the safari front?'

On weekends Tiger Singh was known for clothes of a casual cut – yellow shirts and red checked trousers were a particular favourite – and he was seldom seen out on the golf course without his lucky green tam-o'-shanter. This being a Monday he was in more formal attire of dark suit and grey dastar to match.

'Everything arranged. Ally Dass will be going on Thursday with some of his chaps to set up the kitchen, and Mr Hapula – the club gardener – is taking his men to put up the tents. They'll be going in the minibuses – oh, and my own gardener, Benjamin, has agreed to help too. He'll be travelling with them. I've booked the big coach for Friday morning for the rest of us, so we should all get up there before dark.'

'Splendid,' said the Tiger. 'Have you put your name down, Patel?'

'Yes,' said Mr Patel, 'though I don't think I'll be able to persuade my beloved wife and helpmeet to come this year. "Seen one artiodactyl, seen 'em all," that's what she says.'

'What about you, A.B.?'

'Me? I'm the same – never could tell the difference between a Tommy and Grant's. Still, as Father used to say, they all taste the same in a vindaloo.'

'But are you coming on the safari?'

'Oh yes, I'll be there.' A. B. Gopez took a thoughtful sip from his glass. 'Father used to love going on safari – I'm talking about the old days, of course. Very fond of guns was Father. Spent a jolly fortune on fancy rifles, safari jackets, hats, spats, the whole palaver. When I was growing up it seemed to be all he and his pals talked about – potting the big five.'

'Ah,' said Mr Patel, 'elephant, rhino, hippo, lion and leopard.'

'Hippo? Who ever heard of anyone shooting a hippo? Buffalo, old chap. No more dangerous beast in the whole of Africa.'

'I'm sure it's hippos,' said Mr Patel.

'And I tell you no sportsman worth his sola topi has ever hunted hippos. Sitting ducks. Large ducks, I grant you, but sitting just the same.'

'That's not what I meant.'

'Then why,' said Mr Gopez, smacking his forehead with an exasperated palm, 'did you say it?'

'I meant, A.B., what I said. While I am happy to stand corrected on the composition of the big five as far as shooting the damned things goes, it remains a fact that more people in Africa are killed by hippos than any other animal, so hippos are the most dangerous animals.'

Which is, if I may digress, a sentiment with which my friend Kennedy would agree. Late one night he was driving home from Limuru in the rain. It had been bucketing down for the last two months, this being the end of the short rains. Four miles from Nairobi, where the Matunda River is meant to go under the road, the water had been inches deep for days but his Land Rover had made the crossing a hundred times. He changed down into low gear and put his right foot hard down on the accelerator. Then smartly up again and even harder down on the brake. In a shower of mud and water his vehicle skidded to a stop only inches from a large hippopotamus. I remember him saying that it was not so much its size, nor its presence so near the centre of town, but the insouciance of the beast that particularly impressed him.

'My dear Patel,' said A. B. Gopez, 'though I hesitate to differ, when it comes to hippos I beg to do so. Malik, old chap, you know something about birds and beasts. Wouldn't you agree –?'

'Tiger,' said Mr Malik. 'Any chance of a quick game of billiards?'

3

The ant is eaten by the aardvark, but still the
anthill grows

'Ah, hello, Petula darling – up already?'

A slim, denim-clad figure stepped on to the veranda.
'Good morning, Daddy dear.'

Mr Malik had long had mixed feelings for his daughter
Petula – a mixture of wonder, love and admiration. The
wonder had come first. He could still remember that
moment thirty-three years ago when he first held his baby
daughter in his arms, brown and pink and perfect. How
wonderful that such a strong little being was his own
daughter. How miraculous that his dear wife had produced so lovely a thing.

Love didn't come till later. He wasn't surprised by that.
It had been the same when his son Raj had arrived seven
years earlier. Nearly a year went by before he realized that
he had fallen in love with his first child, a love so strong
that it almost hurt. So it was with Petula. And then, as she
started walking and talking, came the admiration. How
clever a child she was, how special. He loved watching his
two children together. Raj had adored his little sister from
the moment she was born. Mr Malik would find him sitting by her crib gazing at her with a look of pure devotion

while she slept or gurgled or cried. Looking back on it, Raj had always been a very affectionate boy.

Yes, Petula. So intelligent, so strong. And beautiful, just like her mother. He was lucky to have so lovely a daughter – though, if only . . . He glanced over to where she sat across the table from him. If only she wouldn't wear those jeans all the time. But at least she and Salman had finally agreed a date for the wedding. He knew young people did things differently these days but three years was a long engagement by any standard.

Petula picked up the bunch of bananas on the veranda table.

'Will you be coming into the factory this morning?'

'No, not today, dear – it's Tuesday.'

'Oh, of course. The bird walk.'

For the last seven years, ever since his first heart attack and strict instructions from his cardiologist to take things easy, Mr Malik had increasingly left the day-to-day running of the Jolly Man Manufacturing Company to Petula. His father might not have heeded the warning signs but he would not make the same mistake. Besides, Petula was so good at managing and a whizz with all this new technology – kept the firm right up to date with all the latest webs and nets and that kind of thing. Mr Malik, who had never learned to use any machine more complicated than a typewriter or a slide rule, now spent more time at the temple than the business, and was less likely to visit suppliers and customers than visit the patients at the Aga Khan Hospital. Ever since his son Raj had died there, he had gone to the hospital at least twice a week.

Tuesday, though, was his birdwatching day. As usual, he would drive to the museum where his fellow members of the East African Ornithological Society assembled for their weekly walk. After the venue was decided – it might be the arboretum or the agricultural station or even the patch of waste ground behind the army barracks – Mr Malik could be counted on to offer a lift in his old green Mercedes to whoever might need one. A regular passenger was his friend Thomas Nyambe. A government driver in Kenya does not earn enough money to afford a car of his own. The two friends were usually to be seen together on the bird walk talking about the things they saw, Mr Malik making notes in the exercise book he always carried with him. Not all the notes were strictly about birds, though. Many of them were pure gossip – government gossip. And later that day Mr Malik would sit down at his typewriter and write the latest instalment of the newspaper column he sent off anonymously each Tuesday afternoon to the editor of the *Evening News*.

At first glance 'Birds of a Feather' appeared to be a column about the furred and feathered inhabitants of Kenya. Those who read more deeply knew that it was in fact a satirical exposé of Kenyan politics. For lion, read President; for hippopotamus, read Minister of Agriculture and Tourism; for marabou read Minister of Defence; for python, read Secretary of State for External Affairs. The herds of gazelle and zebra and wildebeest that formed a backdrop to the goings-on were the tribal groups of Kenya. The popularity of the column caused a regular spike in sales of the *Evening News* every Wednesday, and much anguish to the ruling elite of the nation.

Over the several years it had been going, more than one minister had been forced to resign – only last month the Minister for the Interior. But while Mr Malik always wrote the column, using the pen-name of Dadukwa – the black eagle who, seeing all but never seen, spreads the news among the other animals – it was Thomas Nyambe who provided the information on which it was based, as well as the traditional, if sometimes cryptic, proverb that Mr Malik liked to put at the head of each column.

Like taxi drivers, government drivers often get the feeling that they are invisible. Their passengers talk to each other or on their mobile phones as if there was no one else in the car. So the drivers pick up all the government gossip which, during periods of waiting around at the depot or outside whatever building their passenger has directed them to, they naturally share with other government drivers. Anything Thomas Nyambe overheard he later passed on to Mr Malik on their Tuesday bird walks, where it would duly appear in the next 'Birds of a Feather' column. If only some government ministers realized that their drivers were neither deaf, mute nor stupid, they would have been saved many a sleepless night.

Petula pulled a small banana from the bunch.

'What about after the bird walk – will you be coming to the factory then?'

'I don't think I'll be able to make it in at all today, dear. The chap's coming round about the marquee at three, and after that I'd better drop into the club and see about the catering. I still have quite a few details to clear up with Ally Dass. What about you? Are you going in?'

'Yes. Still haven't finished the weekly statements. I'll be there all day. Oh, and I'll be home late – CI meeting.'

Petula had recently joined the anti-corruption organization Clarity International. How like her to try to change the world.

'Righty-ho, I won't wait up then. Anything special tonight?'

'A visit from the new Communications Director – from Switzerland, apparently.'

She sat down beside him.

'How did it go at the club last night? Have you found out yet how many people have signed up for the safari?'

'About twenty so far,' said Mr Malik. 'Still room for a few more. I'll give them another day or two.'

'Oh Daddy, all this work and worry. Why not let someone younger do it for a change?'

Someone younger? Hadn't his new doctor told him only last Friday that sixty-six was no age at all? Even as he was listening to his doctor's words, though, Mr Malik couldn't help remembering the age at which his own father had died.

Mr Malik had been away studying in England when news came of his father's first heart attack. He hurried home, and home he stayed. If he had any regrets about not finishing his degree he did not show them. Instead of his studies at the London School of Economics, he now had the family firm. Instead of the pubs of Clerkenwell and Fleet Street, he now had the Asadi Club. His father had been Secretary of the club for nearly forty years. 'Look after the club – and look after your mother too,' was the last thing he had said to his son before he died of that second heart attack, swiftly following the first.

Mr Malik glanced over to where his daughter now sat beside him, nibbling at the small banana, and smiled. It had been four years ago when she had met Salman at the Hunt Club Ball, the very one where he had danced that dance with Rose Mbikwa, and at last she was getting married. Yes, the garden should do nicely for their reception.

'Oh, arranging the safari's no trouble. I've done it so often now. You'll still be able to come, won't you? And Salman?'

Petula paused and looked out into the garden.

'He phoned last night. He can't get away till Friday now.' Petula's fiancé Salman worked in Dubai for an international firm of accountants. 'Looks like we'll have to drive up on Saturday morning.'

'Oh, that's a shame – but you'll still have a couple of days.'

'Yes. Anyway . . . bye, Daddy.'

'Goodbye, dear.'

Mr Malik watched his daughter pick up her keys and heard her climb into her little Suzuki and drive away. That pause. Was it his imagination, or was something wrong?

He took another sip of Nescafé and looked out across the garden. The grass was its greenest, the frangipani and bougainvillea were in multicoloured bloom, and in the flower beds at the end of the garden the canna lilies were just about to flower. With a little judicious pruning now the roses should be at their best for the wedding. Lately, Mr Malik had become very fond of roses. Such a shame, though, about the mango trees.

It was under a mango tree on the coast down at Malindi that, more than forty years ago, Mr Malik had proposed to his wife. Ever since her death he had been trying to get one to grow in his garden at home. Everyone said that Nairobi, though close to the equator, is too high for mangoes, but Mr Malik was at heart an optimist. He was sure there must be one variety of the many hundreds that are grown around the world that would flourish there. Over the last dozen years Mr Malik had collected seeds from any variety he could find that might have a chance. He would clean each seed and score the tough seedcase with an old chisel, then put it in a jam jar half full of water. As soon as the seed sprouted he would plant it in the special mango bed behind the kitchen. Some had survived and grown into fair-sized trees – but though one or two had flowered, not one had ever produced a fruit.

My friend Kennedy told me that when he was thirteen he had the idea of trying to open a mango seed. After attempting to hack it open with his mother's bread knife and crack it open with his father's hammer he was no nearer his goal, but he wasn't going to be beaten. It was time to bring in the big guns. He placed the slippery seed on a chopping block and picked up the seven-pound sledgehammer. Hell no! Why not use the fourteen-pounder? Not taking his eye off the seed, he swung that hammer high over his shoulder and down on to the target. Bullseye. The mango seed shot out from under the sledge-hammer like a rocket, and he told me that he reckoned it might have kept going all the way to the greenhouse if it had not met his right shin. If you have ever had a pain so sudden and intense that you aren't even able to scream, he told me, you will know exactly how it felt. The agonized roar that started in his solar plexus got as far as his Adam's apple but just couldn't find a way out past his clenched teeth. He might, he said, have made a little squeak – a small yip, at most. Tears rose into his eyes. Time seemed to stop. As it turned out, his leg was not permanently damaged. The egg-sized swelling lasted a couple of weeks, the bruise was gone in a month. But that mango seed left an indelible impression on his mind – and I pass his tale on to you for what it's worth.

Mr Malik put down his cup. A dog barked. There seemed to be more and more dogs in the neighbourhood these days – for security, people said. Petula had tried to persuade him to get one, but Mr Malik had always maintained that guard dogs were like guns – more dangerous to their owners than to any potential wrongdoer. While there were bars on the windows of his house – which would, no doubt, keep out the average burglar – they had not been put there to keep out men. They were there to keep out monkeys. Nairobi's few parks, but mainly its suburban streets and gardens, provide food and shelter for hundreds of monkeys which come in two varieties – the common vervet and the Sykes. Both are about the size of a cat, but the vervet is leaner and lighter. If you are still in any doubt, you can recognize the male vervet by its bright-blue scrotum. Both species made occasional visits to Number 12 Garden Lane and, being possessed of the usual simian acquisitiveness, happily reached into any open window to extract whatever they could get their monkey mitts on. Hence the bars, and the necessity of keeping small objects at least the length of a monkey's arm away from them.

From a croton tree at Number 12 Garden Lane came a familiar sound. Even now Mr Malik still got a strange feeling in his bowels whenever he heard the loud three-note call of the large brown bird common in many parts of Africa called the hadada. How long had it been since he had gone on his first weekly bird walk of the East African Ornithological Society, led by the lovely Rose Mbikwa? How long since he had danced that dance with her at the Nairobi Hunt Club Ball? Four years. Ah well, thought Mr Malik, getting to his feet, it wasn't as if he was a good dancer. In his dreams he glided over the dance floor like Fred Astaire; in real life he feared he looked more like a waltzing warthog. It was time to find the binoculars and get on his way. Even if Rose Mbikwa was still away in Scotland, he didn't want to keep his friends at the bird walk waiting.

4

Each aardvark has two exits to its burrow

Rose Mbikwa's mother had long ago expressed her wishes. She wanted to die at home in Edinburgh sitting at the bridge table, having just bid and won a grand slam; failing that, she said, a small slam redoubled and vulnerable would do nicely. Though she had been unsuccessful in this ambition, her husband and daughter agreed that dying in her favourite armchair already on to her second gin and tonic of the evening and more than halfway through the *Times* crossword was almost as fitting a departure. Rose's father, though crippled by rheumatism these several years, assured Rose he could manage. The day before the funeral she flew from Nairobi to Scotland and unpacked her bags in the very bedroom she had grown up in. From now on she would be looking after her father in the big old Morningside house, and that was that.

In truth, this was no burden for Rose. The word 'duty' never entered her head. She was simply doing what needed doing for a man she loved and respected. She would continue to do so for as long as necessary. When her husband Joshua Mbikwa had first been arrested in Kenya all those years ago by order of the then president, she had not campaigned for his release from a sense of duty. It had simply been the right thing to do. After Joshua's death in the plane crash four years later, she had not stayed on in Kenya and started up the tourist guide training programme at the museum out of a sense of duty. It was her small contribution to the land she had fallen in love with. The programme was now going well. Her son, their only child, was grown up and happy and enjoying his job in Geneva. She was needed more in Edinburgh than Nairobi. The choice had not been difficult.

Rose was surprised how quickly she had fitted back into Edinburgh life. Though her father could not get out of the old house much, the door was wide and the world could get in. Friends came to call and stayed to gossip. Her father's sister and her mother's two brothers provided all the family they needed. The two families had always been close. None of them had moved away from Edinburgh, and their regular Sunday get-together at the old house in Glenlockhart Road was a weekly ritual that Rose looked forward to. She would cook the lunch, as her mother had before her. Her father would choose the wine and whisky. Each week the ritual would be completed when Auntie Jean sat down at the piano after the meal. All the family sang – you would almost have thought they were Welsh.

All this is not to say that Rose didn't miss Kenya. Even after four years back in Scotland she sometimes woke up thinking she was in her upstairs bed in Serengeti Gardens. The emptiness of Edinburgh streets disconcerted her still; the streets of Nairobi were always thronged not just with cars and trucks and matatus but with people – people on bicycles, people on foot. She missed the smells of Africa, and the faces and the sound of African voices. The birds? Well, probably best not to think about the birds.

Mr Malik eased his old green Mercedes into a space in the car park of the Nairobi Museum. Quite a crowd had already assembled – the usual mixture of black, brown and white. They were greeted by Jennifer Halutu, who had been leading the walks ever since Rose Mbikwa's departure. Though Jennifer Halutu was a kind and competent woman, Mr Malik missed Rose. He wished he could hear again her loud, clear speaking voice bringing everyone's attention to a chestnut-fronted bee-eater on a telephone wire or a black kite – which is not really black, but brown – soaring over the city.

Before they decided where they would go that day, Hilary Fotherington-Thomas had something to tell them all.

'I have some bad news and some good news. I regret to say that Dr Neil Macdonald, the father of Rose Mbikwa, died six days ago. Many of you will remember Dr Macdonald from his many visits to Kenya. He was eighty-four years old and died at home in Scotland. He will be missed. The good news is that Rose is coming back to Nairobi very soon. I had an email from her this morning. She is flying in tomorrow.'

Though Mr Malik immediately felt a small flutter in his heart, it was overruled by a stern admonishment from his brain. It had been four years. Rose Mbikwa would probably not even remember his name, let alone that dance at the Hunt Club Ball.

After a show of hands it was agreed that, as there were plenty of cars this morning, they would go to the State Agricultural Research Station. A small patch of forest near the entrance to the station, a pond that was used to store water for irrigation, and coffee and tea bushes extending over several acres made for a variety of bird habitats with the chance to see anything from a kingfisher to an eagle. As usual, Mr Malik's old friend Thomas Nyambe rode in the front passenger seat for the journey, and a gaggle of Young Ornithologists – in this case three male and two female – squeezed into the back. Forty minutes later they arrived at the gates of the agricultural station.

'Follow me,' said Jennifer Halutu.

One of the YOs pointed out a pair of augur buzzards circling overhead – one light, one dark.

'Ah yes, buzzards,' said Mr Nyambe. 'That reminds me . . .'

Mr Malik took out his pen, opened his notebook, and began to write.

By the time the walk ended at noon Mr Malik had recorded the names of forty-two species of Kenyan birds – one of the YOs' sharp pairs of eyes had even spotted a rare dwarf bittern standing motionless among some dead rushes on the far side of the pond. He had also noted that the Secretary of State for Development had now dined twice at the Hilton with senior representatives from one of the world's leading producers of GM maize, that the Minister of Finance had again left the country 'on private business' – flying Swiss International – and that despite his assurances that national parks were for people not profit, the Minister of Agriculture and Tourism had given the go-ahead to his wife's cousin for another private development on the shores of the Kiunga Marine National Reserve.

The biggest news that Thomas Nyambe had passed on, though, concerned the new Minister for the Interior. After the previous minister had been forced to resign by revelations in the *Evening News* about unauthorized slum clearing in Nairobi's Kibera district, the new minister had vowed to relocate people only when new housing was available. He would, he had declared, make this his mission. Not only that, he would ensure complete transparency of the process, with open tenders for government housing contracts and a free and fair ballot system for choosing who would occupy the new houses. But according to what Mr Nyambe had heard from one of his fellow government drivers, not only was the building project stalled (despite all that money from the EU), but the list of those eligible for the houses – should they ever be built – seemed only to include members of the minister's own constituency.

'Thank you, my friend, for your company and your conversation,' said Mr Malik, closing his notebook.

'And thank you, my friend,' said Mr Nyambe. 'It is good to share things. Sometimes I think that there should be more sharing in the world.'

Which, by coincidence, is exactly what Petula wanted to talk to her father about at breakfast the very next morning. Mr Malik wasn't sure he understood all the details, but it seemed that the new Communications

Director from Geneva, who she'd met the day before, was keen to set up a local website for Clarity International through which people with interesting inside information – 'whistle-blowers', Petula called them – could reveal what they knew to the world. The tricky thing was to make sure that while anyone could post their information, it couldn't be traced back to them. This was just the kind of thing where Petula, with her passion for all things to do with computers, knew she could be useful. She seemed quite excited.

5

The sand of its digging does not blind the porcupine

'Did you hear, A.B.? Tomorrow's talk has been cancelled.'

'The Thursday lecture, you mean?'

'Yes. Damned shame, I was looking forward to it. "Safeguarding Nairobi's Water Supply in the Twenty-first Century" – should have been interesting.'

Mr Gopez put down his glass and reached for the bowl of chilli popcorn.

'Me too – always like a good fairy story. Chap drowned, did he?'

'Died of thirst, I heard,' said Mr Patel. (Nairobi's water supply, like most of its municipal services, is often a little erratic.) 'Ah, there you are, Malik. Speaking of drowning, you're looking a little damp about the noggin. Raining outside, is it?'

Mr Malik decided to ignore him.

The picture of ourselves that we carry in our minds is seldom the one we see in the mirror. No matter what our age, no matter what our sex or skin colour, few of us view our image in the looking glass with one hundred per cent personal approval. Too short or too tall; too thin or too fat; our eyes too close together or a little too far apart; our nose too big or too small. Of all our physical features, hair seems to give the least satisfaction. Too straight or too curly; too pale or too dark; too thick or too thin – or there is simply not enough of it. Hence Mr Malik's hairstyle.

The classic comb-over is not a matter of sudden whim. A man does not wake up one day, examine his reflection in the mirror and think to himself: 'Right, no more Mr Baldy – it's comb-over time.' He does not decide that from this day forth he will let grow what hairs remain on one side of his head, that he will cherish and nurture them as the vigneron his vines. He does not then begin to coax the hairs with brush or comb, and perhaps a little Brylcreem, to wind their way over his scalp. No man believes that his family and friends, confronted with such a tonsorial transformation, will immediately forget that he was ever bald, that they will think that a miracle has occurred, and the part of his scalp that was once bare has blossomed with hair as the desert blossoms after rain.

No, such things happen slowly, over many years. A man notices a little thinning of the hair. It is the matter of a moment to conceal this by altering the flow of the rest of his hair. As the thinning increases, the time and care taken to disguise it increases. All too soon the man finds himself on the horns of a dilemma. Should he continue with an artifice which is looking more and more unnatural by the month, or should he dispense with it – in effect, go bald overnight? Mr Malik had long ago decided to take the former path. No matter how long it took him each morning or how often the abominably hairy Patel teased him, as long as a single hair grew on his head, that hair would be plastered up and over his scalp in glorious defiance of the effects of age, gravity and male hormones.

'Did you hear?' said Mr Gopez. 'Looks like there's going to be a water shortage tomorrow.'

'Really?' said Mr Malik. 'I thought that new dam on the Thika River was supposed to stop all that.'

'What he means is that the lecture's been cancelled,' said Mr Patel, 'the one about our water supply.'

'Speaking of that new dam on the Thika River,' said Mr Gopez, 'have you chaps read the paper? You don't just need the water, you need the pipes. The old ones all leak, apparently, and according to what I've just been reading in the *Evening News* that aid money from Norway for new ones seems to have leaked too.'

'It's still there, you know,' said Mr Patel.

'I wish I could share your optimism. It'll have been channelled into some secret bank account in Liechtenstein by now, mark my words.'

'Not the money, the gun – the one he shot Erroll with. It's still there, in the Thika River, where he threw it on the way to Nyeri.'

'Oh my God, Patel, you're not still going on about your damned Delves Broughton?'

'Look, A.B., he told that girl all about it. What's-her-name – Carberry's daughter. He told her the very next day. It's all in the book that English journalist wrote, and in the one she wrote too. He admitted that he'd shot Erroll. Not only that, he told her what he'd done with the murder weapon. On the way up to Nyeri he'd stopped at Thika and chucked the gun over the bridge into the falls. You must have read it – *White Handkerchief*, or whatever it was called.' He turned to Mr Malik. 'You've read it, haven't you, Malik?'

'I think you may mean *White Mischief*.' Mr Malik nodded. 'Yes, I've read it.'

'Well, what about the other book?' said Mr Gopez.

'Not that Secret Service assassination thing,' said Mr Patel. 'I thought we'd agreed to ditch the conspiracy theory.'

'No, no. I'm talking about the book by that other woman.'

'You wouldn't by any chance be referring to *Diana Lady Delamere and the Lord Erroll Murder*, would you?' asked Mr Malik. 'By Mrs Leda Farrant?'

'That's the one. Correct me if I'm wrong, but she says that in the 1960s some local journalist chappy came up with some new evidence and got a story published in the *Sunday Nation* putting the finger squarely on Diana. The paper got cold feet, thinking she'd sue. They pulled the story – but not before the first edition had gone out. Much to their surprise, nothing happened. No writ, nothing. A few days later this chap's boss was playing cards at the Muthaiga Club, and who should be on the same table as him? Diana. He thought he should say something – apologize, you know. She waved his explanation aside. "Oh, everyone knows I did it," she said.'

'Yes, A.B.?'

'Well, there you are, that's what I'm saying. She admitted it.'

Mr Patel shook his head in disbelief.

'That is hardly what I would call an unambiguous admission of guilt. Even if she did say it, does it not occur to you that her words might have been intended as ironic?'

'And if I might put in a word here,' said Mr Malik who, being no less fascinated by the case than anyone else in

Kenya, had indeed read all the books about the Erroll case he could get his hands on over the years (and dozens of newspaper articles besides), 'it seems that once again we are faced with the problem of hearsay evidence. The woman who wrote this book – and, as far as I remember, she paints a far from flattering picture of Diana – bases her conclusions on a conversation at which she was not herself present.'

'Exactly my point, Malik,' said Mr Gopez with a triumphant smile.

'What point?' said Mr Patel. 'A moment ago you were saying that Diana did it.'

'The point I was trying to make, Patel, is that Malik is right. Hearsay evidence is like one of those verbal agreements in Hollywood you read about – not worth the paper it's written on. Same with your Delves Broughton.'

At this point, some of you may be feeling just a little confused by all these references to this and that theory by this and that writer. So, while our friends at the Asadi Club order another round of Tusker beers and make further inroads into the bowl of chilli popcorn on the table in front of them, let me summarize.

White Mischief – later made into a film of the same name – was published in 1982 by the English journalist James Fox. The book reads like a true-life detective story and was based on the transcript of the 1941 Broughton murder trial and interviews which Fox and his colleague, the English writer Cyril Connolly, conducted from 1969 onwards with as many as possible of the key players then still alive. His story goes like this.

At about 3 a.m. on the morning of Friday the 24th of January 1941, two African men were driving a milk delivery truck from the then rural settlement of Karen to Nairobi. It was dark and wet. Soon after the two men had turned right out of Karen Road and were heading northeast towards the city, they saw the lights of a stationary car that seemed to have veered across the highway in the direction they were heading. The car had ended up tilted halfway into a shallow pit on the wrong side of the road about 150 yards beyond the junction. They stopped their truck and got out. The car was a black Buick. Though its headlights were still on, the engine wasn't running and the windows were closed. At first the car seemed empty, but when the delivery drivers looked inside they saw a man hunched sideways on the floor under the steering wheel on elbows and knees, his head on the floor, his hands together. He looked dead. The two men immediately turned the truck back towards Karen to go and get help.

Within the hour, four local constables from the police post at Karen were on the scene. They flagged down a white dairy farmer who was also driving towards Nairobi. The dairy farmer later stated that he had earlier passed the spot, heading in the opposite direction, at about 2.40 a.m., but had seen nothing. While talking with the constables, the dairy farmer noticed a wound behind the dead man's left ear. He drove on to the main police station in Nairobi to fetch further assistance while one of the constables fetched Assistant Police Superintendent Anstis Bewes from his nearby home in Karen.

Bewes arrived at 4.50 a.m. He saw tyre marks leading away from the front of the car. When he opened the car door, as well as seeing the body on the floor he noticed blood on the front passenger seat and a strong smell of scent. He also saw white marks on the rear seat – possibly from pipeclay used to whiten gym shoes, he thought – and observed that both armstraps had been wrenched off the inside of the roof and were lying on the back seat. He went off to phone Nairobi, and by 6 a.m. five more police officers were on the scene.

At 8 a.m. a government pathologist, passing by on his way to work, was flagged down. He ordered that the body be removed for examination. It was only when the body was pulled from its crouched position, and he could see the face, that he recognized the dead man as Josslyn Hay, 22nd Earl of Erroll. The body was taken to the mortuary and the car towed away. At the mortuary, Police Superintendent Arthur Poppy confirmed that the dead man had a bullet wound behind his ear surrounded by powder scorch marks. Further examination of the car revealed a spent .32 bullet, bloodstains on the inside of the passenger side window, a hairpin and a lipstick-stained Players cigarette.

Mr Malik admitted to being no less intrigued by the Erroll murder than were his friends, but while part of him – the part that had made him read every book and article on the case that he came across (and recall every detail, clue and theory) – could not help but wonder who did it and why, another part of him thought that there are some questions to which we will never have an answer, and this was one of them. He was relieved to see Tiger Singh approach their table. Perhaps the Tiger would be able to turn the conversation on to another subject. Mr Malik was not

quite so pleased, though, to see another figure behind him
– a white-haired, brown-skinned man dressed in a pale
linen jacket with slacks to match, below which were what
looked suspiciously like a pair of white espadrilles.

'Good evening, gentlemen,' said the Tiger. 'Look who
I bumped into in the Hilton.'

The man stepped forward. Mr Gopez stood and
reached out a hand.

'Harry Khan. Good to see you, old chap – Patel here
told us you were back in the country.'

'Hey, A.B., Patel,' said Harry Khan with a white smile.
'And if it isn't my old pal Malik. What's happening, Jack?'

'Murder,' said Mr Malik.

'Murder?'

'We were just talking about it, Tiger.'

'He means the Lord Erroll murder,' said Mr Patel.

'Don't worry, Harry,' said the Tiger, 'it was a very long
time ago. No reason you should know anything about it.'

'Trial made headlines all over the world,' said Mr Patel.
'But then he got off.'

'I think the word you want, Patel, is *acquitted*,' said Mr
Gopez. 'Broughton was acquitted – found not guilty by a
jury of his peers.' He turned to Harry Khan. 'It was Diana
– Broughton's wife – who did it, you see.'

'Khan, please forgive my friend. He knows not of what
he speaks. Malik'll tell you – he's read the books. Broughton
admitted it, didn't he, Malik?'

'Yes, Patel, but –'

'And please forgive *my* friend, Khan,' said Mr Gopez.
'Whether his mental deficiency is hereditary or acquired,
we can only feel the deepest sympathy for both him and

his family. No, as usual, *cherchez la femme* – and you don't have to *cherche* very far to find all tracks leading to Diana. Wouldn't you agree, Malik?'

'Well, perhaps –'

This time it was Mr Patel who interrupted.

'Perhaps a third-hand account of a conversation twenty years after the event isn't worth much? Couldn't agree more, Malik old chap.'

'Yes, but . . . no. I mean, can't we just agree that no one knows – that it is an unsolved crime? After all, it happened sixty years ago. It's dead. They're all dead.'

'Ah yes, *mortua omnia resolvit*,' said Tiger Singh. 'And yet to the law an unsolved crime is never dead.'

'It's not unsolved as far as I'm concerned,' said Mr Patel. 'Full confession, case closed.'

'*Alleged* confession, Patel. My money stays on the *femme fatale*.'

'Did I hear "money"? Are we talking about a bet?'

Tiger Singh held up a hand.

'If I may say so, gentlemen, it seems to me as if this argument is going nowhere. Each side is simply maintaining a fixed position while trying to denigrate or ridicule the opposing view. And without further evidence a wager is out of the question – wagers demand proof. Now, Khan old chap, what'll you have to drink?'

'Bootleg liquor,' said Mr Gopez. 'That's what *they* used to drink, you know. June Carberry's husband used to brew it up at their place in Nyeri. Isn't that right, Malik?'

Mr Patel shook his head.

'Yes, but that's not what they were all drinking on the night of the murder. There may have been a war on but it was champagne as usual at the Muthaiga Club – crates of it. Isn't that right, Malik?'

'Gentlemen,' said Tiger Singh. 'Will you please allow Mr Khan to tell me what he would like to drink?'

'Yes, A.B., and stop interrupting poor Malik. He's probably dying of thirst too.'

'Better than being shot by a jealous lover.'

Mr Malik cleared his throat.

'If I may make a suggestion, Tiger.'

All eyes turned towards him.

'I've been thinking. You're quite right, Tiger – this argument about the Erroll murder never seems to go anywhere. But on the other hand it does need settling once and for all, and I've just had an idea. What if we could do something here at the club?'

'A re-enactment, you mean?' said Mr Patel. 'You know, I've always thought A.B. could make a very good Earl of Erroll. And I could be Broughton – but where, at such short notice, could I get hold of a loaded pistol?'

'No, no, I was thinking of a sort of trial. Well, not a trial, exactly – more of a debate. Now that the lecture's been cancelled, we could do it tomorrow.'

'That's what I said,' agreed Mr Gopez, reaching into his pocket.

'He said debate, A.B., not a bet,' said Mr Patel. 'Pros and cons, all that kind of thing. Like at school.'

'What exactly did you have in mind, Malik?' said Tiger Singh.

'That we stage a debate about the Erroll murder here at the club. A.B. and Patel each presents his case, the other is then allowed the right of reply. And there'll be an adjudicator, of course – to keep things in order. Then a vote is taken, and the person who gets the most support is considered to have won the argument.'

'What, no money?' said Mr Gopez, removing his hand from his pocket.

'No, A.B., no money. Perhaps you, Tiger, would –'

'Would adjudicate? I'd be pleased to. Well, Patel, A.B. – what do you say?'

'Broughton,' said Mr Patel.

'Diana,' said Mr Gopez.

'Then I take it,' said Mr Malik, 'that we are agreed. Now, I was wondering – would anyone like a game of billiards?'

'Sounds great, Jack,' said Harry Khan. 'Speaking of whom, that'll be a Mr Daniel's on the rocks for me, please, Tiger. Make it a double.'

6

*When thunder rumbles in the sky, the porcupine
seeks shelter under the same tree as the leopard*

The Asadi Club, motto *Spero meliora*, has a proud history.
As the registration certificate above the bar attests, it was
founded in 1903 when Nairobi was little more than a few
tin sheds beside the railway track. It was originally a social
club for homesick immigrants to Nairobi of Indian
descent, most of whom had arrived as indentured labourers to help the British build the 'lunatic line' from the
Indian Ocean to Lake Victoria. Originally built on a mod-
est five acres of ground on the outskirts of what was then
known as the 'Indian Quarter', it was by now surrounded
on all sides by a modern city. Instead of a bare track in
front, there was a sealed road; instead of a wire fence
round it, there was a thick hedge; instead of coffee planta-
tions on three sides, there were the mansions of the rich
and powerful. It boasted a large bar, a dining room and a
purpose-built photographic darkroom (though, with digi-
tal photography, who uses a darkroom these days?), as
well as six squash courts, two tennis courts, a swimming
pool and a billiard room with four full-sized tables (only
one at the Muthaiga Club now, alas).

Those of you unfamiliar with billiards might think that

a game played between two people with two sticks and three balls on a twelve-foot table would not be the most thrilling of pastimes. You might imagine that it would not have quite the excitement of snooker, say, with its fifteen red balls and six colours, or the pizzazz of American eight-ball, with all those spots and stripes and dreaded black ball packed on to a nine-foot table. But billiards is a game of great subtlety and skill. Sinking balls is only part of it; the in-off shot is usually of more value than the straight pot, and you can also score with a cannon (hitting both the other balls with your cue ball). To some extent it is a game of simple physics – of force and momentum, angles and spin. But, above all, billiards is a philosopher's game – and I suspect that this is largely why it has long been the game of choice among members of the Asadi Club. Though billiards may be a simple game, it is by no means easy.

'Foul stroke,' said the Tiger. 'Two points to Khan. Khan eighty-six points, Malik fifty-three.'

'Getting a little excited there, Jack.'

The annoying thing was that Harry Khan was quite right. Mr Malik had no one to blame for the miscue but himself. He had been doing well throughout the game so far – nothing ambitious, nothing rushed. But now, in trying to push his cue ball through for a simple follow-on cannon, he had hit it twice. No, he had no one to blame but himself.

Here's a tip I learned from my friend Kennedy. If you elect to take a spot after your opponent has played a foul, place your own ball one and a half ball-widths from the right side of the D, then line up on the right edge of your opponent's white ball and play your own ball straight – bottom or side spin is not required for this shot. Your ball will bounce off your opponent's and sink neatly in the top right pocket. If you calculate the pace correctly the other white will, at the same time, trickle up the table, bounce off the top cushion and come to rest near enough the red to offer a cannon for the next shot, or even another in-off. Harry Khan must have known this too. He took the spot and calculated the pace correctly. He sank his ball, hit the cannon, then another. Three more reds made the winning score of 101.

'Looks like you lose this time, eh, Jack?'

'Yes. Well played, Khan. Can I buy you a drink?'

'JD on the rocks. No, wait a minute.' He looked at the gold Rolex on his wrist. 'Make that a rain check, I've got to get back to town.'

'Well, come back, won't you?' said Mr Patel. 'Malik can always use another lesson.'

'You know, I might do that. I kind of like this old place.' He looked around the room. 'But ever thought of having it spruced up a bit? Like, modernized?'

Mr Malik followed his gaze. Well, perhaps some of the rooms could do with some fresh paint – though the whole place had been redone after the kitchen fire and that was only . . . gosh, was it really twelve years ago?

'It's not easy to get things changed around here, I'm afraid,' said Tiger Singh.

'That's right,' said Mr Patel. 'There's been a plan before the management committee to turn the old darkroom into a computer centre for nearly a year now, but most of the members think a megabyte is what you get from a large mosquito and hard disks come with old age.'

'Then you need to get some younger members, right?

These old saggy armchairs and that moth-eaten lion by the front door – not exactly hip, know what I mean? Not exactly twenty-first century.'

Tiger Singh looked around him.

'I'm sure you're right, Harry, though we can't get rid of the lion. Club mascot, you know. Guards the door. Keeps the club safe. Isn't that right, Malik?'

'That's right, Tiger. And so far it's never shirked a day's duty.'

'Apart from that time it disappeared,' said Mr Patel.

'Ah yes.' Mr Malik smiled. 'But it didn't really disappear – just went out to get some fresh air.'

'Our friends are referring to an incident a few years ago,' said the Tiger to a mystified Harry Khan, 'when the lion was found on the club roof. No one ever found out how it got there but Sanjay and Bobby Bashu were strong suspects. Anyway, hope to see you here again, Harry. In fact, there's that debate on tomorrow night. Would you be interested in –?'

'That guy you were talking about? Sorry, guys, dead white males are not my scene. Besides, I've got a dinner date.'

Harry Khan racked his cue and with a wave of his hand and a white, white smile bid them all a good night. Pausing on his way through the front door only to pat the head of the stuffed lion, he climbed into a shiny new red Mercedes CLK cabriolet and departed the car park of the Asadi Club in a small shower of dust and gravel.

Inhabitants of Chicago may be familiar with the 'Maneaters of Tsavo', whose stuffed and snarling forms have so long bewitched children and bemused parents visiting the Field Museum of Natural History. The story of these two Kenyan lions goes back to the late 1890s when the railway from Mombasa to Lake Victoria was being built. The tracks had reached nearly halfway to Nairobi when Railway Superintendent Lieutenant-Colonel J. H. Patterson, DSO, began noticing an increase in absenteeism among the Indian labourers. Not known for his enlightened attitude towards his employees, at first he didn't believe the stories the workers told him about screams in the night and blood on the tent flaps. No, he thought, damned coolies were probably sneaking off down the line to open another grocer's shop in Mombasa. But when they brought him a dusty sandal which still contained the foot of its wearer, he realized that something must be done. What happened next you can read about in the lieutenant-colonel's best-selling 1907 memoir *The Maneaters of Tsavo and Other East African Adventures*. In a later chapter of the same book you can read about another maneater – the so-called Kima Killer.

On the 4th of June 1900, Superintendent C. H. Ryall of the Nairobi Railway Police received a telegram that had been sent up the line from Kima railway station, not far from Tsavo. 'Lion fighting with station,' it read. 'Send urgent succour.' Eager for some sport, Ryall ordered that his personal carriage be attached to the next down train and set off, accompanied by two friends. On arriving at the station he arranged that the carriage be left in a siding overnight. He and his companions, well armed with heavy rifles, would take it in turns to stay awake and keep watch from within. But perhaps the night was too hot – or the

47

whisky too strong – because during his watch Ryall dropped off to sleep with the sliding door still wide open. No one in the carriage saw the gleam of yellow eyes in the moonlight; no one heard the pad of four soft paws.

Because the track where the carriage was parked was not well ballasted, the carriage had ended up leaning very slightly to one side. When the hungry lion jumped in, his weight was enough to tilt it a fraction more. The door slid closed, the latch clicked shut, and three men and a lion were locked inside the carriage. The noise was heard by a certain Mohammed Khan, the very man who had sent the telegram in the first place and who was now crouched safely in a water tank opposite the siding, observing the whole business.

His first thought was that this Ryall chap was a genius. To improvise so clever a trap, then to bait it with your very own self. That took a lot of British skill, and a lot of British pluck. What would the brave sahib do now that he had captured the beast – shoot it with his revolver or strangle it with his bare hands? Mohammed Khan heard a commotion but no shots. It looked as though the sahib was going for the bare-handed option.

You can imagine his surprise, therefore, when the next thing he saw was two trouserless gentlemen leaping from a window on the near side of the carriage, followed a minute later by the lion – though the latter was exiting backwards and seemed in less of a rush. The reason for the animal's unusual orientation and unhurried pace soon became clear. The lion was dragging behind him through the window the lifeless body of Superintendent Ryall.

Mohammed Khan was a sensitive soul and knew immediately what he must do. He must find those trouserless gentlemen some clothes quick-smart. Heedless of personal risk, he climbed out of the water tank and in loud whispers indicated that if the two men followed him he would see what he could arrange.

It was not until after eleven o'clock the next day, when the Maasai search party had found what was left of Ryall's body and killed the lion, that his two friends could be persuaded to retrieve their own clothing from the carriage. They returned to Nairobi on the two-forty up train, properly dressed in khaki suits, boots, gaiters and sun hats, though still carrying with them the new red cloaks that had been lent to them by Mohammed Khan and which he insisted they keep as a memento of their adventure. In appreciation of his kindness they, in turn, insisted that he keep the skin of the lion.

It was this Mohammed Khan who three years later, and now the owner of a successful grocer's shop and general emporium in Nairobi, banded together with some chums (including, as it so happened, Mr Malik's grandfather) to form the Asadi Club. As you enter the hallway of the club you will still be greeted by the lion in question. In deference to local African tradition the dead animal is pointing to the north – so that its spirit can find its way to the celestial hunting grounds – and the legend has grown up that as long as it stands guard, the club will continue to prosper. Mohammed Khan stuffed the lion skin himself and didn't do a bad job – though after more than a hundred years of sentry duty the Kima Killer does look a little tired and, despite its lips being drawn back to reveal an impressive set of teeth, it appears to be not snarling, but smiling.

On his own way through the lobby of the Asadi Club later that night, Mr Malik looked around him. Perhaps Harry Khan was right. Perhaps the place was looking a little shabby – but nothing some new chair covers and a lick of paint wouldn't fix. He'd have a word with the manager, get a few quotes to put to the committee. As for the lion, though – no. The lion had to stay.

7

The giant tree falls, and the bush pigs eat its fruit

There was, thought Brian Kukuya, something rather nice about being a government minister. He looked around the spacious room that served as his new office. High ceilings, wide windows, cool tiled floor. In front of the fireplace lay a lion-skin rug (or, to be zoologically precise, lioness-skin rug) of pale tawny hue. He'd had the walls painted to match it and was rather pleased with the result. The painters that his assistant Jonah had organized had really done a first-class job, not like the usual lackadaisical tradesmen you always seemed to get these days – no, not at all. But that is as it should be – nothing but the best for a minister of state. On the wall beside his desk was a discreet but impressive bookcase filled with discreet but impressive books, on the opposite wall a photograph of himself and the President, shaking hands and beaming at the camera. And after years of hustling and hustings, of constituency meetings and barroom meetings and back-room meetings, the Honourable B. Kukuya, Minister for the Interior, had at last reached the position he knew he deserved. Mind you, it had been a close-run thing. At the last minute it had been rumoured that Zakiya Mohutu was going to get the job and he would be left with the Ministry of Transport.

Several favours had to be called in, several promises made. But in the end all had turned out well, and now he could afford to ease off a bit. He could relax. He could delegate.

He pressed a button on his desk.

'Ah, Jonah. What have you got for me today?'

'Just a few letters to sign, Minister, then there's that appointment at ten – it's in your diary and I've put the briefing on your desk. Oh, and I just got a call from the PM's office. This afternoon's cabinet meeting has been postponed. The Swiss delegation's running late again but the PM thinks he should see them anyway as soon as they arrive. Shall I phone the golf club?'

'Thank you, Jonah.'

Brian Kukuya leaned back in his chair and clasped his hands behind his head. Yes, there *was* something jolly nice about being a minister. Not that it was something anyone could do – no, not at all. Delegating, for instance. You had to be sure that the people to whom you delegated were up to the job. Which was why he felt lucky – no, not lucky, far-sighted was a better word – to have let Jonah Litu-mana keep his job as ministerial private secretary after the last minister had been forced to resign. It was important to have continuity, and to have someone who appreciated that a minister does not want to be bothered with details. Big-picture stuff, that was his job, long-term vision. But being in so senior a position had its minuses as well as its pluses. As Brian Kukuya was only too happy to explain to anyone who asked, and many who didn't, he probably worked harder now than at any time in his life.

'Can't switch off, you see. Morning, noon and night – thinking, thinking.'

For instance, a casual observer at the Sandringham Country Club this afternoon might think he was playing golf; afterwards it might appear that he was relaxing in the bar, enjoying a drink. But really he would be thinking, thinking, working, working, all the time.

He glanced down at the desk. Ah yes, the letters. Though he was sure that age and experience had improved his long-term vision, the Hon Brian Kukuya had to admit that the years had done little to improve his day-to-day sight. He was at that time of life when arms seem to get shorter, lights dimmer and print smaller. He was also at a position in life when he was particularly conscious of his appearance. Oh, he didn't mind an expanding waistline and he didn't mind a few grey hairs – his wife told him they made him look distinguished and his mistress told him they made him look trustworthy – but spectacles were out. Last month he had heard about some exercises to counteract the effects of age on eyesight and had asked Jonah to order the book on the internet. Any day now he would start doing them – if he could read them, that is. But it didn't really matter. Jonah always provided a verbal summary of anything important, and he could still see well enough to know where to sign the letters that Jonah put in front of him. He picked up his pen. Only four letters this morning and, judging from the colour of the paper, a couple of departmental memos. He signed each document with care – you had to be careful if you were a government minister – and dropped them into the out-tray. His finger again moved to the button on his desk.

'All right, Jonah. You can send Mr Khan in now.'

Since leaving Kenya in the sixties the Khan family had

prospered. Harry Khan and his two brothers had seen the family firm diversify from the retail business his grandfather had founded into hotel and restaurant franchises and, more recently, into shopping centres. With his good looks and affability, Harry had naturally moved to 'front of house', leaving his brothers to look after the management and accounts. It was Harry who took the investors to lunch, it was he who ran the seminars, it was he who looked after the franchisees' wives. He was very good at looking after the franchisees' wives.

'Mr Khan, delighted to see you.' The minister waved him to a chair with open hand. 'Please, sit down. So, how do you find our country?'

Harry flashed him a wide white smile.

'Kenya will always be the jewel of Africa for me, Minister.'

'How long since you were last here?' Having glanced at Jonah Litumana's briefing, the minister was well aware of the answer to this question – but small talk was small talk.

'Too long,' said Harry Khan. 'But last time, that was a family thing – my mother, you know, she wanted to come back and see what the old place looked like.'

'Of course, I remember now – you were born here. You are as Kenyan as I am. But first, tell me – everything all right at your hotel?'

'Those guys at the Hilton always look after me just fine.'

'Good, good. If there is anything you need – the manager is a personal friend of mine, you know.'

'You are too kind, Minister.'

Harry Khan looked around the room.

'Nice place you've got here. I hear you haven't been in the job very long. Your predecessor – he resigned, am I right?'

'Indeed so. Personal reasons. Very sad.'

'That's not exactly what I heard. Wasn't there something about it in the *Evening News* – that "Birds of a Feather" column?'

'So you've come across Dadukwa, Mr Khan? Then let me assure you that the whole thing is based on nothing more than imagination and innuendo.'

'But some of that imagination and innuendo, it must be coming from pretty high up, right?'

The smile on Brian Kukuya's face slipped a millimetre.

'You are indeed well informed, Mr Khan. And you may rest assured that the government, and I as Minister for the Interior, take all such leaks – such threats to national security – seriously. Very seriously. I have made it clear that any information leading to the unmasking of this unpatriotic scallywag will be well rewarded. It was one of my first directives. You have been reading it, this column?'

'No, not exactly. I met a few guys last night; they filled me in on what's been happening.'

'That would have been at the Asadi Club, I suppose?'

Harry Khan smiled.

'You too seem well informed, if I may say so, Minister.'

'It is my job to know what is going on. Anyway, you may be interested to know that the *Evening News* will soon be closing down.'

'Is that right?'

'Yes – some technicality with its registration, apparently. I don't know if you ever heard of a certain fire in

1940? It started in the office of the then Military Secretary. You may have heard of him – Lord Erroll?'

'Oh yeah. The white guy who was murdered, right?'

The minister nodded.

'Most unfortunate. No one was hurt in the fire, but an awful lot of government records were destroyed.' The minister turned to look out of the window. A jacaranda tree was just coming into bloom. 'Where was I? Oh, yes, the *Evening News*. After my predecessor's unfortunate demise my assistant thought it might be prudent to conduct an audit of newspaper registration documents – just routine, you understand. As I'm sure you know, Mr Khan, all organizations need to be registered – for tax reasons, health and safety regulations, that kind of thing. Unfortunately, he could find no such document in the government records.'

'Don't tell me – it was one of those that got burned in the fire. But they'd have their own copy, right?'

'Yes, you'd think so, wouldn't you? They came up with some excuse, a burglary or something – just last week, they claim. But I ask you, what kind of burglar would steal a company registration document? No, it's quite clear that all this time they have been operating as an unregistered company – completely illegal, of course. We've tried to help. We've given them two weeks to produce the document or shut down. Such a shame – just after they've had their offices refurbished and redecorated and everything. But we really have no choice.'

'I guess not, Minister, I guess not.' Harry Khan nodded towards the fireplace. 'Nice rug.'

'Yes,' said the minister, looking down at the skin of the

lioness, legs splayed, mouth showing teeth that though somewhat yellow were nonetheless fearsome. 'She's quite old too – over fifty now. Shot on the first of February 1956. Does that date mean anything to you?'

Harry Khan shook his head.

'Can't say it does.'

'You have heard of Elsa, Mr Khan?'

'Elsa – you mean Elsa the lioness, Joy Adamson, *Born Free*, all that stuff?'

The minister smiled.

'I see you remember your Kenyan history, Mr Khan. And you no doubt recall that the reason Joy Adamson brought up Elsa and the other orphaned lion cubs was that her mother had been shot – by her husband George, in fact.' He gazed down at the flattened form. 'Ah yes, poor Elsa's mother. I, um, acquired her after George Adamson died – that was after Joy was murdered, of course. He was murdered too – by poachers, they say.'

'Right, another lucky lion skin. Seems quite the thing round here.'

'Lucky?'

'That's what they think at the Asadi Club. They've got a lion skin too – not a rug like that one, but a stuffed one. Not in such good condition either, but I guess it's even older than yours. Anyway, according to club tradition, as long as the lion's OK, the club's OK.'

'Oh, what a quaint idea. But tell me, Mr Khan, what brings you to Nairobi this time? Visiting family again?'

Harry Khan leaned forward in his chair.

'No, Minister – and hey, call me Harry – this time it's business, straight business.'

'Business? Tell me more.'

'As you may know, our company is quite a big player in the shopping centre game over in the US; mostly eastern seaboard, but we're moving into the west – San Diego, Seattle. After my last visit here, I got to thinking. Maybe we could use some of the lessons we've been learning over there, over here.'

'I wonder, Mr Khan, could you be a little more specific?'

'I'm talking megamalls, Minister. I'm talking one-stop. I'm talking food, clothing, entertainment. I'm talking thirty, forty, fifty thousand square metres of air-conditioned retail space with car parks to match – maybe residential too. We've been looking at the market here in Nairobi pretty closely. We think now could be the right time.'

'What you propose sounds most interesting, Mr Khan, but surely this is simply a commercial venture? I don't quite see –'

'Where you come in? The way I look at it is this – and correct me if I'm wrong here, Minister. We're talking about a large investment. I won't bother you with the details of finance and stakeholders and all the boring stuff, but we're talking – OK if I use US dollars? – we're talking millions, tens of millions, maybe even nine figures.'

The minister sat back in his chair.

'Go on, Mr Khan.'

'Like I say, it's a pretty big wad. It's going to be big for Nairobi, and what's good for Nairobi is good for Kenya – right? That's why I'm here. I thought I should start by getting the advice of someone high up, someone at the top. There's going to be money in this for a lot of people. That's why I came to you.'

'I see. And this . . . er . . . advice?'

'What I'm looking for is local knowledge. People who know how the system works, people who know the people who know the right people. For instance, the first thing we're going to need is a site.'

'Site?'

'A building site. Somewhere to build – somewhere big, somewhere central.'

'Oh,' said the minister. 'Well, I happen to know that there will be tenders out soon for redevelopment of some of the area around Kibera –'

'Kibera – isn't that the slums? With all respect, Minister, I'm not sure that's quite the place for a five-star retail facility.'

Brian Kukuya smiled.

'We prefer to call it "unofficial housing", Mr Khan. But I think I can see your point. Something a little more central?'

'Right. So what I'm really asking is that if you do get any ideas, you give me a call. Like I said, for the good of the country.'

'I think I understand you, Mr . . . Harry. Yes, I think I understand you perfectly.'

It has sometimes been said that Kenya is not so much a nation as a collection of tribes. When nineteenth- and twentieth-century European invaders decided to carve up Africa, the borders between their agreed spheres of influence were not decided by nature or (strange thought) by the people who actually lived there. They were decided by merchants and soldiers and men with maps in the faraway capitals of another continent. The border between British East Africa and German East Africa was a straight line with a small kink round Mount Kilimanjaro. The border between British East Africa and Italian East Africa similarly owed more to geometry than geography. The result of this is that even today the Maasai of Kenya have more in common with their brother Maasai of Tanzania than they do with their fellow Kenyan Kikuyus, and the Cushitic speakers of the north converse more easily with their Ethiopian cousins than with their Swahili-speaking coastal compatriots.

The Hon Brian Kukuya was a Luo man and, if you could have delved into his soul, you would find that his loyalties were to his family, his tribe and his country – in very much that order. Had you been able to delve deeper still, you would have discovered that even above loyalty to family was a great love of and concern for the well-being of Brian Kukuya.

'Ah, there you are, Jonah. You have shown Mr Khan out? Now, tell me, is there any more news about the *Evening News*?'

'Ha ha, news about the news, Minister. The Minister is most clever and amusing.'

Yes, thought Brian Kukuya, he supposed he was.

'How is your – *our* – little plan going? I suppose there is no chance that the editor will be able to produce this certificate of registration?'

'None whatever, Minister. You may be sure of that. I have taken care of it. It is already in my personal possession.'

'Good, good. That will certainly be a thorn removed from the flesh of the government's side.'

'A most poetic and apposite analogy, Minister.'

Apposite? Poetic? Yes, perhaps it was.

'Well now, I have another little matter I would like to discuss with you.'

By the time Jonah Litumana had left the minister's office, he knew about the minister's brilliant plan for a new megamall in Nairobi and was in no doubt that the building of this edifice would be good for the country, the city and the people. It would also be good, he was quite sure, for the minister. And he was sure that with a little constructive meditation he would think of just the right spot to build it.

8

If the rock falls on the melon or the melon on the
rock, it is not the rock that is smashed apart

Benjamin Ikonya had grown up on a small family farm
many days' walk from Nairobi and been just sixteen when
he first came into Mr Malik's employ. He liked looking
after Mr Malik's garden. He liked the morning ritual of
first selecting and cutting some twigs to bind to his broom
handle, then sweeping the lawn clean of the night's fallen
leaves. He enjoyed mowing the lawn, and pruning the
shrubs and bushes. He especially liked making and light-
ing the bonfire outside the front gate every afternoon
(small bonfires are the main rubbish disposal system of
Nairobi, and give the city its special smell). For the first
time in his life he had his own room, with electric light
and running water, and three meals a day. And he could
send money home and still have enough left over to buy
bonbons and Coca-Cola – every day, if he wanted.

It had taken him some time to get used to city people.
They had a strange direct way of talking – no respectful
preliminaries, they just got right on to the subject. His
cousin Emmanuel said that was the way *wazungu* talked.
Not only that, city people seemed surprised when you
only answered the questions they asked. It was as if they

really expected you to be so disrespectful as to venture your own opinion, or to give information that was not specifically asked for. Benjamin had been brought up much too well to ever feel comfortable doing that. But Mr Malik was always polite to him. He didn't call him a shamba boy; he said that Benjamin was his gardener. He always asked Benjamin's opinion if he thought an old plant needed removing, or a new one should be planted. Whenever anyone complimented Mr Malik on his garden he would always say that it was Benjamin who should take most of the credit. And Benjamin not only looked after the garden. From growing up in the country he was familiar with much of the wildlife of Kenya and was once able to help Mr Malik when there was a birdwatching competition at the club. In the course of this competition they visited Benjamin's home village, and on the way back they'd been held up at gunpoint by Somali bandits. Benjamin said that Mr Malik had saved his life, and Mr Malik said that Benjamin had saved his.

It had been Mr Malik's inspiration that Benjamin go along on the safari. 'Ah, Benjamin,' he said to him one morning as Benjamin came sweep-sweep-sweeping past the veranda. 'I've had an idea.'

At these words Benjamin's heart sank. This was not the first time he had heard one of Mr Malik's ideas. Only a couple of weeks ago Mr Malik had come up with the theory that if Benjamin shook each tree every day before he swept beneath it, he would have less work to do.

'Any loose leaves will fall down, you see, so you won't have so many to do the next day.'

To Benjamin it was clear that in the long run this would

make absolutely no difference. The number of leaves falling from any tree was dependent on the natural leaf cycle of the tree, and no amount of shaking would change that. But he went along with it. He liked Mr Malik, and he wanted him to be happy. Then there had been the idea that instead of burning the garden rubbish every day he could save time by letting it build up for a week and have one big bonfire. Which Benjamin did, with the result that instead of a very little smoke curling up into the Nairobi sky every afternoon there was an enormous plume on Friday that sent hadadas screeching from the trees and brought all the neighbouring askaris rushing round with buckets of water. But Benjamin tried his best to be an optimist. Perhaps this idea would be different.

'As you may know, Benjamin, I have agreed to once more organize the annual Asadi Club safari. This year I have arranged a surprise, but I will need some help to set it all up.'

Benjamin was not sure about surprises. There was, he thought, a lot to be said for a life without surprises.

'I'll show you what to do, then I'd like you to go on ahead to the campsite and get it ready. It's in the garage.'

Benjamin had indeed been wondering what was inside the two large crates that had been delivered the day before.

'I realize that this will mean working on Sunday, but I thought that in exchange you might be willing to take Monday and Tuesday off – and Wednesday too, if you like. Perhaps we could drop you off at Embu on the way back. Then you'd be able to get the bus from there to your village and visit your family. How does that sound?'

Benjamin's mother and father – not to mention any

number of brothers, sisters, cousins, uncles, aunts and both grandmothers – still lived in the village where he had grown up, and he never seemed to get home often enough. A few days with his family was a tempting offer.

'But, Mr Malik, what about the wedding? I must get the garden ready.'

'Benjamin, the garden is as ready as it possibly can be. You have been working very hard all month. It has never looked better.'

'Thank you, Mr Malik,' he said. 'In that case, I think your idea is a very good idea.'

'Excellent, Benjamin. You have eased my mind.'

And he took Benjamin into the garage and showed him exactly what he wanted him to do.

Rose Mbikwa flicked through the stack of LPs, still in the box beside the sofa. The house was just as she'd left it. For most of the time that Rose had been away it had been let, staffed and furnished, to a Canadian entomologist researching army-worm control in maize crops. The woman seemed to have spent most of her time in her laboratory or in the field – so the staff had had little to do, except keep things just as they had always been. Elizabeth polished and dusted, Reuben pruned and mowed, and the three askaris took turns to guard the house and garden from thieves and rascals. Now Rose was home again, and all that remained of her tenant was the faintest smell of naphtha and balsam.

Elizabeth had said dinner would be ready in an hour. What would it be – Chet Atkins, Anita O'Day, Peggy Lee? Rose paused, pulled a vinyl disc from its sleeve and put it on the turntable. The orchestra swelled, and from the stereo speakers came a sweet, slightly breathless voice. Rose flopped down on the old sofa and looked up at the portrait hanging over the fireplace. A handsome black face smiled back at her. It was her husband Joshua.

Rose Macdonald had been twenty-five when she first came to Kenya from Scotland and twenty-six when she walked down the aisle of the Holy Family cathedral in Nairobi to wed the handsome aspiring politician Joshua Mbikwa. Those were turbulent years. Just before their only son Angus turned eighteen and was due to start university at St Andrews, Joshua was dead – killed when the light plane he was in fell out of a blue sky. By now on the Opposition front bench, he had been returning to Nairobi from a political meeting in Eldoret to vote on a censure motion against the government. Though the Prime Minister (who, by a single vote, survived the motion) ordered an immediate and thorough enquiry, the Minister of Aviation was unable to deliver a definitive result to parliament. The cause of the crash is still officially unknown.

One of the many surprises awaiting the young bride Rose Mbikwa when she moved into the house in Hatton Rise with her husband was to see that his record collection contained every disc that Doris Day had ever recorded. Doris Day? That American epitome of all things nice and normal? That blonde-haired, pink-lipped, tightly corseted symbol of fifties domestic womanhood? Rose (who as a sixteen-year-old pupil of Edinburgh Presbyterian Ladies' College had made a point of reading *The Prime of Miss Jean Brodie* though it was banned at school, who in her bedroom had rocked to Little Richard and rolled to Chubby Checker, and who had made it a point of teenage honour to hitch her skirt up at least four inches above her knees as soon as she was out of the house on a Saturday night) had always thought of herself as more of a Ruth Brown girl. But once she'd got over the shock of discovering that someone younger than forty could actually like the sight and singing of Doris Day, she mellowed. And now whenever she found herself in a nostalgic mood she would put one of the old LPs on the turntable and find herself back in those happy, hectic days of her marriage to Joshua Mbikwa.

Mr Malik pulled back the garage doors of Number 12 Garden Lane.

'There you are, Ally. Mind out, though, they're heavier than they look.'

Ally Dass ordered his truck to back up and his men to load the two wooden crates, each about seven-foot square by two-foot deep, that were lying on the floor. From the dents and scratches that covered them, they were clearly not new. The men heaved them into the truck, finding just enough room for them behind the blackened gas range and assorted crates of food and kitchen equipment.

'Benjamin's coming up with you. He'll show you what to do with them when you get there. As I mentioned to you at the club, Ally, it's going to be my little surprise for this year's safari. Now, Benjamin, have you got everything you need?'

'I have remembered all that you showed me, Mr Malik. First the erection cranks, then the draw-bar extender screws, then the spirit adjustment.'

'Good. And remember that there's an instruction book in the left-hand case if you need it. Oh, I nearly forgot – here's something for you all on the journey.'

Mr Malik handed Benjamin a large round tin on whose side were colourful sketches of lions, giraffes and elephants. On the top was printed in large lettering: JOLLY MAN ASSORTED BONBONS.

I once spent a Christmas in Australia, where I was surprised not so much at the novelty of sitting down in a hundred degrees in the shade to an alfresco lunch of hot roast turkey with all the trimmings and plum pudding to follow, as being asked by my bikini-clad hostess to pull her bonbon. It was only when I noticed the beribboned paper tube in her hand that I finally caught on and was rewarded with a bang, a paper hat and a joke – about a chicken, I seem to remember (though now I come to think of it, it may have been the one about the cockatoo). At home we had always called them 'crackers', you see. I suppose that to Americans crackers would be what we called 'fireworks' – or perhaps even 'biscuits'. And they would think a biscuit was a 'scone' and – oh, the complexities of the tongue that binds us. When it comes to edible confectionery, things get even more confusing. What are 'sweets' in England are 'candy' in America and 'lollies' in Australia and New Zealand. In Kenya they have always been 'bonbons' – but wherever you are and whatever you call them, these small lumps of flavoured sugar have long proved a hit with young and old. Equipment to manufacture these delights is not complicated to make or operate, and the items produced are easy to pack, store and distribute.

Among the confectionery manufacturers of Kenya, few take their business more seriously than the Jolly Man Manufacturing Company.

Like many a commercial enterprise in Kenya, the Jolly Man Manufacturing Company has been through many ups and downs. Begun by Mr Malik's father in the 1930s as a maker of cigarettes, it was badly affected in the 1940s by wartime tobacco restrictions, then by competition from cheap imports from the US. When Mr Malik Senior had made the move from cigarettes to cigars, the company had done well, mainly as an exporter. Since Mr Malik had taken over the running of the firm on his father's death in 1964, it had continued to prosper. But about three years ago Mr Malik began to notice orders drying up. The problem, as his daughter Petula soon discovered, was China.

'They are cutting into our markets, Daddy. I've been looking into it – similar product, cheaper price. It's the labour costs, you see.'

'But can't we –?'

'Improve our product? There's only so much you can do with rolled-up leaves, Daddy, and I think you'll have to agree that we've done it.'

'What about –?'

'Cutting costs? We can't compete on wages, so the only way we can cut costs is to improve efficiency. The only way we can do that is to shed labour and invest in new plant.'

'Shed labour? You mean, sack people?'

At the last count the Jolly Man Manufacturing Company had 132 people on the payroll, each of whom Mr Malik considered as more or less part of his larger family.

'Out of the question. Isn't there something else we can do?'

Petula thought.

'What we might be able to do, Daddy dear, is diversify.'

When four old but still serviceable Brückner and Gabell confectionery production machines came up for a good price in Kampala, Petula bought them and had them shipped by rail to Nairobi. The new venture took off like a rocket.

Much of its success was due to Mr Malik's reputation. His staff liked him, his suppliers and distributors trusted him. It was also due in large part to Petula's inspired idea to use African animal names for the new products. Although jelly babies have a worldwide following, what African child could resist biting the head off a Jiant Jelly Jiraffe? And while lollipops are lovely and gobstoppers are great, wouldn't you rather get your tongue to work on a Lion All-Day Licker or suck on an Elephant Ball (available in a handy two-pack)?

And so the Jolly Man Manufacturing Company began winding down its cigar operations and winding up production of bonbons.

9

The rhino eats the melon, but kills the lion

'Gentlemen, and ladies.'

Other than at the regular Sunday curry tiffin, ladies were still an unusual sight at the Asadi Club. Tonight was an exception. News of the Lord Erroll debate had spread and though it was being held on the evening before the annual Asadi Club safari, the dining room was packed with members and their wives. Even Petula, who never came to the club, had sounded interested but at the last minute had phoned her father to say she wouldn't be able to make it – another CI meeting.

Tiger Singh stood. The room fell silent.

'This is, as you know, an unusual event. Tonight at the Asadi Club, rather than our usual lecture, we are going to examine a crime. The crime is murder. This is not, of course, a trial – it is a debate between two of our members, Mr Gopez and Mr Patel. But it is in many ways like a trial, with you, ladies and gentlemen, as the jury. As in a court of law, you will not be called upon to make a moral decision, though morality may well be discussed. You will be called upon to make a decision of fact. Certain facts are undisputed, and I will outline them shortly. Other facts are disputed, and I will allow the debaters themselves to describe to you whichever of these they think you will find pertinent.'

The Tiger adjusted his gold-framed spectacles low on his splendid nose.

'The people involved in the case are, with one exception, now dead. No new witnesses will be called, no new evidence presented. Such evidence as will be presented is in the public domain. I'm sure many of you will be familiar with much, if not all, of it. Some of you may even have formed your own judgement about the guilt, or innocence, of one or more of the parties involved. Should you have done so, I urge you to put away your prejudices and to listen with open minds to what Mr Gopez and Mr Patel have to say. Our two protagonists will soon be presenting their arguments, but before they do so they have agreed that I should read out a summary of the background to the case, and of the evidence produced in the trial of the only person prosecuted for the murder on the twenty-fourth of January 1941, of Lord Josslyn Hay, the twenty-second Earl of Erroll.'

The Tiger turned towards the two men seated beside him and, after receiving a nod from each, began outlining the facts of the case – the crashed car, the discovery of the body, the police investigation. He described the clues the police had found at the scene of the crime – the broken armstraps, the lipstick-stained cigarette and the white marks on the back seat of the car – and how when the investigating officer visited Sir Jock Delves Broughton at his house on the afternoon of the murder, he noticed a pair of half-burned white gym shoes on a bonfire in the garden.

'And now, to the trial. The prosecution alleged that Broughton, on hearing Lord Erroll dropping off Diana at the house in Karen at about 2.20 a.m. on the night of the murder, put on a pair of gym shoes and climbed out of his first-floor bedroom window armed with a pistol. He hid in the back seat of Erroll's car. When the car slowed down at the junction with Ngong Road, Broughton shot Erroll, pulled him on to the floor, drove the car into a murram pit, ran home, climbed back up the drainpipe and got back into his bedroom without being seen by anyone in the house – though one person in the house gave evidence that she heard a dog barking sometime in the night. As corroboration the prosecution hoped to show that the bullet that killed Lord Erroll matched bullets previously fired from Broughton's own gun.'

The Tiger pursed his lips.

'I have to say that their case was not a strong one. In a fine example of the barrister's art, the counsel for the defence, Mr Morris, showed conclusively that Broughton's gun could not have been the one that fired the fatal bullet, thus demolishing the ballistic evidence on which the prosecution largely relied. As a house of cards will fall after one card is removed, their case collapsed. In a unanimous decision the jury acquitted Broughton of the murder of Lord Erroll. I will now leave Mr Patel to explain to you why he thinks they were wrong.'

Tiger Singh bowed towards Mr Patel, who now stood.

'Thank you, Tiger.' He turned to face the audience.

'The Tiger has said that I will try and convince you that the jury was wrong to find Sir Jock Delves Broughton not guilty of the murder of Lord Erroll. On the contrary, I think they were right. Why? In the light of the evidence – or lack of evidence – and in the light of Broughton's plea of not guilty, they had no choice. But we, ladies and gentlemen, are privy to information that the jury did not have. We know what happened *after* the trial.'

If Mr Patel had been wearing a waistcoat, thought Mr Malik, at this point he would undoubtedly have stuck his thumbs into its pockets.

'Since the trial and acquittal, there have been many theories about who was the murderer. Means and motives abound. There were, apparently, many people in Kenya who would have been quite happy to see Erroll dead – as well as, if you believe one theory, the British government. But after the trial no new witnesses came forward, no new and reliable evidence was found.'

Mr Patel reached for the glass of water in front of him and took a small sip.

'But many years later – in 1982 to be precise – one of the people involved in the story made an astounding claim. Juanita Carberry, at the time of the murder fifteen years old and stepdaughter of Erroll's friend and former lover June Carberry, told the English journalist James Fox that two days after the murder Broughton had arrived at the farm where she lived near Nyeri. Finding her alone, he confessed to her that he killed Lord Erroll.'

Though most had heard the story before, there was still an audible gasp from the audience.

'Yes, my friends, by his own confession, Broughton was indeed the murderer. The story Juanita Carberry told was this. Immediately after the inquest into Erroll's death, Broughton drove to where his wife was staying with June

74

Carberry at her house on the Nyeri farm. He arrived to find Diana and June were out. Only young Juanita was at home. When she had first met him at his house in Karen on the afternoon of the murder, he had taken her to see his horses. Now she took him to see her own horse. On the way to the stables he told her that he had shot Erroll. He added that on the way up to Nyeri he had stopped at Thika and thrown the gun into the Chania Falls.

'James Fox revealed all this in his book *White Mischief*. But not only this – he also discovered that Broughton made other confessions. After his return to England in September that year, Broughton confessed to an old friend called Marie Waterhouse, later again to an old horse-racing acquaintance called Alan Horn. Fox also unearthed second-hand evidence of even more confessions. For instance, Prince Windisch-Graetz – an Austrian resident of Nairobi at the time – heard from a doctor who visited Broughton while he was in jail before the trial that Broughton had confessed to him.' Mr Patel turned to Mr Gopez and smiled sweetly. 'But that is, of course, hearsay evidence and not admissible in this debate.'

He held up three fingers of his left hand. With his right hand, one by one, he bent the fingers down.

'Confession one, Juanita Carberry. Confession two, Marie Waterhouse. Confession three, Broughton's old racing friend. Three independent confessions. A most interesting story, is it not? But James Fox was not the only person to whom Juanita Carberry revealed her secret. According to the writer of another book on the subject, Juanita Carberry had already described the events of that day in Nyeri to her as early as 1977. And Miss Carberry narrates much the same story in her own autobiography – this last book published only eleven years ago.

'So, ladies and gentlemen, Sir Jock Delves Broughton may have been found not guilty of murder by a jury of his peers, but it was he who had the motive, he who had the means, and he who later confessed – on at least three separate occasions – to that dark deed. It was he who killed Lord Erroll. Your Honour, I rest my case.'

A moment's silence was followed by a burst of applause during which Tiger Singh leaned towards him.

'Mr Patel – you should have been a Queen's Counsel.'

Mr Patel smiled.

'Thank you, Tiger – praise indeed. Let's see A.B. get out of that.'

The Tiger stood up.

'I think we all agree that Mr Patel has presented a most persuasive – and, may I say, eloquent – argument. Though the confessions he describes would not necessarily be admissible as evidence in a court of law, I must remind you – and myself – that this is not a court of law. It is simply a debate. I would now like to introduce to you Mr Gopez who is, if I am not mistaken, ready to sow one or two small seeds of doubt in your minds.'

10

The lion does not approach the buffalo from the front, the zebra from the back or the snake from any side

Mr Gopez stood.

'Thank you, Tiger. Ladies, fellow members. My good friend Mr Patel has already told you that the journalist James Fox unearthed evidence that Sir Jock Delves Broughton made three confessions to the crime of murdering Lord Erroll – one while he was in Kenya, and two more after returning to England. What he neglected to point out is that the confessions differed in small but important details. For instance, Juanita Carberry said that Broughton told her he'd thrown the gun into the Chania Falls. According to the journalist James Fox, however, Broughton's later confession to his old friend Marie Waterhouse included the detail that after the murder he gave the pistol to a friend to hide. To his old horse-racing acquaintance in England he said he had not himself pulled the trigger but had arranged and paid for the murder on behalf of a third party – a man called Derek. So you see, ladies and gentlemen, three confessions – but three different stories.'

Mr Patel stood up.

'With your permission, Tiger, I would like to point out that the journalist interviewed each of these people many years after they heard Broughton's confession. Any differences between their accounts can simply be put down to the effects of time on memory.'

'Of which, I am sure, many of us are all too aware, Mr Patel. But shall we let Mr Gopez continue?'

'Thank you, Tiger,' said Mr Gopez. 'Now, with Mr Patel's permission, I would like to ask *you* a question.'

The Tiger raised an enquiring eyebrow.

'In your long and distinguished career in the law, have you ever come across a case of someone confessing to a crime they did not commit?'

Tiger Singh nodded.

'I have indeed, Mr Gopez.'

'And leaving aside confessions made under threat or coercion, is it not the case that the more serious the crime, the more likely it is that someone will falsely confess?'

'In serious crimes – such as murder, for instance – I can almost guarantee one or more people will turn up at the lawyer's office or the police station falsely claiming to be the culprit.'

'Thank you, Tiger.'

'Mr Gopez, I think you will have to explain to the jury – the audience – the relevance of this phenomenon to the subject of this debate.'

'Certainly, Tiger, I will be pleased to.'

Mr Gopez turned again to the audience.

'Many of you will be aware of the legal principle of double jeopardy. Briefly stated – and I'm sure the Tiger will correct me if I stray too far from the correct definition – it is a principle enshrined in law which prevents a person from being tried twice for the same crime. I bring up this point because, as I think you will see, it has a strong bearing on the case under discussion.'

The Tiger again nodded but said nothing.

'Let us get back to Sir Jock Delves Broughton,' said Mr Gopez. 'Let us examine the character of the man. An Englishman, he inherited a fortune from his father but by the time he arrived in Kenya in 1940 he had lost most of it through gambling and other wanton extravagances. He avoided fighting in the First World War by claiming to have suffered sunstroke as his regiment was leaving for France. Many people thought he faked it. I ask you, ladies and gentlemen, does this sound like a bold man, a man who would not hesitate to shoot a rival dead? No, it is a picture of a weak man, a cowardly man. And Broughton was not only weak in spirit but in body – a car accident many years before had left him with a limp and a crippled right hand. Yet because of lack of any other evidence, this is the man who, it is claimed, climbed down a drainpipe from an upstairs room in the dead of night, crept unseen into a car, shot a man, manhandled the corpse, ran a mile back to the house and climbed up the drainpipe without being seen. This is the man who on the tenth of March 1941 was charged with the murder of Lord Erroll.'

Mr Gopez paused to survey the audience.

'Now let me, if you will, indulge in a little specula-tion. Broughton denies the charge and is acquitted. He knows about double jeopardy – with no new evidence he cannot be charged with the same offence. But at the same time he has come to realize that murder, shooting a man – especially, if I may say so, a lord of the realm, the Hereditary Lord High Constable of Scotland, no less – is quite a glamorous crime. Indeed, he can hardly fail to be aware of this – the trial made headlines for weeks in newspapers throughout the world. Add to this the fact that Lord Erroll was thought by many to be a cad and a bounder, and that there were many people in Kenya who were quite pleased to see him dead – why, that made killing him almost seem like a selfless act of public service. If Broughton can somehow make people think that he did it and managed to get away with it, think how he will rise in their estimation. What a clever fellow, what a brave chap that Broughton is. Hooray for Broughton.'

'Let me get this clear, Mr Gopez,' said Tiger Singh. 'You are suggesting that Broughton did not murder Lord Erroll, but later – for reasons of self-aggrandizement or bravado – claimed to have done so?'

'I raise the matter as a distinct possibility.'

'But if Broughton didn't really kill Lord Erroll, Mr Gopez, then who did?'

'That, my dear Tiger – ladies and gentlemen – is what we shall now explore.'

Mr Gopez again turned to his audience.

'If not Broughton, ladies and gentlemen, then who? Long after the crime, long after the suicide of Broughton himself, another person confessed. It happened in 1966 at the Muthaiga Club, the very place where Lord Erroll had first met Diana Broughton. Twenty-five years after the murder and the trial, four people were sitting round a table at the club playing cards. One was the Managing

Director of the *Sunday Nation*. Also at the table was Diana – who by her fourth marriage had now become Lady Delamere, no less. Though the room was cool, the Managing Director was sweating. Two weeks earlier his paper had printed a piece by an investigative reporter which clearly stated his belief that Diana was the murderer. The law says that you are not allowed to call someone a murderer in print – it is gross libel. The Editor had managed to pull the story before the second edition, but the Managing Director had been in daily dread of a letter from Diana's lawyer ever since. Finding himself seated next to her at the card table, he thought that perhaps it might not be too late to apologize. He had hardly begun when Diana interrupted him. "Oh," she said, "everyone knows I did it."'

In front of the packed audience in the dining room of the Asadi Club Mr Patel again rose to his feet.

'Look, A.B., how many times do I have to tell you? What she said – if she said it – was no more than an ironic joke.'

Mr Gopez turned towards him. He smiled his biggest smile.

'Patel, I completely agree with you.'

Mr Patel sat down as if he had been pushed. Mr Gopez paused and leaned forward, both hands resting flat on the table in front of him.

'As any detective will tell you, ladies and gentlemen, the investigation of a crime always starts with what might be called the big five – who, what, when, how and why? But there is a sixth question. Sometimes we not only need to know why this person did what they did, but why is this person telling me about it? With that in mind, let us look again at the confession of Sir Jock Delves Broughton to Juanita Carberry. We have heard much about him, but what about her?'

Mr Gopez picked up a book from the table.

'From her own autobiography we learn that this fifteen-year-old girl had already suffered much in life. Her father John Carberry was a sadist and a bully – known to local Africans as *Msharisha*, after the long whip he used freely on both animals and men. Her mother had died in a plane crash when she was three, her stepmother June was one of the most notorious of the so-called Happy Valley set of the time – free, with her husband's apparent connivance, to indulge her tastes in extramarital sex, drink and drugs. This was the early world of Juanita Carberry. June encouraged the adolescent Juanita to smoke cigarettes and wear make-up, so perhaps it was no surprise when Juanita revealed in her memoir that by the time she was fifteen she was – how may I put it? – already a woman. Indeed, for more than a month before the murder she was being locked in her bedroom every night at the farm at Nyeri after being caught with a soldier in her bed.'

Mr Gopez paused to allow the mixture of shocked gasps and shocked laughter to fade.

'Yes, and a few months after the murder of Lord Erroll she ran away from her father and stepmother to live with her uncle. But let us return to Juanita's account of the days before and after the murder – not the one that she gave to James Fox or to later writers, but the one she gives first-hand, the one in her autobiography. In essence it is this. At the time of the murder she is at home in Nyeri – a good three-hour drive away from Nairobi. Her stepmother June is staying with the Broughtons near Nairobi at their house in Karen, her father is overseas. On hearing by telegram of the death of Lord Erroll, whom she had never met, she and her governess drive from Nyeri to Karen. Here at lunch she meets for the first time Broughton and Diana. While going for a walk in the garden with the avuncular Broughton to see his horses she notices on a smouldering bonfire some half-burned gym shoes. She drives back to Nyeri with June and Diana. A couple of days later Broughton turns up and, finding her alone, confesses that he killed Erroll and has just thrown the gun into the waterfall at Thika. He then tells her how he had hidden in Erroll's car and shot him when the car slowed down at the road junction. Feeling sorry for him because of his wife's affair – everybody, it seems, knew about the affair – she decides to tell no one of this confession.'

Mr Gopez paused. Through the open windows of the club dining room could be heard the noises of the night. Inside the room, silence – no laughter now.

'Now, let us compare this with the account Juanita gave to James Fox some years earlier. In most ways the story is the same, but in her earlier version there is an additional element. You may remember that when Lord Erroll was found dead in his car by the milk delivery drivers that dark and rainy night, the armstraps usually attached to the inside of the roof were lying on the back seat. Juanita had a theory about this. She told Fox that on the day before the murder she had visited the hairdresser in Nairobi with

June and Diana. They had gone in Erroll's car, and she was sure that at that time the armstraps were in place. Her theory was that Broughton had shot Erroll from the back seat while the car was moving. He'd then grabbed the straps as the car ran off the road, pulling them off when the car crashed.'

Mr Gopez held up the book that was still in his hand.

'In her autobiography, you may remember, Juanita Carberry said something slightly different. She said that when she arrived at the Broughtons' house at Karen on the morning after the shooting she had never met Diana. Here she is saying that the day before that she went to the hairdresser in Nairobi with Diana and June. So, had Juanita Carberry met Diana before, or hadn't she? Was she in Nyeri on the day before the murder, or was she in Karen?'

Mr Gopez put the book back down on the table.

'It was while considering these interesting inconsistencies that the question occurred to me – the sixth question. Why, I began to wonder, why after keeping the secret of Broughton's confession for over forty years, did Juanita Carberry at last decide to tell other people? I think I have already demonstrated that Juanita's version of events is sometimes contradictory, and I've raised the possibility that she may not always have been telling the truth. This made me think, ladies and gentlemen. What if the whole story of the confession was not the truth? What if Broughton had not, on the way to the stables at Nyeri, told her that he killed Lord Erroll? But why make up such a story? The simplest answer was that she wanted to hide something, to divert attention from what really hap-

84

pened that night in January 1941. She wanted to protect someone – but who?'

Mr Gopez again leaned forward over the table.

'Ladies and gentlemen. I suggest the person Juanita Carberry wanted to protect was none other than herself.'

The snake smiles before it strikes

Mr Gopez had to allow several minutes for the tumult caused by his words to die down.

'Now,' he said, 'with our adjudicator's permission, allow me to share with you what really happened that night.'

Tiger Singh rose to his feet.

'In a court of law, Mr Gopez, I would have raised several objections by now. But in the spirit of this debate, and looking at the rapt faces in front of us, I cannot but let you continue.'

Mr Gopez bowed his thanks and turned once more to face the audience.

'As she let slip to James Fox, Juanita Carberry *was* staying at the Broughton house at Karen on the night of the murder. Like June Carberry, she would have heard Erroll and Diana arrive back from the dance. Slipping on her gym shoes and taking one of her father's guns that she had brought with her from Nyeri – you will remember that he was away at the time so she knew it would not be missed – she climbed out of the bedroom window. While the two lovers were taking their leave, she concealed herself in the back of the Buick – just as she later claimed Broughton had done. And just as she said Broughton had done, she waited until the car slowed down at the junction and shot him. As the car veered across the road she grabbed at the armstraps, which came away in her hand. That was another slip she made – how else could she know what happened to those armstraps? She switched off the car engine and made her way back to the house unseen.'

'An interesting and by no means impossible theory, Mr Gopez,' said the Tiger. 'You have certainly raised and answered an important question – why did the girl tell? But you have not yet answered one of your "big five" questions, perhaps the most important one. You have not told us *why* she killed Lord Erroll. You have not given us a motive.'

'It is simple. Juanita was an attractive girl. She was sexually precocious and clearly fond of men. Perhaps she found Erroll as attractive as so many other women did. She approached him and was rebuffed. If she couldn't have him, she could at least make sure that no other woman could. It has happened often enough before. Or perhaps the reverse. He made an unwelcome pass at her – or went even further. In her anger she killed him.'

Mr Patel rose to speak.

'All very interesting, I'm sure. But, A.B. old chap, this is pure speculation.'

'Speculation, my dear Patel, which just happens to fit the facts. You have proposed your theory. I have proposed mine. Shall we leave it to the audience to decide which is true?'

Who would you have voted for? I must admit that Mr Patel made a very strong case for Broughton's guilt, and even though I noticed a few discrepancies that he tried to brush under the debating carpet, he certainly had style. On the other hand, you may have been impressed with the way in which A. B. Gopez first demolished the opposing theory and then came up with a counter-theory – even if it was somewhat, shall we say, imaginative. As for first bringing up the Diana confession and then agreeing with his opponent to dismiss it, that was a very nice touch. Judging from the general hubbub after Mr Gopez sat down, much the same thoughts were being entertained and discussed by the audience. It took some time for the adjudicator to call the meeting to order.

'Ladies, gentlemen – quiet, please,' said Tiger Singh for the second time. 'You have heard the arguments from our two esteemed speakers. It is now my task to sum up each of them, and then to call for a vote. Mr Patel has said that, despite the acquittal of Sir Jock Delves Broughton in a court of law, his subsequent confessions to the murder of Lord Erroll leave no doubt that he was the guilty party. Mr Gopez has explained that these confessions may have been the result not of guilt but of bravado. He has also suggested that certain irregularities in the statements of another person, Juanita Carberry, lead to the conclusion that not only did she fabricate the story of Broughton's confession to her, but that she was herself the murderer. I will now ask you to vote. All those who support Mr Patel, please raise your hands.'

The Tiger counted and wrote down the number.

'All those who support Mr Gopez, please raise your hands.'

A second number was written beside the first. The

Tiger looked over his glasses towards the expectant crowd.

'As might be expected in a debate of this nature and with debaters of this calibre, the count is a close one. The result is as follows. Mr Patel, forty-one votes. Mr Gopez . . .' he paused. 'Mr Gopez, forty-two.'

Mr Malik was the first to congratulate both parties on their inspired performances.

'Yes,' said Tiger Singh, 'I would not like to come up against either one of them in a court of law. But I noticed that you didn't vote, Malik – didn't want to offend either party, I suppose.'

'No, not so much that,' said Mr Malik. He paused. 'It's just there are some aspects of the whole thing that still worry me. But as I say, it's all in the past now – as I feel sure is the dispute between our two friends. Let me again thank you all for stepping into the breach. I don't think even a lecture on Nairobi's water supply could have attracted such a crowd. Now, if you'll excuse me, I should go home. Early start in the morning, you know.'

'Sure you wouldn't like to stay for another billiard lesson?'

Mr Malik turned to the figure who had just appeared behind him.

'Oh, hello, Harry. I wasn't expecting you tonight.'

'I've been out to dinner at Tusks – just business – so I thought I'd drop by on my way back into town. So, what do you say, Jack, how about a game?'

'Now, Harry, we really must let Malik go,' said the Tiger. 'It is indeed a busy day tomorrow – the club safari, you know. Which reminds me, Malik. I'm going to have to be in court again tomorrow morning. I'm afraid the case I've taken on is lasting longer than expected – in fact, I've still got a bit of work to do on it tonight. Don't keep a place for me on the coach. I'll drive up in the afternoon and join you there.'

'What about you guys?' said Harry Khan, turning to the other two. 'Can I buy you a drink?'

'Not for me, thanks, Harry,' said Mr Patel. 'It's been quite a night.'

'You missed an excellent debate,' said Tiger Singh.

'Oh yeah, right – the debate. Well, what about you, A.B.?'

'Just a nightcap perhaps, Harry. Though sweet be victory, it is sometimes rather thirsty work.'

It turned out that after so closely fought a contest Mr Gopez needed not one restorative but three, and in the course of consuming them he was interested to discover that Harry had had a very busy day. Not only had he met the Minister for the Interior that morning, but that evening he'd been dining with the Minister of Transport.

'Oh really? He lives round here, you know, just over the back fence as a matter of fact. Once tried to persuade us – the club, I mean – to sell him some land. Nothing came of it, of course. Didn't I read something about him and his secretary in the *Evening News* yesterday?'

'Yeah, but he explained it to me. Seems like some kind of spider or insect fell down her dress and he was just trying to help her get it out. But he's still not sure how the photographer got there.' Harry chuckled. 'Those guys, they sure don't like that newspaper – and boy would they all like to get hold of that Dadukwa guy. But from what

I've been told, the *Evening News* will be closing down any day. Anyway, got to go. Have fun on that safari.'

By the time Harry Khan arrived at his hotel the several clocks above the reception desk revealed that, while the sun was rising over the Sydney Opera House, it was approaching midnight in Dubai and most of the office workers of New York were looking forward with mixed feelings to the subway ride home. On his way past the Jockey Bar he did notice an attractive woman in tight-fitting jeans sitting by herself, and thought perhaps a final nightcap might not be such a bad idea, but he had second thoughts when he saw her being joined by a tall man carrying two long glasses of what appeared to be ginger beer. As he changed direction and headed for the lift, he heard the woman thanking the tall man.

'My pleasure, Petula,' said the man.

12

The chameleon does not dance before the snake,
nor the beetle before the chameleon

Isn't that good news? Petula's fiancé Salman has managed to get some extra time off. He must have taken the afternoon flight from Dubai and Petula has picked him up from the airport after her CI meeting. Perhaps he has already checked into the hotel, and the two love birds are enjoying a drink together before a night on the town – or somewhere more private perhaps.

Actually, no.

Salman, I have to reveal, is still sitting at his desk in his office on the thirty-second floor of the TransAsia building in downtown Dubai. He is double-checking the week's spreadsheets, and by the look of them he will soon be burning the midnight oil (of which, despite all Salman's long hours, Dubai still has a reasonable supply). You will be pleased to hear, though, that this is not too much of a chore, for Salman has always loved figures – especially when those figures represent large sums of dollars, euros, pounds or yen. But if Petula's fiancé is still in Dubai then who, I hear you ask, is this other chap – this tall, rather good-looking chap – sitting next to her in the Jockey Bar of the Hilton Hotel late on a Thursday night in downtown Nairobi?

'Yes, but where do you start?'

The tall man put down his glass.

'The way I look at it is this. It's no good just trying to tackle the problem from the top down, and it's no use just trying to do it from the grass roots up. We have to attack corruption at every level.'

'But aren't we just whistling in the wind?' said Petula. 'Surely poverty is the real problem.'

'I can't argue that poverty and crime aren't connected. Just as poverty leads to crime, crime – and I'm including corruption here, of course – surely leads to poverty. Look at this country. Nominal per capita annual income less than eight hundred dollars – by most standards that's pretty low. And within those figures, huge disparities of wealth. Corruption has to be one of the factors behind that.'

Petula sighed and nodded.

'Yes, I've been looking at CI's own figures. We're right up there with places like Paraguay and the Democratic Republic of the Congo. But how do you tackle it? I mean, take the police. They get paid a pittance. The only way an individual policeman can survive is on bribes and dodgy fines –'

'Most of which they have to pass up the ladder anyway.'

'Right, and we all know how far up that ladder reaches. Corruption has become an institution. So where do you start trying to dismantle it?'

'Remember what we were talking about at the meeting on Tuesday? Publicity. Let the people know who's taking the bribes – and not just the small ones. As I said, you've got to attack this on every level. How much does the average man in the street –?'

'Or woman . . .'

The man smiled.

'Or woman . . . have to pay every day? We're not just talking about direct bribes, but indirectly – in the things they have to buy.'

Petula nodded.

'People forget about that. Every time a matatu driver has to pay a bribe at a police roadblock, that puts the fare up.'

'Every time a butcher has to bribe the health inspector, up goes the price of meat.'

'So what are we going to do about it?'

They raised their glasses.

'Publicity!'

'And if I may say so,' continued Petula, 'I thought that point you raised at the end of the meeting was spot on. The internet has got to be the way to go. The government can try to gag the press as much as they like – I even heard a rumour that the *Evening News* is going to be shut down – but let's see them try to control the internet.'

'That's right,' said the man. 'Let's see them try.' He drained his glass. 'Another ginger beer?'

'Thanks, but I'd better get home.'

'What about another meeting tomorrow then – same time, same place?'

'Sorry. I promised to go with my dad on his club safari this weekend, and I have to be up early on Saturday. I'm meeting Salman – my fiancé – at the airport in the morning and we're driving up.'

The man smiled again.

'Sounds great. You know, that's one thing I really missed while I was away. Camping out under the stars, seeing all the wildlife.'

'Yes, of course. I forget you were born here. When they said our new director was coming from Geneva, I just assumed you were Swiss. How long have you been away?'

'That's kind of difficult to say. I started school here in Nairobi, at St Edward's, but I went away overseas to boarding school when I was thirteen – I came home for holidays, of course, but that was never for more than a few weeks at a time. Then college in the UK and then I joined the UN. I was working for them for eleven years – mostly in Geneva. I've always tried to come back to the old family home as often as I could – my mother still lives there.'

'Will you be moving back there then?'

The tall man smiled.

'She hasn't asked me, so I haven't had to say no. I think we both know that we're too old for that to work. But I've been looking forward to living in Nairobi again. It's one of the reasons I applied for the job.'

'So it's good to be home?'

'Good,' said the man with a grin, 'and getting better.'

Over the many years that he had been running the annual Asadi Club safari, Mr Malik had come to accept that no matter how many times you tell everyone that the coach will be leaving from the club car park at eight o'clock sharp, at least one of them will be late. Who would it be, he thought with an inward smile, this time? Would it be Shivraj Prasad, unable to find his sun hat or binoculars *anywhere*? Or, mused Mr Malik, would the youngest teenage child of the Dev family (what was her name?) once again refuse to get out of bed at so unearthly an hour? Perhaps, like last year, the coach would be kept waiting by Ali Hilaly's mother's missing medicine. In the end, it turned out to be Mrs Lakshmi (who forgot her pills and had to send her husband home to get them), but by eight thirty-five all of the twenty-two names had been ticked off the list. Mr Malik suffered a small moment of panic when another car pulled into the car park, but it was only two men from a painting firm come to give an estimate for redecorating the clubhouse – Mr Malik was pleased to see the manager had wasted no time. With some relief he climbed aboard the coach.

'Everybody ready?'

'No, no, just a minute.'

Mr Lakshmi whispered something to Mr Malik and scurried into the club. Three minutes later, as he climbed back inside, it was Mr Malik's turn to whisper something. After Mr Lakshmi had made the necessary sartorial adjustments, Mr Malik tried again.

'Everybody ready?' he repeated. 'Righty-ho. We're on safari.'

At these magic words the coach driver pulled the handle to close the door and released the big black brake lever. The coach crept slowly out of the car park of the Asadi Club into the Nairobi morning traffic.

'What about your daughter, Malik?' said Mr Patel from

the second row of seats. 'I thought you said she was coming with that fiancé of hers?'

'Petula – they – will be coming tomorrow,' said Mr Malik. 'Salman couldn't get the day off, but he'll be flying in from Dubai on the early flight. She's fetching him from the airport and they'll drive straight up.'

To travel from Nairobi to Meru there is little choice but to take the Thika road, known to generations of Kenyan drivers as Pothole Alley. Some potholes have now been there so long they have acquired affectionate nicknames – the Big Splash and Lake Victoria come to mind. Very occasionally they are filled in – if, for example, the President leaves Nairobi on one of his five-yearly 'meet-the-people' tours – but their location can still be identified, sometimes years later, by the way the traffic parts round an apparently smooth piece of road as the drivers automatically swerve aside to avoid the phantom pothole.

The going was good until just past Ruiru, where the coach had to squeeze past a broken-down truck right in the middle of the road. A few miles further on they came across an accident between two matatus. It seemed that at least a hundred people were sitting and standing beside the road – thank goodness, thought Mr Malik, that none of them seemed hurt. So it wasn't until eleven o'clock that the bus finally passed through the small town of Thika and crossed the Chania Falls.

Mr Patel leaned over A. B. Gopez to point at the still-swollen waters of the Thika River surging over the rocks below the bridge.

'It's still there, you know.'

'It? There? What?'

'The gun, the one that Broughton used.'

Mr Gopez turned to Mr Malik in the seat in front.

'Malik, old chap, remind me – what was that score last night?'

'Patel forty-one, Gopez forty-two. I say, look. Isn't that a hippo?'

'So it is,' said Mr Patel, gazing down at the water below. 'One down, four to go.'

'Now what are you talking about?' said Mr Gopez.

'The big five, of course, A.B. Elephant, rhino, hippo, lion and leopard.'

'Hippo? I've told you before, hippos are not one of the big five. Buffalo.'

'So you did, so you did. But still, hippos kill more people.'

'What do you mean, kill more people?' said Mr Gopez.

'That's what they do. In boats.'

'How, may I ask, do you get a hippopotamus into a boat?'

It was Mr Patel's turn to roll his eyes.

'Hippos in water, A.B. *People* in boats. The things swim underneath and tip them over. Then – chomp. Happens all the time, apparently. I read something about it in the *Evening News* just the other day.'

'Malik, would you mind telling Patel here that he's spouting balderdash? He seems deaf to my voice.'

Mr Malik, it has to be said, had not been following his friends' conversation with all due diligence, his thoughts not being on murders or hippos but on the surprise he had planned for the safari. If everything had gone according to plan, Benjamin should have it up and ready at the campsite by now.

'Hmm? What did you say, A.B.?'

'What would you say was the most dangerous animal in Africa?'

'Er . . . lions?'

'No, no, Malik. Your lion, it is generally accepted, is at heart a cowardly beast. Think harder.'

'Zebra!'

This ejaculation was uttered by neither Mr Patel nor Mr Malik but by young Imran Hilaly in the back of the bus, who thus claimed the traditional Asadi Club safari prize for spotting the first zebra of the trip. With some relief, Mr Malik excused himself, stood up and reached towards the luggage rack for the large tin of Jolly Man assorted bonbons.

13

The beetle on the elephant's back cannot say there
is no dew on the ground

The sight of Imran Hilaly demolishing four Cheetah
Chews and a Lion Licker had made Mr Malik feel a little
peckish. He looked at his watch. Yes, lunchtime. The
driver found a place to stop the coach under some thorn
trees beside the river, and everyone piled out. Tiffin packets were passed round – chapatti wraps, cutlets and
samosas – and Mr Malik opened a case of mixed sodas.

'Lemonade, cherry fizz or cola?'

'What, no beer?' said Mr Gopez.

'Mmmm,' said Mr Patel, swallowing a large bite of
samosa. 'I'd know Ally Dass's cooking anywhere. Plain
soda for me, please, Malik old chap. Have you booked
him for the wedding yet?'

'All arranged – mchuzi, marquee, mosque.'

'Mosque, eh?'

'Salman said he wouldn't mind temple but his family
wanted mosque. Petula doesn't seem to care one way or
the other.'

The thorn tree in whose shade they now sat was, Mr
Malik noticed, adorned with several weaver birds' nests,
each with an attendant male advertising its nuptial cre-

dentials with loud songs and vigorous waving of wings. From their black eye masks and dark backs Mr Malik recognized them as Baglafecht weavers. How long ago it seemed since he had last heard Rose Mbikwa say those words on the Tuesday morning bird walk – 'Bag-la-fecht weavers'. What had she seen while she had been away in Scotland? he wondered. In the 1960s he had spent two years in England but he had never crossed the border. Were there Scottish swans, Scottish sparrowhawks, Scottish skylarks?

Mr Malik gazed up past the thorn tree to the wide blue sky. High overhead flew a skein of birds – probably pelicans, he thought, on their way to Upper Reservoir. As if from nowhere a pair of black kites appeared and began circling above the coach. Amazing how even in an out-of-the-way place like this they could spot a picnic within minutes. He looked around. Everyone seemed to have finished their lunch packets and sodas. It was time to get back on the bus. Next stop – the equator. For just as it is a tradition on the Asadi Club annual safari that the first child to spot a zebra wins a prize, it is a tradition when heading north to stop at the equator to stretch the legs and watch water go down the plughole.

Though I cannot claim to have learned much from my Geography lessons at school, I arrived in Africa with the firm belief that the equator is an imaginary line around the earth equidistant from both poles. I wasn't much good at Science either, but I do remember our Physics master making a convincing case that, contrary to popular belief, the Coriolanus effect, while ensuring that large fluid systems on the scale of hurricanes and ocean currents tend to move clockwise in the southern hemisphere and anti-clockwise in the north, has no effect on the way the water turns as it goes down the plughole in the bath (or should that be the Coriolis effect? I fear English was not a strong subject either). On both counts I was wrong. The equator is in fact a white line drawn across the road just south of Meru, where you can find a dozen cheerful locals with buckets of water and small bowls ready to demonstrate for a few shillings that – look! On this side of the equator the water goes round this way. We step over the line, and – look! It goes round the other way.

'Of course, it's all nonsense,' said Mr Gopez once they were back on the bus. 'I tried it in my house once, all the baths and sinks and washbasins. Some went one way, some went the other. It's all to do with the plumbing, they tell me.'

'They do, do they?' said Mr Patel, sitting down beside him. 'Then it's a pity that "they" didn't tell you which is the most dangerous animal in Africa.'

'Buffalo,' said Mr Gopez.

'Hippo,' said Mr Patel.

'Oh, look,' said Mr Malik. 'Over there, near that bush. Isn't that a dik-dik?'

There is a story told in many parts of Africa about an elephant and the little antelope called the dik-dik. One day a dik-dik was trotting through the bush when it ran head first into a huge mound of fresh elephant dung. So fresh was the dung that the elephant who dropped it was still only a few feet away – and on seeing the dik-dik's distress, it burst into laughter. The dik-dik, though it may be small in others' eyes, is large in its own. Right, it thought, I'll show that elephant. Which is why even today the tiny dik-dik always deposits its dung all in one place. This may grow into a pile many feet tall, and the dik-dik is hoping that one day it will have made a pile big enough for the elephant to walk head first into. All of which was of some interest to Mr Malik, as the location chosen for the Asadi Club campsite was, according to the man at whose house he was now paying a courtesy call, prime dik-dik country.

'Dik-dik? Absolutely. Scores of 'em.'

'And elephants, Mr Johnson?'

'Tembo? Rather. Find dik-dik, and tembo won't be far away.'

Mr Malik looked around the room where he was now sitting. From what he had seen so far tembo seemed to be the only species of large mammal not represented by a stuffed and mounted head hanging on one wall or other of the sprawling bungalow.

'You are a hunter, Mr Johnson?'

'Hunting? Good God, no. Won't have a gun on the place. Know what you're thinking. All these animals, no guns – just dropped dead, did they? My father. Guns everywhere. Rifles, pistols, shotguns – even had a 1914 Lewis gun, tripod and all. Boy Johnson, last of the great white hunters. Meet a man, fight. Meet a woman, flirt. Meet an animal, fire. Lot of bloody good it did him. Got drunk, hit my mother. Savaged to death by his own bull mastiffs.'

He nodded towards one wall that must have contained the heads of twenty assorted big game. 'Too late for them. Still, old friends. Can't chuck 'em out, not now. Ever shot?'

'No, Mr Johnson, I myself have never held a gun.'

'Good. Live and let live.'

Mr Malik smiled.

'I must say that is my own belief.'

'Thought so. Like 'em alive, not dead. Asked young Hilary. Said you were a good sort.'

'Thank you. And as Mrs Fotherington-Thomas told me, this is indeed a beautiful place. It is most generous of you to let us stay here. I very much hope you will be able to join us for dinner one evening, Mr Johnson. Would tonight, perhaps, be suitable?'

'Better not. Beryl. Needs attention. Ha. You know what they're like.'

Mr Malik was sure Hilary Fotherington-Thomas had said that her friend was not married, but this clearly did not preclude other female company.

'Tomorrow perhaps?'

'Love to, but I've got a visitor. Old pal. Got to fetch him in the morning.'

'Then please bring your visitor.'

'Really? Splendid.'

'Are you picking him up from Meru? If I can be of any help . . .'

'Nairobi.'

'That is a very long drive.'

'Drive? No fear. I'll take Beryl. Following wind, just over an hour.'

It took Mr Malik a moment to work out what Dickie Johnson was talking about.

'You fly, Mr Johnson? You mean that Beryl is an aeroplane?'

'One of the best. Like to see the old girl?'

He led Mr Malik outside, to a large shed behind the bungalow. After some heaving and cursing the door was opened to reveal an old Land Rover and, beside it, a single-engined Piper Cherokee. Though Beryl was a little scratched and dented for Mr Malik's liking, he didn't say so. What he did say was that he hoped very much Mr Johnson would come the following night at six, and that he would bring his visitor.

'Excellent. Love to.'

'Now, if you will excuse me, I should be heading down to the campsite myself before it gets dark.'

'Like a lift?'

'No, please, I'd rather walk.'

'Good man. Only a mile or so. No buffalo, but watch out. By the river. Hippos. Dangerous beasts, hippos.'

'Indeed so,' said Mr Malik.

'Well, anything else, let me know.'

'Thank you, Mr Johnson. You are too kind.'

His host held out a hand.

'Good. Tomorrow then.'

By the time Mr Malik had made his way back to the campsite the sun was just setting. He found his friends already started on the beer and chilli popcorn, but before joining them there was one more person he had to see. He spotted him near the seventh tent.

'Ah, Benjamin, how did it go – all according to plan?'

'The surprise, you mean, Mr Malik? I had a little trouble with those very big screws – but then I read the instruction book, as you told me. I had forgotten that they must be turned against the clock. Now everything is fine.'

'Good. And the lamps?'

'All filled up and ready.'

'Excellent. Thank you, Benjamin.'

'We were just saying, Malik old chap, that this,' Mr Patel waved one hand around to encompass the campsite while using the other to hand Mr Malik a glass of beer, 'is a damned fine spot.'

The camp had been set up on a flat area of coarse sand beside a small lake, left behind when the nearby river had changed course. Shaded by thorn trees and surrounded by soft clumps of maru, the campsite already felt friendly. Ally Dass had set up his kitchen slightly away from the main camping area, but not so far that they could escape the smells of barbecued meat and simmering spices.

'Thank you, my friends,' said Mr Malik. 'I am so glad you like it. Now, Ally told me he'd have dinner ready by half past seven. That gives us just over an hour.' He looked over towards the seventh tent, then back towards his friends. 'So who's for a game?'

'What – cards, do you mean?' said Mr Gopez.

'Tiddlywinks?' said Mr Patel.

'No, not cards, and not tiddlywinks. Not even snakes and ladders. Come, follow me.'

Up he got and, without seeing who might be following

him, strode to the seventh tent. His friends were right behind. When he pulled back the flaps they were amazed to see, glowing green beneath the light of four hissing gas lamps, a full-sized twelve-foot billiard table.

'String for break, A.B.?' said Mr Malik.

14

When elephants fight it is mice that suffer

As the Tiger had surmised, the legal case of Hareesh vs Hareesh (no relation) for which H. H. Singh, LLB, MA (Oxon.) was engaged to represent the plaintiff had indeed taken longer than expected. What should have been a simple out-of-court settlement – after all, how much damages can a courier company expect to be awarded just because its business competitor decides to use the same shade of pink for its delivery bicycle? – had turned into a detailed and protracted argument about ethics, economics, family and justice. In the Tiger's experience it is seldom wise to raise the question of justice before a court, especially in a civil case. But as so often happens both plaintiff and defendant seemed determined to win at any cost, and there was nothing that either counsel – nor even the judge – could do about it. The Tiger could only be thankful that at twelve-thirty Judge Kafari decided to adjourn the case until the following Monday (Friday afternoon, as the Tiger was well aware, was the judge's golf afternoon). As soon as the Tiger was out of his wig and robes he phoned the garage to see if there was any news on his Range Rover.

*

When it comes to having a car repaired, Kenyan motorists have three basic options. The most expensive choice is to take your vehicle to the MORF, or Manufacturer's Official Repair Facility. Not only will a MORF almost certainly have the appropriate repair manual for your vehicle, but you can be reasonably sure that someone there will be able to read it. And while one can never be certain that spare parts used in a MORF are exactly as specified by the manufacturer (and not some cheap pirated copy thereof), said parts will probably do a fair approximation to the job required. The second choice is to go to your friendly local AVA – All Vehicles Accepted. There is no pretence here at using genuine new parts – second-hand parts are the norm. But you know that the savings are being passed on to the customer, and while the mechanic's overalls may not be spotless, each grease stain can be read as a badge of experience. Third on the list of choices is the *jua kali* – Swahili for 'hot sun'. Such repair facilities are common on the outskirts of every city and town throughout Kenya. They consist of a man standing beside the road with an adjustable wrench and what my friend Kennedy insists on calling an 'Irish screwdriver' – and when it comes to straightening a steering rod or unbending a side panel you'd be amazed just how much a clever and determined Kenyan can do with one spanner and a large hammer.

For the repair of the malfunctioning fuel pump on his Range Rover, Tiger Singh had put the vehicle into the capable hands of Rhapta Road Repairs – All Vehicles Accepted. The old fuel pump had come off easily enough, the manager assured him when he phoned, and the new one would be on 'in a jiffy'. He would call back the minute it was ready. By five o'clock that minute had still not come, and another phone call revealed that in fact the new pump had not yet arrived. Ah well, worrying about that would have to wait until the morning. Right now, what Tiger Singh needed was a drink. He was already on the street outside his chambers on Mama Ngina Street and about to raise an arm to hail a cab to take him to the Asadi Club when he heard a voice calling his name.

'Hey, Tiger!'

The voice seemed to be coming from a red Mercedes sports car that had just pulled up on the other side of the road. Its driver – brown-skinned, white-haired, wearing a white shirt unbuttoned far enough to show a large gold medallion – was waving to him in a most familiar way.

'Hey, Tiger – need a lift?'

Of course, it was Khan – Harry Khan. After looking both ways twice, then once again to make sure, the Tiger crossed the road.

'Hello, Khan old chap. Good to see you.'

'You too. So . . . can I give you a ride?'

'That's very kind of you. I was going to take a taxi over to the club – my car's being repaired.'

'The Asadi Club? Jump in.'

The Tiger opened the shiny red door and sank into the soft leather seat.

'In this baby I'll have you there in no time flat.'

Though in ideal conditions the Mercedes-Benz SL roadster that Harry Khan was driving can accelerate from 0 to 100 kph in about the time it takes to read this sentence, and you can be cruising at something over 200 kph very soon thereafter – not in Nairobi. A combination of a complete absence of road rules, and the frequent absence of what in other cities goes by the name of 'road', means that the duration of any journey in Nairobi is known only to the gods of traffic – and whether you are in a Mercedes or a Morris Minor seems to make very little impression on them. On this particular Friday evening the longest delay was caused by a couple of thulu boys, enterprising young men who adopt a pothole, fill it in, then cheerfully stand beside it soliciting payment for their public spirit from every motorist who passes. What with that, and the usually heavy traffic, it took Harry Khan and the Tiger a full forty minutes to cover the five kilometres from downtown Nairobi to the Asadi Club. By the time they had parked the car and pushed through the front door of the clubhouse, both were in need of a long drink.

'Where the hell is everybody?' said Harry, glancing to his left as they entered the bar. 'I don't remember ever seeing the billiard room empty when I was here last time.'

'Oh, didn't anyone tell you? The safari – the annual club safari. It's this weekend.'

'Safari? Oh yeah, sure. I remember.'

'I would have been there myself,' said the Tiger as they took their drinks from the bar to the table by the window, 'but I had to be in court this morning and my car's being fixed. Malik's found somewhere near Meru this year. I'm still hoping my car will be ready to drive up tomorrow. Anyway, Harry, you haven't told me yet what brings you to Nairobi – visiting the family again?'

'No, not this time. This time it's business.'

'Don't tell me the Khans are going to start up in Kenya

again. Does this mean we'll be seeing the old signs going up – "Khan's for Kwality"?'

Before selling up and moving to Canada – before the Idi Amin thing had blown up in Uganda – the Khan family had owned a string of general stores throughout East Africa. Their advertising signs were a common sight on hoardings from the coast to Kampala.

Harry Khan smiled and shook his head.

'I'm talking business with a capital B.' He patted his briefcase. 'Could be one of the biggest things to hit Nairobi for quite a while. I was telling the minister about it just yesterday.'

'Really? I'd have thought things were a bit, how shall we say – uncertain? – for investors here at the moment.'

Harry laughed.

'Yeah, well, that's Kenya. But now could be just the right time. Sure, confidence is down – but so are prices and costs. Me and my brothers are thinking this could be the moment for a smart guy to make a move.'

'And what exactly is the business you are suggesting?'

'Shopping centres, Tiger baby. Retail. I'm not talking about your Sarit centre or your UKAY. I'm talking big, I'm talking about something like Nairobi has never seen before.'

'Sounds impressive, Harry, and I dare say Kenya can do with all the investment it can get.' The Tiger raised his glass. 'Good luck to you.'

'Thanks, Tiger. But, believe me, it's nothing to do with luck. When I want to gamble, I go to Vegas. Planning, preparation, knowing how the system works – that's how you get things done.'

'So, the minister was . . . er . . . helpful?'

'The Honourable Brian Kukuya promised me his full cooperation. Like I always say – what Harry wants, Harry gets.'

The Tiger raised an eyebrow.

'And you promised him . . .?'

'Hey, no promises.' Harry Khan's smile widened. 'But I think you could say we understand each other.'

The Tiger was fairly sure he knew what Harry Khan meant. As happens everywhere in this world, the men with the power can use that power to be helpful or not helpful. If you wanted to get things done in Kenya (sometimes, as the Tiger well knew, even in the Kenyan court system), you had to play by their rules.

'I should warn you, though, Harry. I'm afraid ministers tend not to last very long in office at the moment.'

'Yeah, so I heard. This Dadukwa guy, right? I've met a few people out there who'd like to see *that* eagle grounded for good – though from what I've been hearing, the *Evening News* may not be around much longer anyway. But don't worry. Harry always keeps more than one iron in the fire.'

The Tiger nodded.

'So where will it be, this shopping centre?'

'That's one of the things I'm doing right now – scouting out sites. I've already got a couple of possibilities lined up. The other thing I'm trying to do is put together a local team. In fact, that's one of the reasons I'm pleased to be talking to you right now, Tiger,' continued Harry Khan. 'We'll be needing a lawyer – and from what I hear, you're the best.'

The Tiger held up his hands.

'Sorry, Harry, I'm flat out at the moment. Believe me, the last thing I need is more work. As I say, I would have been on the club safari right now, but I had to appear in court this morning, and then my car . . . Anyway, I'm not really sure it's my area. I could probably put you in touch with someone . . .'

'Come on, Tiger. Name your price.'

'It really isn't the money, Harry. I just don't have time for any more work.'

'OK, OK.' Harry Khan raised his glass. 'Cheers. I guess I'll just have to find some other way to persuade you. So, this safari. I guess old Jack'll be there, right?' Seeing the look of confusion on Tiger Singh's face, 'You know, Malik – that's what we used to call him at school.'

'Malik? Oh yes, he'll be there. He's arranged the whole caboodle.'

'You remember last time I was here – that bird thing?' Harry Khan looked down into his glass. 'I guess he really liked that broad. Anything come of it – him and Rose?'

'Not as far as I know.'

Harry Khan smiled.

'Then maybe I'll give her a call later. Her number should still be in my little old black book. But right now, how about another drink? And seeing how there's no one in that billiard room, what do you say to a game?'

It was the Tiger's turn to smile.

'For a small wager, perhaps?' he said.

15

The mongoose that hunts both mouse and squirrel
catches neither

'I say,' said Mr Patel.

'Golly-gosh,' said Mr Gopez.

Mr Malik entered the tent first. He slid open a shallow drawer at the side of the table to reveal a pair of five-foot wooden cues. From a smaller, deeper drawer he removed a set of three billiard balls. He placed the red one on a mark near the end of the table.

'So, A.B. – plain ball or spot?'

Mr Gopez realized that his mouth was still open.

'Er . . . plain, thanks,' he said, closing it.

Mr Malik passed him one of the two white balls. In the time-honoured fashion of billiard players the world over, each man placed his cue ball on the baulk line and hit it towards the top of the table. The one whose ball ended up closest to the bottom cushion would decide who should take first stroke in the match.

'Damn and blast!'

Mr Gopez, having won the string, attempted the classic safety shot of sending his cue ball up the table to hit the red at half-ball and bring them both down behind the baulk line. As you are not allowed to play backwards from the baulk line when your ball is in hand, this meant that Mr Malik would be forced to try an indirect shot off one of the cushions. But Mr Gopez misjudged his angles. Though his own ball ended up behind baulk, the red ball rolled to a stop only inches below the middle pocket.

'This table of yours is all very fancy, but are you sure it's level?'

After bringing his opponent's attention to the four built-in spirit levels with which the table came equipped, Mr Malik was able to sink his cue ball off the red into the middle pocket with little difficulty. And he judged the strength of the shot well. The red ball came to rest nicely positioned for a straight pot into the left-hand top pocket.

'Seems pretty level to me, A.B.'

Mr Malik took the red ball from the pocket and put it back on its spot. Another pot, perhaps?

It took a full forty minutes for the first player to reach 101 and so take the game – that player being, in this case, Mr Malik. He felt he had never played so well. By the time he had made the winning stroke, quite a crowd had gathered round the table and many comments and congratulations were being given to him.

'Well done, Malik,' said Mr Gopez, shaking him by the hand. 'You certainly seem to be on form tonight. Those spirit levels, though – are you *sure* they're all right?'

The dinner gong sounded.

'Yes, A.B.,' said Mr Malik. 'Positive. Benjamin, would you mind turning down the lights? Now, let's see if Ally's food tastes as good as it smells, shall we?'

*

By any gastronomic measure the first camp dinner was a triumph. From his eight-burner gas range and an assortment of pots and pans Ally Dass had coaxed great bowls of spicy beef pasanda and fragrant dahi wala, tender rogan josh gosht and lamb bhuna. His undui featured vegetables all the colours of the rainbow, while the perfume that wafted from the alu chole and tarka dhal and mountains of steaming basmati rice made mouths water and lips smile in anticipation of each and every mouthful. From the clay tandoori half buried in the river sand and fired up with wood from the nearby fever trees the master chef pulled kebabs sizzling by the score – prawn, fish, meatballs – then whole chickens on long spits, including his famous murgh hariyali (which had been marinating in its sauce all the way from Nairobi). And still he found room in that oven for more nan breads than fifty hungry people could eat.

'Delicious, quite delicious,' said Mr Gopez, adding the last kebab stick to the pile beside his plate. 'That chicken was – well, words fail me.'

'Ah,' said Mr Patel, wiping his hands on a napkin, 'the simple life. It's a pity the Tiger isn't here – you know how he likes a good undui. Damned shame . . . that legal case of his must have taken longer than he expected.'

Mr Gopez sighed and agreed how good it was to get away from the old hustle and bustle – to which Mr Patel replied that was no way to refer to one's wife. Mr Malik put down his napkin and pushed back his chair.

'Well, chaps, might I suggest we see if the billiard table is free? As A.B. said earlier, I may well be on form. Yes, I'm sorry the Tiger isn't here yet – tonight I think

I might give even our club champion a run for his money.'

The game between Harry Khan and Tiger Singh at the Asadi Club was soon over.

'How about the best of three?' said Harry. 'One game just doesn't seem fair.'

The best of three turned into the best of five. By the time they were finished, the club was empty. Harry insisted on dropping his opponent home before driving back to the Hilton. They made their way out of the front door towards the car park to find the manager outside, admiring the red Mercedes.

'Beauty, isn't she?' said Harry. 'Want to go for a spin?'

The manager nodded.

Harry patted his pockets.

'Whoops, looks like I left my keys inside somewhere. Hey, I remember – they're in my briefcase. I must have left it in the bar. Wouldn't want to forget that.' It took him only minutes to retrieve his case and keys and reappear at the front door. Closing it behind him, he skipped back down the steps. 'OK. Who wants a ride round the block?'

'Excuse me, sir,' said the manager. 'Did you just close the door?'

Harry looked behind him.

'Close it? Sure, I think so.'

'Ah,' said the manager. 'Then there is a problem, sir. My keys, my door keys, they are inside.'

'You mean you can't get in? But what about the back door?'

'The kitchen staff are gone, sir. The door will be locked.'

'Don't worry,' said Tiger Singh. 'The club president always has a spare set and it just happens I'm club president. I'll just pop home and –'

The Tiger was about to say that he'd bring the keys back when he realized that he was without a car.

'Hey,' said Harry Khan, 'no problem.'

He was able to persuade both men that it would be a simple matter for him to take Tiger Singh home, pick up the keys and bring them to the manager at the club. Within half an hour, having delivered the keys and declined the manager's offer of a nightcap before he left, he was back at the Hilton. On his way to his room Harry thought he might take a quick look in the Jockey Bar. Perhaps that woman would be there again. Perhaps this time she'd be alone.

16

When the squirrel argues with the monkey, it
should not ask the baboon to act as judge

Rose Mbikwa awoke to see the early sunshine streaming
in through the bedroom window. Outside a bird was
singing a familiar song. An olive thrush? A Cape robin?
Or was it a bulbul? Silly, she just couldn't remember.
Never mind. Surely what was important was to hear the
song and enjoy it, not to know what kind of bird was
making it. There had been a time, early on in her birdwatching days, when the most important thing to her by
far was seeing a new kind of bird – the rarer the better.
These days she found herself taking as much pleasure
in watching a sparrow as a Prince Ruspoli's turaco. For
several minutes she lay awake, luxuriating in the sweet
sound of the unknown bird and the feeling of being
back home in her own bed. But there were things to do.
She got up and pulled on her dressing gown. Breakfast
– and after breakfast she might even try to set up her
new computer.

'Good morning, Mother. Will you join me?'

She had forgotten Angus had said he might drop in for
breakfast. He gestured to the second seat at the table on
the veranda and continued attending to his toast.

'Thank you, dear,' said Rose, sitting down opposite him. 'I see you found the honey.'

Since childhood Angus had always been fond of the dark Ogiek honey from the Mau Forest, and as soon as Rose had told Elizabeth that he was coming back to Kenya she had gone out to the market to buy a brand new jar.

'Mmm.' He took a bite from his toast. 'And it's great to have proper Kenyan coffee again. Can I pour you some?'

As she watched him fill the second cup, she could hear the song of that bird again from the jacaranda tree behind her.

'How did it go at the new office yesterday?'

'OK,' said Angus through another mouthful of toast. 'Still trying to get the phone lines and internet sorted out – though I don't suppose I've got much hope of getting anything done on a Saturday. I'd forgotten how long these things take in Kenya.'

'Yes, I was lucky the phone line's still on here. I thought I'd try and hook up my new computer this morning – goodness knows what the connection speed will be like.'

'Need a hand?'

'No, thank you, dear. I've been getting quite good at this computer business recently, you know.'

Which was true. Before she left Kenya to look after her father, Rose had never owned a computer. But life was quiet back at the old house in Edinburgh with mostly just the two of them there. Why not try connecting with the world through the internet? Rose bought herself a desk-top machine and was surprised to find that she took to the whole thing like a duck to water. She soon mastered the software, and within days she knew her ethernet from her wi-fi and her USBs from her scuzzies and could defrag a disk in a matter of moments. She'd even added extra RAM to her computer all by herself. It was all rather fun.

'Are you sure you won't come with me to the Thanandu this afternoon?' said Angus. 'I'm sure there'll be room, and I know Uncle Dickie would love to see you.'

'No, no, I expect I'll make it another time. Besides, I've already got a date tonight with a friend. I don't think you've met Harry, have you – Harry Khan?'

At the campsite of the annual Asadi Club safari, day did not dawn so bright.

'Where's the bloody mountain gone?'

Mr Malik poked a sleepy head out of the tent. The view to the west was not, he had to admit, promising. Where yesterday Mount Kenya had loomed on the horizon like the head of a white-haired giant, he could now see only a thick bank of cloud, dark as dusk.

No one is quite sure how Mount Kenya acquired its name. Was it from the Kikuyu word *Kirinyaga* – shining mountain? Did it come from the Embu word *Kirenia* – mountain of white? But soon after Dr Johann Ludwig Krapf clapped his missionary eyes on the mountain in 1849 and recorded its name in writing, it became generally known as Mount Kenya (pronounced Keen-ya) and in 1920 the surrounding part of the British East African Protectorate was christened the Kenya Settlement. The mountain also gave its name to a man.

Kamau wa Ngengi was born in 1894, in a small village not far from an uninhabited swamp that would five years later be the site of a supply depot for the Mombasa to Uganda railway. By the time he finished school the supply depot had become Nairobi. Kamau found work as an office clerk in town and soon became a rising star in local politics. His friends and colleagues sent him to England, where he studied at the London School of Economics and lobbied for African rights. By the time he came to write a book based on his academic thesis he had chosen a new name – Jomo Kenyatta. When his country became independent in 1963 he became its first prime minister and, one year later, its first president. The new nation was named after the mountain: it was pronounced, like his name, Ken-ya. And just as the shadow of Mount Kenya reaches for miles around it, so Jomo Kenyatta's influence on his country is still felt more than thirty years after his death.

'Oh, just a bit of dry-season mist, A.B.' said Mr Malik. 'I'm sure it'll burn off when the sun's up.'

He looked at his watch and yawned. He had not slept well – but on the first night on safari he never did. He could always blame it on the unfamiliar bed or the sound of his companions snoring, but it was not that. He had slept well in many an unfamiliar bed and would do so tonight. And though the sound of one person snoring may not be conducive to a good night's sleep, Mr Malik always found that a chorus of snoring (to which, he liked to think, he would contribute a harmonious baritone if he could only drop off) could be quite soporific. No, he just never slept well on the first night under canvas, and that was that. He had to lie there awake, and let his mind wander where it willed.

Though it had tall mountains and thick forests and the wide unfenced savannah to roam through, that night his mind kept coming back to two things. One was the wedding of his daughter Petula. What if it rained? Would there be enough food? Was the marquee big enough? Was everything all right between Petula and Salman? The second subject to which his recalcitrant mind returned was the murder of Lord Erroll. A.B.'s ingenious and innovative explanation was so much more convincing than any he'd yet come across – but still something didn't seem quite right. The frustrating thing about all this was that both he and his mind knew that thinking about these things would not provide any answers. He would find out from Petula tomorrow the state of play with the wedding, and no new facts about the Erroll case were about to appear out of the thin air of mere thought. But admonish it as he might, his mind would just not let go of the subjects, and it was a tired and slightly grumpy Mr Malik who sat down next morning at the breakfast table.

The Mr Malik who arose from the table was a different man. Ally Dass had once more worked his culinary magic. A selection of fresh fruit – bananas (three varieties), pineapples, pawpaw and slices of sweet mango – had begun Mr Malik's transformation. A cup of hot Nescafé and a plate of string hoppers with chopped chillies and fried garlic – an innovation to the breakfast menu which Ally Dass had picked up from a Sri Lankan cook he had been introduced to at the Nairobi races the previous November – completed the transformation.

Mr Gopez was feeling similarly restored.

'Ready for a spot of "find-the-fauna", Malik?' he said.
'Ready, A.B.? Abso-jolly-lutely.'

Over the many years he had been going on safari, Mr Malik had come to the conclusion that there are basically two ways to find animals – you go to them, or you let them come to you. The trouble about going to them is that you are so busy trying to see where you're going that you don't have much time to look around. Not only that, you're making so much noise that most animals either hide or scarper. But sit still in one place, stay quiet, and though the local fauna will be sure to notice your presence, they may eventually decide that you look harmless enough and start going about their normal business. Does this not lessen your chances of spotting species? you may wonder. Surely the more ground you cover, the more different creatures you will see?

My friend Kennedy once told me that on a trip to the US, a few years ago, he met a chap who was very fond of running. Few weeks went by when his name didn't appear in the paper as the man who had just run from X to Y, or Y to Z (where X, Y and Z were always several hundred and often more than a thousand miles apart). When my friend met him, he had just run from Amarillo to Salt Lake City (the hard way) and was getting ready for the main event – a trot to Fresno across Death Valley and the Sierra Nevada. He had become known as the Power Runner. After some thought, and by steady application, my friend Kennedy developed a less strenuous version of this activity – and while Power Sitting may not have quite the cardiovascular advantages of its more vigorous counterpart, he claims it is much easier on the shoe leather and very much easier on the knees. It is also excellent for watching wildlife.

For you don't just power sit anywhere, you choose your position with care. The first essential is good visibility. Two birds in the bush will always be worth less than a bird in the hand if you are in the bush too. In front of the bush or beside it is where you want to be – and if the bush happens to be in flower or fruit, so much the better. Secondly, a certain level of comfort – while not essential – is desirable. Perching on one buttock on a rock, or hanging from the branch of a tree, is not Power Sitting (though while a flat rock is preferable to a pointed one, and a smooth log beats a knobbly one, the use of cushions is to be discouraged – the nodding head and the drooping eyelid are not conducive to wildlife watching). Thirdly, my friend Kennedy insists it is best to power sit alone. We humans are social animals and it is hard to keep quiet in company. But conversation is for comfy chairs and coffee shops. The true Power Sitter, though not wishing to be taciturn, tends to silence. Anyway, try it somewhere near where you live – and if you aren't satisfied with the result, my friend Kennedy will give a full refund, no questions asked.

Safari operators, I have found over the years, are in general not in favour of the practice – and who can blame them? You don't make your money by telling someone to go and sit on a rock. What you tell them is that they need to drive around the wide savannah in an open-topped van, fly over it in a light plane or drift over it in a hot-air balloon and that will be eighteen hundred and twenty-five dollars per person thank you very much. But when it comes to sitting still and watching, Mr Malik is of the same opinion as my friend Kennedy. So while the three minibuses head off from the campsite in search of the big five, plus however many of the smaller species of African animal are out and about and visible after breakfast on this particular Saturday morning, we find Mr Malik strolling towards the river, trusty Bausch & Lomb 7 x 50 binoculars swinging from their leather strap round his neck. The sounds of Ally Dass rattling his breakfast pots and cursing his assistants grow ever fainter. Mr Malik is on the lookout for a nice comfy spot to sit down.

17

The sleeping leopard opens one eye for a mouse,
two for a baboon

'Eyes like a hawk,' said Mr Gopez, taking a bite from a cold chicken leg. 'He spotted a couple of cheetahs half a mile away – and all you could see was their ears.'

'Oh,' said Mr Patel, 'running away from him, were they?'

'Most amusing, Patel, most amusing. But, you have to agree, young Benjamin here certainly knows his stuff.'

'Yes, he's quite right, Malik. And did you know cheetahs are the only cats that can't retract their claws? That's what Benjamin said. So they get blunt, you see, like a dog's. That's why you never see one up a tree.'

Even if you haven't been to Africa, you may have seen pictures of tourists on a game drive. The favoured vehicle for such excursions is a Nissan minibus with a canvas roof that can be rolled back to allow the passengers to poke their heads out and point their optical instruments – be they cameras, binoculars or video recorders – at whatever animals of interest come into view. There is a driver in the front and often a guide who not only keeps an eye out for said animals of interest but is in radio contact with other guides in the area. Just as African vultures swoop in from unseen miles away to a kill, flocks of safari buses head from all points of the compass towards any lion, cheetah, leopard or other large mammal that shows itself (among the large and diverse fauna of Africa, it is the bigger carnivorous mammals that the average tourist most wants to point a Nikon at). It is from such a drive that the members of the Asadi Club safari have just returned, satisfied but hungry.

'See anything else?' said Mr Malik.

'Giraffe, buffalo, lions,' said Mr Gopez, 'and lots of antelope, of course. But you know I can never remember their damned names. What were they again, Benjamin?'

Benjamin stepped forward.

'Thomson's and Grant's, and bushbuck, kudu, eland, waterbuck, topi, hartebeest, wildebeest –'

'Good gracious – that many, were there? Shame you didn't come, Malik. Yes, I think I'll be sticking with your Benjamin this weekend.'

Benjamin thanked Mr A.B. very much.

'And he's pretty good on the birds too – though I can never remember their damned names either. There were some little chaps actually on the neck of a giraffe, shinning up and down like monkeys.'

'Those were oxpeckers, Mr A.B. And, Mr Malik, there were yellow-billed oxpeckers and red-billed, both together on one giraffe. That I have never seen.'

'Benjamin here says that they eat the ticks on the animals. Is that right, Malik?'

'Absolutely right. Anything that Benjamin says about birds is the full shilling, A.B. – you can be sure of that.'

Mr Patel tore a chunk from his chapatti.

'That business last year with the warthogs,' he said. 'That was something to do with ticks, wasn't it?'

Mr Malik gave a small cough.

'So I discovered later.'

'Ticks?' said Mr Gopez. 'Warthogs? What on earth are you talking about?'

Mr Malik could see he was going to have to explain.

'On the last safari – of course, you weren't there. I thought the burrow was disused, you see. I'd seen the mongooses going in and out, so I thought the warthogs must have abandoned it.'

'What on earth's all this got to do with ticks?'

'I discovered later,' said Mr Malik, 'that mongooses are a bit like oxpeckers. Warthogs will let them come into their burrow and nibble off any ticks they have.'

'So he puts the latrine not five yards away from this burrow,' explained Mr Patel, 'right across what turns out to be Warthog Highway. A bit of blue canvas is no obstacle to a determined warthog, let me tell you. Poor old Ma Haniff – never been the same since.'

'Ah,' said Mr Gopez. 'Yes, that would explain it. Anyway, what about you, Malik – what did you get up to this morning while we were out on safari?'

'Oh, I just went and sat down by the river.'

'River, eh? See much?'

'Well, I saw a troop of baboons. And then some colobus monkeys came along, and a bush pig, and a pack of mongooses – dwarf ones. That kind of thing.'

'Colobus, eh?'

'Yes, the black and white ones, you know. And I saw

quite a few birds too, and – oh yes – a three-horned chameleon. It was on the bush right beside me, but I didn't
notice it until I saw a grasshopper vanish before my eyes.
Big one too.'

'Excuse me, Mr Malik – the *juali*, did you touch it?'

In many parts of Kenya, to touch a chameleon is to die.

'Yes, I did, Benjamin – I even picked it up. Beautiful
thing. But please do not worry for me. I have touched
many chameleons and no harm has come to me. And, of
course, I put it back again on the bush.'

'No, Mr Malik, I know that they are not dangerous.
That is just a foolish superstition. But now it will rain.'

'I do hope not, Benjamin. I was rather looking forward
to the night drive.'

There is nothing quite like driving around the African
savannah after dark. It both shrinks and expands. Though
vision is limited to how far your torch or headlights shine,
the darkness becomes an infinity of the unknown. The
animals that you see then are very different from the ones
you may see in daylight. Most birds have disappeared to
their roosts – most, but not all. Now is the time you may
see a little scops owl pounce on a cricket, or a giant eagle
owl swoop down on a hare. If you are lucky, you might
spot a nightjar hawking for moths – if you are exception-
ally lucky, you might even see a male pennant-winged
nightjar, trailing from each wing a long white feather twice
the length of its body in contravention of all the princi-
ples of sensible aerodynamic design. But what you will
mainly see are eyes.

Wherever you shine your torch, the eyes shine back.
On the flat grasslands these will mostly be the yellow eyes

of spring hares. These small burrowing rodents are never seen in daylight, but at night they bound about the grassland in their hundreds like mobs of miniature kangaroos. Many other animals that live in burrows during the day emerge at dusk. Aardvarks and pangolins begin their nightly search for termites, porcupines dig for roots and tubers, honey badgers roam in search of not just honey but insects, eggs, fish and frogs, carrion and any small mammal they can catch up to the size of a young antelope (if you are on safari with honey badgers about, make sure your rubbish receptacles are strongly built). This year Mr Malik very much hoped to see a pangolin. He had never seen a pangolin.

'Look,' said Mr Gopez, 'there's a car coming. Must be the Tiger.'

'No,' beamed Mr Malik. 'That isn't the Tiger's car, it's Petula's.'

She had come, he soon noticed, alone.

To say that Petula had been a bit cross that morning when she read the text message from Salman would be like calling Mrs Guptarani's Double Dynamite Chilli Chutney 'baby food'. Petula was seething with anger, she was red with rage, she was incandescent. The message (message, mind you, not even a proper phone call!) said that he couldn't make it back to Nairobi until the next day. How long ago had they planned this holiday? How many times had she told Salman to make sure he got weekend leave? (Only weekend, mind you, not even a single weekday!) How often had she told him how important this would be to her, to her father? She phoned him straight back, so there was no danger of Salman Mohammed being unaware that he was the most unreliable, selfish, thoughtless – BORING – man she had ever had the misfortune to meet. In vain did he try to explain that the figures just had to be in Sydney by start of business on Monday. He couldn't make the Saturday flight, and that was that. What if he came down to Nairobi on Sunday? That would be all right, wouldn't it? By great act of willpower Petula summoned enough self-control to explain that the safari would be over on Monday, so thank you so much for your very kind offer – but you know where you can put it. The worst thing was that there was nothing she could do. She couldn't fly to Dubai and drag him on to a plane. No, it is true to say that on Saturday morning Petula Malik was not a happy fiancée. But she was damned if she was going to miss the safari.

'Hello, Daddy darling.' She gave him a big kiss. 'I'm afraid Salman couldn't make it – some work thing.'

'Oh, I'm sorry to hear that. Any chance of him coming up later?'

'I don't think so, Daddy, and it doesn't really matter. Mmm, is that Ally Dass's devilled chicken? I'm famished.'

'It's just that I was rather hoping to talk over the arrangements with him.'

'Oh,' said Petula through a mouthful of chicken, 'what arrangements would those be?'

'The wedding, you know.'

'Wedding?' said Petula. She swallowed the chicken and smiled a sweet smile. 'What wedding?'

On his hatless head, Mr Malik felt the first raindrop fall.

18

As raindrops wash away the leopard's spots, so
wishes blunt its teeth

What he really needed, thought Mr Malik, was an umbrella.
He looked out of the tent – no, make that twenty umbrellas. The rain that started just after lunch had turned into a
steady downpour. Not that there was any problem with
the tents. They were fine and waterproof – just as Godfrey Amin had promised they would be. It was getting
between them that was the problem. But everyone seemed
to be taking the bad weather in good spirit. Seated round
one end of the table that had now been cleared of lunch
things, Petula was discussing events international, national
and domestic with several of the other women. Had Mimi
Hassan really gone to the UK for a distant cousin's wedding, or was it for another facelift? When would the
Nairobi City Council do something about parking near
the central market? If you sew six kangas together can
you really call it a sari? At the other end of the table young
Henry Vanshu had brought out a pack of playing cards
and was instructing some of the other children in the
finer points of Bombay hold 'em. Over in the seventh
tent a noisy crowd of teenagers had started up a game of
team billiards. Some of the girls were surprisingly good.

The duet of snores that could now be heard coming from the men's tent suggested that Messrs Gopez and Patel had each achieved a satisfactory state of post-prandial somnolence. What with their chorus and the noise of the rain on canvas, Mr Malik didn't hear the Tiger's Range Rover arrive.

'Hello, Malik.' Tiger Singh closed his striped umbrella and leaned it against the side of the tent. 'I'm glad I made it before dark. Wouldn't want to drive at night in this kind of weather. I would have been sooner except something came up at the club. And what's all this rain, anyway? It was blue skies all the way up, then as soon as I got through Chuka – splosh. I thought it was supposed to be the dry season.'

'Oh. Hello, Tiger. Yes, sorry about that. Just a summer shower, I expect.'

Mr Malik was not far from the truth. Though they were fifty miles from Mount Kenya, the massive mountain can still affect the weather. Local downpours are common even in the dry season. One theory is that they are caused by warm wet winds blowing in from the east meeting cold air that flows down from the top of the mountain. The other theory is that Mr Malik should never have touched that *juali*.

'So, Tiger, sit down. Can I get you a tea, coffee or anything? But you were saying something – something about the club.'

'Yes, strange thing. The manager phoned me this morning just as I was about to leave. Would you believe it? The lion's disappeared.'

'The lion – the Kima Killer?'

'Yes. Just a prank, no doubt. Are the Bashu boys here?'

'No. Sunny said they couldn't come this year. Something important on at the coast, he said.'

'There you are then – look no further. A glass of passion juice would be nice, then a beer perhaps.'

'Were you at the club last night?'

'Yes, as it happens. Had a drink with Harry Khan – wanted to get me to work with him on some new project he's dreamed up.'

'Really?'

He took the glass from Mr Malik and drained it in one. 'Mmm, that's better.'

'So you'll be working for Khan Enterprises.'

The Tiger gave him a pained look.

'No, no. I told him I was much too busy. They'll have to find someone else to do their law work. Not my kind of thing, shopping malls. Not my kind of thing at all.'

Mr Malik handed him a bottle of Tusker.

'Have a game of billiards with him, by any chance?'

'I did, as a matter of fact.'

'Good. I'm afraid he beat me rather badly the other night, but no doubt you thrashed him.'

'Well,' said the Tiger, pouring the beer into his glass, 'I wouldn't say that. The margin was really quite close.' He peered out of the dining tent. 'Very close, in fact. What on earth's happening over there?'

Yells and laughter could be heard even above the rain.

'Why don't you come and have a look?' said Mr Malik.

Under cover of the Tiger's golf umbrella the two men dashed over to the brightly lit tent and pushed through the flaps. Lined up along the walls of the tent stood a crowd of young and old. At the far end a girl was leaning over the green baize of the billiard table, lining up for a shot, her chin almost touching the wooden cue. She made a couple of dummy strikes then hit one of the white balls hard. Up the table it went, clipped the red ball, clipped the other white and disappeared into the right top pocket. Up went a cheer.

'Four points,' said a youthful voice.

'There,' said Mr Malik, beaming. 'My special surprise for the fifty-second annual Asadi Club safari.'

'Well, I'll be . . .'

They stayed to watch the end of the match – the girls' team won – then returned to the dining tent to find Mr Patel and Mr Gopez sitting at one of the tables with two open bottles of Tusker between them.

'Hello, Tiger,' said Mr Gopez. 'Couldn't see the sun but we thought it must be over the yardarm.'

Mr Patel gestured to the rain still falling outside the tent. 'Did you bring this?'

'It was here when I arrived,' said the Tiger, 'I'm sure of it. May we join you?'

More seats were pulled up round the table. Tiger Singh brought them all up to date with events in the metropolis – with all agreed on the Bashu boys as the most likely suspects for the missing lion. The new arrival was informed of what had happened on the safari so far.

'Have you seen the big five yet?'

Mr Gopez spread the fingers of one hand and counted them off.

'Lion yes, buffalo yes, leopard no, elephant no, rhinoceros no.'

'Funnily enough,' said Mr Patel, 'we were only talking about buffalo on the way down. For some reason, A.B. here thinks they are the most dangerous animal in Africa. I've told him that it's hippos, but he won't believe me.'

'Of course they are,' said Mr Gopez. 'You've only got to look at those horns.'

'Never mind horns, it's teeth that cause the damage. Isn't that right, Tiger?'

Tiger Singh took a small sip from his glass of Tusker beer.

'I cannot claim to be an expert on these matters, but before this discussion goes any further, gentlemen, might I ask you to clarify your terms? For instance, exactly what do you mean by "animal"? Is a human an animal? In which case, he is surely the most dangerous. Is a snake an animal? I would guess snake bites cause a large number of fatalities.'

'Is a crocodile an animal?' added Mr Malik. 'Is a mosquito? Is the Aids virus?'

Mr Patel thought for a moment.

'I suppose what I meant was a mammal, non-human.'

'Look here, Tiger,' said Mr Gopez, 'never mind your legal-eagle nit-picking. We know what we meant. And I say that buffalo kill more people in Africa than hippos.'

Mr Malik thought to ask why a buffalo would want to kill a hippo but decided against it.

'And I say,' said Patel, reaching for his wallet, 'that they don't.'

The Tiger looked first at Mr Patel, then at Mr Gopez, then back at Mr Patel.

'Are you suggesting a wager?'

138

'I am. And a proper bet this time, not a damned debate.'

'What do you have to say to that, A.B.?'

'If our friend here wishes to put his money where his mouth is, I should be delighted to indulge his desire.'

Mr Patel counted out some notes.

'What shall we say – ten thousand?'

Mr Malik held up a hand.

'My dear friends, if you will forgive me for interrupting, I can foresee a problem here. I mean, how do you know? How can we find out how many people are killed by these animals – or any others, for that matter? I doubt that there are government statistics. And even if there were, how reliable would they be, exactly?'

'Good point, Malik,' said the Tiger. '*Rem acu tetigisti* and all that.'

'But I read about it,' said Mr Patel, 'that's what I've been saying. Just the other day, in the *Evening News*.'

'A very fine newspaper, no doubt,' said Mr Malik, 'but where exactly do they get their figures from?'

'I don't know – from their own files, probably. You see stories all the time: "Suspicious Death at Lake Naivasha: Hippo Helping Police with Enquiries".'

'No, no, Malik is right,' said the Tiger. 'If there is going to be a wager between two members of the Asadi Club, then strict guidelines must be drawn up to enable a fair outcome, and sound evidence is top of the list. It occurs to me that what we need is an expert witness.'

'Someone who's seen it happen, you mean?'

'I was using the expression in its legal sense, A.B. Someone who knows all about the subject, who's studied the statistics and so on, and is prepared to testify.'

'Sounds all right to me,' said Mr Gopez. 'What do you say, Patel?'

'If we can find one, then that's fine by me.'

'I say,' said Tiger Singh, 'who on earth are those two chaps?'

19

A hungry leopard has more teeth than a well-fed
crocodile

Mr Malik had no difficulty recognizing one of the men
who had just pulled up in an old Land Rover as Dickie
Johnson, nor in surmising that the other darker-skinned
man – the rather tall and good-looking and much
younger man – must be the guest he'd flown to Nairobi
to pick up. The two of them hurried through the rain to
the tent.

'Ah, Malik. *Chakula* – still on?'

'Most certainly, Mr Johnson. We were expecting you.
Dinner is nearly ready – and this must be your guest.'

'Yes, meet Angus Mbikwa.'

Mbikwa? Mr Malik was vaguely aware that Rose
Mbikwa had a son. But of course, what more natural
than that as an old friend of Hilary Fotherington-
Thomas, Dickie Johnson would also be an old friend of
Rose, and of her son? After shaking the tall man by the
hand, Mr Malik introduced the two new arrivals to his
friends.

'You have a wonderful place, Mr Johnson,' said Mr
Patel. 'We all like it very much.'

The older man gave a short sniff.

The tall man smiled.

'Yes, it is special, isn't it? And Uncle Dickie has always been most generous with sharing it. I've been coming here since I was a boy.'

'As you may know, Mr Mbikwa, this is our first visit,' said Mr Malik.

'Well, it's been a while since I was last here, Mr Malik, but I can assure you it hasn't changed a bit. Nor, I have to say, has its owner.'

Another sniff.

Mr Malik saw Petula coming towards them from the other end of the tent.

'Gentlemen, may I introduce you to my daughter Petula?'

'Hello, Mr Johnson.' Petula shook the older man's hand, then offered her hand to his companion. 'And hello, Angus. How good to see you again.'

'Petula. What a lovely surprise. So this was the safari you mentioned.'

Mr Malik was finding all this rather difficult to follow.

'You know each other?'

'Yes, Daddy darling. Angus works for CI – he's the new director I told you about. We had a meeting on Thursday night, at the Hilton.'

'I'm so sorry, Mr Mbikwa, I was sure my daughter said you were from Switzerland.'

Angus Mbikwa smiled.

'I was working in Geneva for many years before I got this job – so yes, I suppose you could say I came from Switzerland. But I was born here. So, Petula, do I also get to meet your fiancé?'

'Salman? I'm afraid Salman couldn't make it.'

'That's a shame.' He turned to her father. 'You have a wonderful daughter, Mr Malik. The work she is doing for Clarity International – for the country. You must be very proud of her.'

'I am indeed, Mr Mbikwa. Thank you. Now, dinner should be ready in about half an hour, I think. Can I offer you both something to drink?'

Dickie Johnson thought that a whisky might fit the bill – just a 'chota peg' – while Angus asked if he might have a ginger beer.

'So, Mr Malik,' he said, 'have you and your friends seen much game so far?'

'Well, yes – I suppose if you added them all up we have. That was this morning, of course, before this rain.'

From Dickie Johnson came a different noise this time, something between a sniff and a grunt.

'*Juali rasha*, that's all. Couple of hours, gone.'

'I hope so, Mr Johnson.'

'So, game. Not disappointed, Malik?'

'Indeed no, it has been as you said it would be. My friends have seen cheetahs and lions, and many antelopes and gazelle and buffalo and whatnot.'

'Buffalo, eh? Dangerous beast, your buffalo.'

Mr Malik could not help noticing a distinct I-told-you-so look pass from Mr Gopez to Mr Patel.

'Yes,' he said, 'we were . . . er . . . talking about it earlier.' He had a sudden thought. 'I don't suppose that you'd happen to know, Mr Johnson, which animal – which *mammal* – kills the most people in Africa, would you? It's so hard to get reliable figures.'

Angus laughed.

'There's not much Uncle Dickie doesn't know about African animals, Mr Malik.'

'Most interesting,' said the Tiger. He turned towards their guest. 'Mr Johnson, I wonder if you would be willing to help us. You see, there has been a small difference of opinion between our two friends here. One says the most dangerous animal is the hippopotamus, the other says buffalo. They are even willing to bet money on it. Would you be willing to settle the matter for us?'

Dickie Johnson thought a bit, then smiled.

'Delighted.'

'Then, gentlemen, it appears we may have our expert witness. All right with you two?'

Mr Patel looked at Mr Gopez. They both nodded.

'Excellent. But before we ask Mr Johnson to adjudicate, perhaps it would be well to make sure the details of the wager are clear and unambiguous.'

Taking from his pocket a fountain pen and notebook, Tiger Singh took the two participants aside. From his years of experience both in court and at the Asadi Club, he knew that when it comes to adjudicating such disputes it is always best to get things down in writing.

'So tell me, Daddy,' said Petula. 'The surprise – everything went all right?'

'Why don't you come and see?' said Mr Malik. 'And perhaps our guests would like to see it too.'

'Stap me vitals!' Dickie Johnson ran his eye over the full length of the billiard table. 'Heard of 'em. Never thought I'd see one.'

'Heard of what, Uncle Dickie?' said Angus.

'Churchman's Portable. Yes, look,' he said, pointing to where two mahogany covers were leaning up against the side of the tent. 'Removable tabletop – right, Malik?'

'Absolutely and completely right. So you know about these tables, Mr Johnson?'

'London maker, two-part construction, steel frame, three-sixteenths-inch Welsh slate, gutta-percha cushions. Only made about a dozen. Where on earth did you get it?'

Mr Malik explained how he had come across the table in Nairobi at Amin and Sons. All he knew was that Godfrey Amin had bought it some years ago at auction.

'It is in what seem to be its original crates, but the labels on them are so torn and faded you can't really make out much. Do you play, Mr Johnson?'

'Used to. Not for years.'

'Well, perhaps after dinner you would like a game. And speaking of dinner, I think it might be time to head back to the dining tent. Tonight we will be having something special – murgh hariyali. Our cook Ally Dass marinades the guineafowl in the sauce for two whole days.'

'Sounds wonderful. Plenty of piri-piri? Can't stand bland food.'

'In that case, Mr Johnson, I think you will enjoy your dinner.'

Mr Malik was not wrong. After just one mouthful Dickie Johnson assured him that everything was indeed *kizuri* and that he hadn't tasted anything quite so delicious in years. Angus Mbikwa, sitting between Mr Patel and Mr Gopez, also seemed to be enjoying himself.

When the plates had been cleared and the glasses refilled, Tiger Singh proposed a toast of thanks to their host.

'And, ladies and gentlemen, I would also like to thank Mr Johnson for agreeing to help us in another matter concerning the habits of African animals – two, in particular. This is a subject of which he has acquired an intimate knowledge through a lifetime of study. We are now honoured to be able to call upon that knowledge. Malik, would you explain?'

Mr Malik picked up a sheet of paper from the table.

'As many of you will know, two of our club members have made a bet. I have the terms here before me, drawn up earlier this evening. Mr M. Patel and Mr A. B. Gopez, as members of the Asadi Club, make the following wager. Mr Patel claims that the common or river hippopotamus is, at this time, responsible for more human deaths in Africa than any other mammal. Mr Gopez claims that the wild or cape buffalo is responsible for more human deaths in Africa than any other mammal. Death is here defined as intentional or accidental, immediate or within one year due to injuries inflicted. Mammal is here defined as including all animals which suckle their young, whether terrestrial, amphibious or aquatic, but excluding humans. The stake of the wager is to be ten thousand shillings from each party, winner take all.'

'Gentlemen,' said Tiger Singh, 'are you still happy with these terms, and do you agree to be bound by the opinion of Mr Johnson, now before you, as expert witness in the matter?' Both men nodded their agreement.

'Then, Mr Johnson, will you kindly settle the argument for us?'

Dickie Johnson stood. He looked first at Mr Patel, then at Mr Gopez.

'It is,' he said, with just the faintest of smiles, 'neither.'

20

The wise frog does not count the teeth of the
crocodile

Although, as Mr Malik suspected, firm statistics are hard
to come by, the claim that buffalo are the most dangerous
beast in Africa seems mostly to come from people who
have upset them. A reliable way to upset a buffalo is to aim
a gun at it and shoot. Buffalo are sociable creatures; upset
one and you will find that you have upset several. It is the
wounded buffalo, often assisted by sympathetic family
and friends, that seems to do the damage. Even so, and
despite the fact that the African buffalo is common and
widespread throughout much of the continent, death by
buffalo is still a rare event. I have only been able to find
one confirmed report of a man killed by a buffalo in
Africa in the last five years. He was visiting the continent
from Idaho with his wife – and yes, she shot at it.

Hippos are also common and widespread, spending
most of their days lolling about African lakes and rivers
and coming out to feed on grass, reeds and other such suc-
culent herbage only after sunset. The first time I saw a
hippopotamus in the wild was on a trip to Lake Naivasha.
What has stayed with me even more than the sight of the
animal itself, picked out in the dim beam of my torch not

fifty yards away, was what it did. After heaving itself from the water and munching away at some papyrus for a while, it looked towards me and stood quite still. I knew what was about to happen – I remembered years ago seeing exactly the same look on the face of my own eighteen-month-old nephew. Sure enough the animal turned round and, with its back to me, began to pooh. What did surprise me, though, was the role of the animal's tail in this procedure. Most animals with tails – even long tails like horses or cows or greater kudu – lift them out of the way. Hippopotamuses have short tails. But rather than lifting it, this hippo began whirring its tail from side to side like a demented windscreen wiper. Dung flew everywhere and, as I say, it's not a sight you'd forget. I later found out that this – combined with retromingent urination – is the way that hippos mark their territory. And that's the trouble, you see. Because while other hippos recognize and respect these markers, humans, on the whole, don't. Which goes a long way to explaining why a not insubstantial number of them get attacked and killed by indignant hippos every year in Africa. But although I have been able to find a total of twenty-one reliable references to humans being killed by affronted hippos, both in Kenya and other African countries over the past five years, I must agree with Dickie Johnson that another mammal kills many, many more.

'Dogs?'

Mr Gopez's eyes bulged.

'Woofers?'

Mr Patel seemed to be choking on his beer.

'Man's best friend?'

'Yes,' said Dickie Johnson. 'Dogs. Dozens, every year, in Kenya alone. Bites, infection, rabies. Whole of Africa? Hundreds.'

'That must be ten times the number killed by buffalo and hippos combined,' said Tiger Singh.

'But, Tiger . . . they're not –'

'Mammals? Yes, they are.'

'But they're –'

'Domestic?' Tiger Singh turned to Mr Malik. 'Am I right in thinking that the terms of the wager said nothing to exclude domestic animals?'

Mr Malik nodded.

'The terms are quite clear.'

'But . . .'

'But . . .'

'As Malik says, the rules are clear,' said Tiger Singh. 'I see no grounds for an appeal.' He drained his glass. 'The only question that now remains is what happens to the stake monies.'

'Wager null and void.' Mr Patel held out his hand. 'Dogs indeed. I'll have my ten thousand back, please, Tiger.'

'All bets off,' said Mr Gopez. 'Mine too, please.'

'I fear,' said Tiger Singh, 'that the matter is not quite so simple, gentlemen. There has been no irregularity, you see. What has happened is simply that you have both lost your bet.'

'Exactly. Come on, Tiger, cough up.'

'I wish I could, Mr Patel, I wish I could,' said the Tiger. 'But this presents a most unusual ethical conundrum.'

'Hand it over, Tiger. This isn't a case in one of your bally courts of law.'

'Indeed not, A.B., though that reminds me that I do seem to remember a precedent. Not in the annals of law, but in the annals of an equally august institution – the Asadi Club.'

'Precedent?' said Mr Patel.

The Tiger nodded.

'Cast your minds back to the Christmas of 1992.'

'Ah yes, of course,' murmured Mr Malik. 'The Great Tombola Fiasco.'

'Exactly, Malik, exactly. You may all recall that somehow or other half the tickets for the Christmas tombola disappeared.'

'Sanjay Bashu lost them, you mean,' said Mr Gopez.

'Aspersions were indeed cast, A.B., but the evidence was never sufficient to make a watertight case. And nobody knew whose numbers they were.'

'Yes, I remember,' said Mr Malik. 'The Tombola Committee couldn't return the money because they didn't know who to give it to.'

'That's right, Malik,' said Tiger Singh. 'It was decided that the only thing to do was to give the whole lot – the money and all the prizes – to charity.'

Mr Gopez stared at him.

'Are you suggesting that my ten thousand shillings – our twenty – goes to charity?'

'That is exactly what I'm suggesting, A.B. In the spirit of the Asadi Club, it seems the obvious solution.'

The two men looked at Tiger Singh, then at each other.

'And may I further suggest that as an independent party, Mr Mbikwa might decide which charity? What do you say Patel, A.B.?'

'Oh, all right,' said Mr Patel.

'Oh, all right,' said Mr Gopez.

It did not take Angus Mbikwa long to decide.

'The Aga Khan Hospital?' said Mr Malik, getting up from the table. 'An excellent choice. Now, if you'll excuse me, gentlemen, I have to go and see a man about a –'

'Don't say it, Malik,' said Mr Gopez. 'Don't say it.'

'About a . . . game of billiards.'

On his way out of the dining tent with Dickie Johnson, Mr Malik heard one of his friends – he couldn't be sure which – muttering that this would be the last time he asked Malik to help with a wager, and he realized, with a smile, that those were exactly the words he had been hoping to hear.

'Wondering . . .' said Dickie Johnson. The red was back on its spot after he'd made a tricky long jenny into the top right pocket, and now he was lining up for a cannon. 'Tomorrow, first thing.' He stroked his cue ball past the red and other white, clipping both of them but moving neither far. 'Four seats.' He repeated the stroke in the opposite direction, scoring another cannon and lining up for a third. 'Like one?'

Mr Malik had heard Angus suggest over dinner that Uncle Dickie might take Beryl on a joyride the next day and had heard him persuade Petula to go too. Now it seemed that Dickie Johnson was asking him if he'd like to accompany them.

Mr Malik was not a cowardly man. Should duty summon, he was ever ready to heed the call. The Malik head was steady and the Malik heart was strong – but it has to be said that the Malik stomach was neither. A joyride in a single-engined aircraft – and he had seen the aircraft – was not, on reflection, a duty. But perhaps . . .

'That is very kind of you, Mr Johnson. Could I, by any chance, accept your offer on behalf of a friend of mine?'

'Of course.' Dickie Johnson scored a third cannon and now looked set up for the couple of reds that would win him the game. 'First thing. Before it gets bumpy.'

'Then I will tell my friend Benjamin to be ready by dawn.'

The gates to the large house in Serengeti Gardens swung open, the red Mercedes crept up the driveway and stopped beside the front door.

'Thank you, Harry,' said Rose Mbikwa, getting out of the passenger side. 'It was a wonderful evening.'

'You still dance like a dream, Rose baby – like a dream. Do it again sometime soon, right?'

'Sometime soon.'

'Great. Hey, I've just had an idea. What are you doing next weekend?'

'Nothing planned. I've only just got back, remember.'

'I was thinking of going down to the lake – my cousin's got a place there. And Saturday night –'

'The band still plays at the old hotel?'

Harry Khan grinned.

'You bet. Why don't you come down and spend a couple of days. There's loads of room. I could pick you up Friday afternoon, bring you back Sunday.'

Rose thought for a moment.

'No, I probably shouldn't. My son Angus has just come

back to Nairobi for a new job and I'd like to spend some time with him. He's so busy during the week.'

'Hell, bring him along too. Like I say, there's loads of room.'

'Well . . .'

'Ask him. I'll phone you Thursday.'

The front door was not locked. Rose let herself into the house. She did not feel like going to bed. She had been home only three days and it was not yet nine o'clock in Edinburgh. And as Harry had pointed out, in New York it would be four o'clock in the afternoon – why, he'd only just be getting out of bed. She was pleased she had said yes to his invitation when he'd phoned up out of the blue. It had been fun, just as much fun as when she'd been out with him the last time he'd been in Nairobi. Now she was home it brought back happy memories of dancing around the house with Joshua all those years ago. And she thought of Mr Malik, and dancing with him that evening four years ago at the Hunt Club Ball. She smiled. Oh, how fast the years went by. Rose wandered over to the record player. Doris Day? No, not tonight. She pulled a record cover from the pile and put the disc on the turntable.

'Is that all there is?' sang Miss Peggy Lee. 'Is that all there is?'

Rose Mbikwa curled up on the sofa.

'If that's all there is, then let's keep dancing.'

2 1

The frog needs no string to tether it to water

'What's that?' said Mr Gopez. 'There, did you hear it?'

'Hear what, A.B.?'

'Shh. Listen.'

As the guests departed, so had the clouds. The Milky Way now stretched clear across the African sky. Though it was now too late for a night drive Mr Patel, emboldened by the cool night air and his third bottle of Tusker beer, had challenged the Tiger to a game of snooker and in the seventh tent was already fifty points behind. Sitting on stools round the campfire, enjoying a postprandial Johnnie Walker beneath the stars, sat Mr Gopez and Mr Malik. There is something about sitting out under the stars. You don't have to be an astronomer, you don't need a religion. To gaze up at the heavens on a clear Kenyan night is to be aware of something else, something other, something beyond. The fly in this celestial ointment, though, is the noises.

'There – hear it? Hyenas, I'm sure of it. Sound pretty damned close too.'

Mr Gopez looked around him at the darkness beyond the light of the fire and the lanterns, and shivered.

Those of you who grew up as I did in the English

Home Counties may think yourselves inured to the sounds of the wild creatures of the night. The long sad screech of the barn owl or the mournful hoot of the brown owl will barely register on your consciousness. The scream of a vixen on heat will not curdle your blood, nor the sharp high bark of the dog fox send shivers down your spine; the diabolical snuffle of the marauding hedgehog will cause you to neither blanch nor quail. But even Buckinghamshire men may feel, if not disturbed, then far from turbed by the sounds of the African night. For there are things out there that want to eat you.

'Hyenas?' said Mr Malik. 'Are you sure?'

'Yes. I saw a programme about them on the Discovery Channel. They're not the cowards everyone thinks they are. They don't just chew on lions' leftovers, they like fresh meat. Damned clever too.'

Mr Malik thought he had been on enough safaris to recognize the vocal repertoire of a hyena in all its variations. This was not one of them, but he knew better than to contradict his friend straight out.

'I wonder if it could be anything else,' he said. 'I know, let's go and ask Benjamin.'

Benjamin had not, of course, grown up in the English Home Counties. He had been born in Kenya's Eastern Province, where he spent his early childhood playing in dust or mud according to the season and had later been given the responsibility of first looking after the chickens and then the goats (on the whole, he preferred the chickens). When the village judged him old enough, he was sent to school. He learned to read and write English and

Swahili and still had lots of time on his three-mile walk to and from school to climb a tree and look into a bird's nest, or watch a wasp dig a hole and fill it with comatose caterpillars, or confuse a mongoose by imitating its chattering alarm call. Each morning he looked forward to seeing which animals had crossed the road or walked along it the night before. The tracks of four-footed beasts were not too difficult to work out, but how to tell the difference between a millipede and a centipede, a python and a mamba, was a source of endless fascination. Mr Malik and Mr Gopez found him in the cooking tent, where Ally Dass was piling up his plate with rice and curry.

'Very good food, Mr Malik.'

'Indeed it is, Benjamin. I was wondering, though, if you heard that noise just now. We weren't sure what it was.'

It is widely known among naturalists that as soon as you ask someone if they can hear a noise, the creature that has been making the noise stops making it. The bullfrog that has been calling solidly since dusk to attract a cow-frog to his patch of pond glances at his wristwatch and sees it is time for a coffee break; the bittern that has been booming away in the bulrushes beside him decides on a whim to give up the musical stage and join a silent order. For some reason the creature Mr Gopez had heard decided not to play by the rules. They heard a soft whistle, gradually getting louder and turning into a sound not unlike the one an eight-year-old child might make while being slowly garrotted.

'That noise?' said Benjamin through a mouthful of biriani.

'That one,' said Mr Malik. 'My friend Mr Gopez thought it might be a hyena.'

'No, Mr Malik, it is much smaller than a hyena.'

'Is it a jackal?'

'No, Mr Malik, much smaller than a jackal. It is the little dassie, the one that lives in the trees.'

Dendrohyrax arboreus, usually known in Kenya as the tree hyrax, is a mammal about the size of a small cat – though being without a tail it more resembles an inflated guinea pig. Unlike its more sociable relation the rock hyrax, the tree hyrax prefers to spend life with just a single member of the opposite sex, and whereas groups of its promiscuous cousins can be seen scampering round their holes and burrows during the hours of daylight, tree hyraxes emerge from their hiding places in hollow trees only at dusk. They wander through the night munching leaves, gazing at the moon and scaring the bejesus out of anyone unfamiliar with their impressive vocalizations. By the time the sun has risen they will have retired to their tree hollow to rest and digest. They are slow, unremarkable animals. The hyraxes' main claim to fame is to be found in their family tree which, if you follow it back fifty million years or so, reveals that their closest relation is neither the cat nor the guinea pig but the elephant – an interesting fact that you seldom hear the latter mention.

'Ah yes. Thank you, Benjamin. And oh, I nearly forgot. Would you like to go up in a plane tomorrow morning, first thing? If the weather's fine, that is. Mr Johnson says he has a spare seat.'

'Mr Malik,' said Benjamin, grinning from ear to ear, 'I

very much would.' He thought for a moment. 'Mr Malik . . .'

'Yes, Benjamin?'

'In that case . . . please be careful. If you see another *juali*, perhaps not to touch it.'

22

A raindrop has no memory

Rose Mbikwa rubbed her eyes. Though it was only just getting light outside, she had already been sitting an hour in front of her computer. Shouldn't she still be sleeping in rather than waking early? She sat back in her chair and looked around the sitting room. Yes, nothing had changed – yet after four years away everything was different. Life in Nairobi used to be so simple. Monday, correspondence. Tuesday, bird walk. Wednesday and Thursday guide training at the museum. Friday, shopping – with Elizabeth to help with the bargaining and Reuben to help with the carrying. But now?

She had already decided not to go back to leading the bird walk. It wouldn't be fair on Jennifer Halutu – from what Hilary had told her, Jennifer had been doing a fine job (and though numbers had dropped at first, they were now up again). And the guide training programme at the museum that she had started nearly twenty years ago – well, it had clearly been running smoothly enough without her. Perhaps it was time to start something new. Or perhaps, thought Rose, she should slow down. Those last few months looking after her father had not been easy. Maybe it was time to hand on the baton to the next runner in the relay race of life. Time to sit and watch the flowers. As she gazed out of the window at the brightening sky, she heard in her mind the voice of her father. She was not surprised to hear it – she had heard it often enough since his death. She was, though, slightly surprised at what she heard him say.

'Slow down?' said the broad lowland voice she loved so much. 'Away, lassie.'

Mr Malik was woken by what sounded like rain on the roof of the tent, which was strange as he was sure he hadn't touched another chameleon, even in his dreams. But as his brain shook off its blanket of sleep he realized that dawn had broken and the sound was growing louder and nearer. It was an aeroplane. He put his head out of the tent just in time to see Beryl roar overhead with a saucy waggle of wings, leaving behind not silence but the chatter and screech of a hundred invisible but nonetheless indignant bush creatures.

By the time the joyflying party made it back to camp the sun had risen high into a blue sky, showing Mount Kenya in all its majestic glory. The mountain looked so much closer than the grey glimpses of yesterday. The hungry flyers headed straight for the dining tent, where Mr Malik watched another mountain appear as Ally Dass piled rice and dhal on to Benjamin's plate. In between mouthfuls, Benjamin told him of his aeronautical adventure – the elephants, the huge herds of wildebeest, the leopard they saw right at the top of a thorn tree.

'That reminds me. Last night, did you by any chance hear a leopard near the camp?'

The sound of a leopard, once heard, is unmistakable –
a sort of cross between a grumble and a roar and a sigh.

'Yes, indeed, Mr Malik. There were two.'

'Really?' said Mr Malik. 'I could only hear one.'

'Yes, you are right. Only one of them made a sound.'

Which to Mr Malik didn't really seem to make any
sense.

'Er . . . forgive my asking, Benjamin,' he said, taking a
small sip from his glass of fresh passion-fruit juice, 'but if
you could only hear one, how do you know there were
two?'

'Their feet, Mr Malik.'

'They were close enough for you to hear their foot-
steps?' Leopards are notoriously light on their feet. 'That
sounds a bit too close.'

'No, Mr Malik. I mean I *saw* their feet, this morning,
just now. Come, I will show you.'

Putting down his plate, Benjamin led Mr Malik, now
joined by Mr Patel and Tiger Singh, fifty metres down the
sandy track still damp from the previous day's rain.

'There, you see,' said Benjamin, pointing to some marks
in the sand. 'First one leopard, walking slowly. Then
another behind, walking faster. The first one woman, the
second one man. I think the man is chasing the woman.'

Mr Malik stared down at the marks on the sand. If he
concentrated hard, he could make out that there were
indeed two sets of prints. But why Benjamin thought one
was going faster than the other, or why he thought they
were different sexes, he had no idea.

Nor, it seemed, did Tiger Singh.

'How on earth do you know that?'

'The first track is here – do you see, Mr Tiger? The prints are flat – walking feet.' Benjamin pointed to four prints, then another four in a regular pattern. 'Then the second leopard comes along – see, here, second leopard steps on track of first leopard.' He pointed to four prints that they now saw made a separate pattern overlaying the first one. 'The second prints have moved the sand backwards just a little, and they are further apart – hurrying feet. And look, they are wider than the first prints. The first is a woman leopard, the second is a man leopard.'

'Now that you have shown us, Benjamin, I think I can see it,' said Mr Malik. 'But why do you think the male is chasing the female?'

Benjamin grinned.

'I think man is always chasing woman – is that not so, Mr Malik?'

My friend Kennedy told me he often used to go and stay with a Maasai friend in his village – somewhere out near Kilimanjaro, I think it was. The Maasai have a very special relationship with cattle – in fact, believe that all the cattle on earth are rightfully theirs. Lions and leopards have traditionally disputed this claim, and around this time one animal in particular had been making a regular nuisance of itself by sneaking into the brushwood enkang at night, always around the new moon, and making off with a goat or newborn calf. No matter how carefully the men of the village wove the fence, no matter how many fires they lit, this sneaky predator would find a weak spot, creep in and manage to make off with its booty without being seen. In the morning the crime was only too clear, but there were never any footprints. Whatever animal it was entered and left through the same weak point in the enkang and, in dragging its prey behind it, erased any trace of its identity. For months all attempts at excluding or capturing this marauder had failed. Rumours had even started that supernatural agencies were involved. Though Irish by ancestry, my friend Kennedy holds strictly rationalist views. Could it be, he suggested to his friend, that the calf-killer was neither lion nor leopard nor leprechaun – but human?

And so it turned out. Two nights later, a moran from a neighbouring village was caught in flagrante with one of his friend's young female cousins. He soon admitted that after each previous visit he had taken home with him not only sweet memories of love but, in an attempt to throw a false scent, a small article of portable livestock. The young man was duly chastised, reparations agreed and the marriage arranged. My friend Kennedy was quite the man of the hour and was offered the traditional Maasai hon-ours of a bowl of fresh milk mixed with cattle's blood and the nocturnal company of his host's wife. He told me that as he hardly deserved such generous thanks for so trifling a service, he only felt able to accept one of them – though he never did tell me which.

The leopards were, it seemed, not the only animals that had been wandering around near the tents that night. Ben-jamin was able to identify the tracks of a kudu, a couple of dik-diks, a family of bush pigs and a troop of monkeys. '*Tumbili*, I think. The feet of the *mbega* look the same but they would cross there up in the trees, not on the ground.'

Mr Patel spotted what he thought was another leopard footprint.

'No, this one is the little leopard, the *mondo*.'

Benjamin followed the tracks to where they seemed to end abruptly.

'What happened?' asked Mr Patel.

Benjamin scouted round a tuft of grass. From about three yards away he picked up a feather and returned to where the others were still standing at the spot where the animal seemed to have vanished.

'Here, do you see these deep prints, and the marks of the claws?' He squatted, pointing to the pair of footprints. '*Mondo* is walking slowly. He hears something over there. He turns. He jumps. There he lands, right on top of a bird.'

'And what kind of bird would that be, Benjamin?' said Mr Malik.

Benjamin turned the pale grey feather round between his finger and thumb.

'I am sure that you know more about birds than me, Mr Malik. I think perhaps a plover.'

Mr Malik took the feather from his hand.

'Benjamin, I am sure you are right.'

On their way back to the camp Benjamin pointed out to them other, smaller tracks. Here the fussy trail of a hurrying beetle, there the little bunches of four small prints widely spaced that had been made by a mouse. They saw the sinuous trail of a snake which, as Benjamin pointed out, must be very fresh. It had gone over the prints their own feet had made only minutes before.

*

Back at the camp Petula described more of their early morning flight. Beryl had taken them all the way to Mount Kenya.

'Not to the top. Dickie – Mr Johnson – says that's too high for an unpressurized plane. But we flew right round it. And because we were low we could see so much. We saw a family of elephants with two babies – the small one must have been only a few weeks old. They were drinking down by the river. And we saw a black rhino and two white rhino, and we saw an ostrich on her nest. Then a huge line of pelicans flew along the Tana River, just a few feet high, with the sun on their backs. They were so beautiful.'

For someone whose three-year engagement had just ended she seemed remarkably cheerful.

'I believe,' said Mr Malik, 'that it is the male ostrich that sits on the nest. But indeed, how wonderful to see all this from above. And where is Mr Johnson now – did you not ask him to join us for breakfast?'

'Uncle Dickie's just putting Beryl to bed,' said Angus Mbikwa.

Petula laughed.

'Yes, he says she gets tired when she has to get up so early. And we saw a leopard up a tree – oh, Benjamin told you about that – and a family of warthogs all in a line, and thousands of zebras, and . . . What else did we see, Angus?'

'Oh . . . many, many things. But I have to agree that those pink-backed pelicans were something special, flying so low in the early light. That is a sight I shall never forget.'

Mr Malik smiled. Of course, any son of Rose Mbikwa would be able to tell a pink-backed pelican from a great white, even from a hundred yards.

23

When you give water to a monkey, do not expect
to see again your coconut shell

Are we like monkeys, thought Mr Malik, or are they like
us? As Hilary Fotherington-Thomas had mentioned, a
troop of baboons had taken up residence in the old abandoned homestead down by the river. Mr Malik had asked
the driver of the safari bus to pull up outside it. Most of
the baboons were taking it easy in the shade of the wide
veranda – couples grooming, mothers feeding babies,
young baboons playing in pairs or small groups. It was
perhaps the younger ones that seemed most human, chasing and quarrelling like children in a playground. Perched
on the roof was the old dog baboon. Though Mr Malik
couldn't see its eyes, shaded beneath deep brows, he could
feel them watching him, watching everything. For at least
half an hour the safarists stayed there – nobody wanted to
leave – until from the distance came a loud hiccup.

'A zebra,' whispered Benjamin. 'Alarm call. Mr Malik,
shall we go and see?'

Mr Malik signalled to their driver to start the engine.

They found the small herd of zebra near the river, no
more than a few hundred yards away. The animals seemed
nervous. One of them, a stallion, was staring at a patch of

bushes. The driver stopped the bus. After a couple of minutes, the stallion seemed to relax and put its head down to graze with the rest of the herd. Mr Malik saw a movement out of the corner of his eye. It was a lioness. Crouched low, moving just one leg at a time, she crept out of the bushes to take up position right behind the vehicle.

'She is using us to hide, Mr Malik,' whispered Benjamin, 'hide from the zebra.'

It is strange but true that whereas the smallest human on foot will be the signal for every zebra and lion within a half-mile radius to hot-hoof or hot-paw it towards the distant horizon, ten people in a minibus seem not to arouse the slightest suspicion. They and their vehicle are seen by the resident wildlife as some kind of large but harmless fellow creature. The other two buses arrived a minute later. Neither zebras nor lioness took the slightest notice of them. The lioness had now crawled to a position not two feet from where Mr Malik was sitting in the passenger seat. She was so close that he could see only her left flank. Then, like a racehorse out of the gates, she was off. Before the zebras could even think about reacting she was halfway towards them. With snorts and brays they scattered.

It was clear that the lioness had already chosen her victim. All that watching and waiting had been to see which among the small herd was the youngest or oldest or weakest – which would be the easiest kill. The watchers saw her catching up with one of them, getting closer by the second. The zebra headed for the river. Both animals disappeared behind a dense patch of meru, the zebra only inches ahead of the big cat. In the three minibuses twenty-eight people held twenty-eight breaths.

'Look, there.'

Benjamin pointed towards a dark shape from the other side of the bush. It was the zebra's head. Its eyes were wide, its tongue flopped from open jaws. It was dead. The head of the lioness appeared. Her jaws were still round the zebra's throat where she had clamped them as soon as she had bowled her prey to the ground, cutting off the air to its lungs. There were gasps from the minibuses, both at the shock of the death that had just happened almost before their eyes and at the magnificent strength of the lioness, dragging by the neck an animal twice her own weight – or more – as if she was doing hardly more than carrying home a shopping basket.

'If she is moving it, she must have young cubs,' said Benjamin. 'Otherwise she would eat it right there.'

And sure enough, after the lioness had dragged her prey a few more yards, two cubs, still with the spotted coats of infants, emerged from another low bush.

'Where are the rest of the pride?' asked Mr Gopez.

'When she has her cubs, Mr A.B., the female leaves the pride. Usually just for a few weeks, though sometimes it is for ever.'

'But those cubs, they are not old enough to eat that zebra, are they?'

'No, they are still drinking their mother's milk. But I think here it is easier to guard. She can feed herself and her cubs, and keep other animals away.'

The lioness, after greeting her young with a small but no doubt affectionate snarl, lay down next to the dead zebra and began to feed.

I know that the question now on most minds is exactly

which species of zebra was the mother lioness now munching on? Of the two species common in Kenya my money is on Burchell's zebra *Equus quagga*, subspecies *burchellii*. The size and location of the herd, and the fact that it was a stallion rather than a mare who seemed to be the boss, suggest this species rather than Grevy's zebra *Equus grevyi*. Of course, if we knew whether the animal killed was white with black stripes, or black with white stripes, there would be no doubt. Without this vital piece of information it is impossible to be sure.

A little further upriver the safarists had excellent views of a troop of black and white colobus monkeys coming down from the trees to drink. According to Benjamin, this was most unusual – these monkeys usually get all the water they need from the fruit and leaves they eat, and if they do find themselves thirsty will look for water in a tree hollow. But this particular troop didn't seem at all worried by being on the ground. With much whooping and crashing of branches they followed each other down in two-tone confusion. Some of the smaller, and presumably younger, ones seemed to think it a great game to leap from the tip of one branch fully sixty feet above the ground into a low bush beneath them, all emerging unscathed from the fall.

'Can they swim, do you think?' said Mr Patel.

As if in answer to this question, one of the younger colobus ran at full speed up a rock beside the river and launched itself into the air, landing in the water with a most satisfying splash. No sooner had it paddled ashore than it was ready to repeat the exercise, for all the world like a teenager at a swimming pool. This time it was followed by another young one. Both swam to shore and chased and frolicked in the shallows.

'My God,' said Mr Gopez. 'Look over there – isn't that a crocodile?'

Not twelve yards from the young monkeys something was moving through the water – and yes, those eyes and nostrils were unmistakable.

A large African crocodile can kill a zebra or even a buffalo. While not quite up to this challenge, this one was without doubt big enough to swallow a young colobus in a single gulp. One of the male adult monkeys stood up on its hind legs and gave a scream. But rather than running away, the first young colobus picked up a small stone and threw it towards the crocodile. Within seconds the others were lined up along the bank beside it, showering the water with stones. The occupants of the safari buses saw the crocodile stop swimming. Perhaps reasoning in its slow reptilian way that there's really very little meat on a monkey these days, it turned and swam away.

Monkey meat was notable only by its absence on the lunch menu back at the campsite. The hungry safarists had to make do with a simple assortment of freshly cooked pakoras followed by crispy murgh masala, a large bowl of mattar paneer and a creamy koya gobi mattar with cauliflower and mushrooms, and plain old navratan rice. The plates cleared and cleaned, it was time to leave.

There was no doubt that the Churchman's Patent Convertible billiard table had been a great success. It really was the most marvellous contrivance, thought Mr Malik, as he helped Benjamin pack it up. When the two halves were together you could hardly see the join, but after a few clockwise cranks of the 'draw-bar extender screws' (the ones that Benjamin had that small problem with) the halves came apart, while operating another mechanism caused the legs to begin folding under, each running on wheels along a steel track attached to the packing case into which each half of the table fitted. When both halves were flat in their cases, the two of them replaced the mahogany tops and lifted the lids on to the cases. The cases were built to the same quality as the table. Thick felt and a tight fit ensured that their contents were well protected for transport back to Nairobi. At one o'clock the coach turned up as arranged.

Tiger Singh wondered whether Angus Mbikwa would like a lift back to Nairobi in his Range Rover.

'Thank you, Mr Singh, but I am already being looked after.'

'Oh, of course – you'll be flying back with Mr Johnson.'

'No, I am being driven back by Ms Malik.'

'Oh, please,' said Petula. 'If you would rather go in Mr Singh's Range Rover, I'm sure it would be much more comfortable.'

'But, Petula, we still have to discuss next week's agenda. So thank you, Mr Singh, but I will go with Ms Malik.'

'Nice chap,' said Mr Patel, joining Mr Malik to wave the two of them off in Petula's little Suzuki. 'I was chatting to him at dinner last night. He told me all about his new job, so I asked him to give the talk at the club on Thursday week. Said he'd be delighted. Know anything about it, this Clarity thing?'

'Clarity International? Yes, it's all to do with keeping governments honest. Petula's on the local board. That's how she met him, you know.'

'Oh, I thought it must have been through his mother. Pal of yours, I seem to remember.'

At the Nairobi Hunt Club Ball four years ago Mr Patel had not been the only person surprised to see Mr Malik dance, nor to remark on his dance partner. The sight of him waltzing round the ballroom of the Suffolk Hotel with the lovely Rose Mbikwa caused many a tongue to wag – and to continue wagging for some weeks afterwards.

'Well, sort of,' said Mr Malik, 'but I haven't seen her for some time. She's been looking after her father in Scotland, though I heard she's just got back.'

'Speaking of getting back,' said Tiger Singh, 'any of you other chaps like to come with me? It'll be quicker than the coach. Might even have time for a game of billiards at the club before the others arrive.'

'No thanks, Tiger,' said Mr Patel. 'I . . . er . . . promised to help young Imran with his homework on the way back.'

'Jolly kind of you to offer, Tiger,' said Mr Gopez, 'but I think I might go in the coach and have a bit of a snooze. Why don't you go, Malik?'

'I would be pleased to,' said Mr Malik. He was somewhat surprised at the alacrity with which his friends had refused the offer of a lift, but this could be a chance to have a chat with the Tiger about a few things that had been on his mind. What did he think were the chances the club mascot would turn up again, and what were his thoughts about A.B.'s theory on the Erroll case? The

Tiger might even have some advice on mending broken engagements. 'But would it be possible to drop Benjamin off on the way? He's having a few days with his family.'

Mr Malik had never before driven with Tiger Singh. Never in his life did he want to again. When I tell you that even after taking the B6 and leaving Benjamin at the bus stop in Embu they reached Nairobi in under five hours, you will be able to make a good guess at how many trucks were overtaken on blind corners, how many village dogs escaped death by the width of a whisker and how many chickens survived by just the skin of a beak. When they arrived at the club a game of billiards was out of the question – it was all Mr Malik's shaking hands could do to hold on to a glass without spilling its contents.

He had noticed the absence of the Kima Killer as soon as he'd walked in the door. Once he was halfway into his second drink and felt that his heart rate and adrenalin levels had subsided below the critical range, he asked Tiger Singh to again go through the events leading up to the disappearance of the club mascot. The Tiger had been there on Friday night. Harry Khan had given him a lift from town and stayed on to play billiards. In fact, they were the last to leave.

'Can you remember who else was here that night?' asked Mr Malik.

Tiger Singh thought hard.

'There was no one in the billiard room – I remember Harry Khan remarking on that – but I think there were a few people in the bar when we arrived. Whether anyone was in the dining room, or anywhere else, I really couldn't say. But there definitely wasn't anyone else here when we left – apart from the manager. I told you about that business with the front door getting accidentally locked, didn't I? Harry had left his keys inside – in his briefcase, as I remember. He went back inside to fetch it from the bar, pulled the door closed behind him and locked us all out. But it was all right, I had a spare back-door key at home and Harry took it back to the club for the manager after he'd dropped me off.'

'If it *was* the Bashu boys, then they must have been hiding somewhere in the club.'

'But even so, how could they have got away with the lion? It's not something you could hide under your hat.'

Nor even, thought Mr Malik, in your briefcase. Nothing more could be done about the matter for the moment. Tiger Singh at last managed to persuade Mr Malik that a relaxing game of billiards was just what he needed and had time to win two games before the coach arrived with the rest of the safari party.

'Place doesn't look the same out there,' said Mr Gopez as he joined them in the bar. 'Has anyone worked out yet how they did it?'

As Mr Malik shook his head, he noticed a pale mark on the wall.

'That's strange,' he said. 'Isn't that where the registration certificate usually hangs?'

24

The monkey bitten by a snake fears a vinestem

Mr Malik awoke with a startling thought. Oh my God, what about the loos? There might be enough room in the garden for 170 people, but he had only one loo – two, if Benjamin didn't mind guests using his. Wait a minute, what was he worrying about? There was not going to be a wedding. Oh dear, oh dear, oh dear. Not even the Tiger had been able to suggest how to get Petula and Salman back together. He sat up in bed and shook his head. He supposed Petula knew what she was doing. He gave a long sigh. It was all too difficult. He reached for one of the stack of books on the bedside table.

On the cover a white man in a short-sleeved shirt and slouch hat lounged on a lawn sloping down to some water. Beside him was an enormous deerhound. It was a picture of Lord Erroll taken at Lake Naivasha sometime in the 1930s. Mr Malik picked up a second book. Looking back at him was a young woman dressed in shorts and a short-sleeved shirt. She was lying on bare ground beneath some trees. Beside her, its head in her hand, was a cheetah. In the black and white photograph the young woman looked about sixteen. This was the girl who claimed Sir Jock Delves Broughton admitted to her he had murdered his rival in love, Lord Erroll. Was A.B. right? Could Juanita Carberry really have been the killer? There was no doubt that he had put his finger on something. There *was* something strange about the timing of her revelation, so long after the event. If she had decided to keep silent at the time, why change her mind, and why do it then? Then there were the inconsistencies in her own accounts. Was she in Nairobi at the time of the murder or wasn't she?

He could see problems, though, with A.B.'s theory. If Juanita *had* shot Erroll, how had she managed to get his car into the ditch, and how had she manoeuvred his dead body on to the floor of the car all by herself? There was something strange about the position of the car too. If the murderer – whoever it was – waited for the car to slow down at the road junction, why was it on the Nairobi road, a good 150 yards beyond the junction, when it was found by the milk delivery drivers? Something was still not right. But why, thought Mr Malik, was he wasting his time thinking about the Erroll case? It was over, it was finished, it was all in the past. Like the wedding.

He put the books back on the pile beside the bed and looked over at the clock. That must be Petula he could hear bustling about in the kitchen. Time to get up. It was going to be a busy day.

'Ah, there you are, darling.' Mr Malik levered open the tin of Nescafé with a teaspoon. 'How was the drive home yesterday?'

'Fine,' said Petula, taking the jug of passion-fruit juice

from the fridge. 'Was that you we saw in Mr Singh's car?'

'That's right, he gave me a lift back to Nairobi.' Mr Malik spooned just the right amount of powder into his cup, added a dash of water from the tap and stirred. He'd found that if you mixed in a little cold water before you added the hot it seemed to taste better. 'I didn't see you, though.'

'You overtook us and another couple of cars rather fast on the hill just outside Muranga. As far as I could see you seemed to have your eyes shut.'

'Really?' said Mr Malik, filling the cup from the kettle. 'Just having a bit of shut-eye, I expect.' Mr Malik took a sip from his cup. 'You know, darling, about the wedding . . .'

'Daddy dear – the wedding is on.'

Mr Malik put down his coffee.

'Really? I'm delighted to hear it.'

'You know – that's just what Angus said you'd say. It was good to have that chance to talk – to someone outside it all, if you know what I mean.'

'So you didn't just talk about Clarity International all the way home then?'

'We talked about lots of things – we even talked a little bit about you. But he made me see that perhaps I was a little hard on Salman. After all, his work is important, and important to him. So I'm going to give him a second chance.'

Mr Malik thought back to his own work and marriage. How many times had his own dear wife missed out on evenings out or weekends away when something came up at the factory? Too many. She had never complained. Though Mr Malik knew that he could not undo all the

178

mistakes he had made in his life, sometimes he found himself wishing that he had done things differently.

'Work isn't everything – but yes, perhaps you were a little hard. So I don't have to cancel the marquee, uninvite all the guests?'

His answer was a small kiss on the cheek. The telephone rang.

'The Tiger called you two as well, did he? Do you know what it's about?'

'All he said to me was something about a letter, A.B.,' said Mr Patel. 'Did he mention anything else to you, Malik?'

'No, but he sounded worried – and you don't often hear the Tiger worried.'

When Tiger Singh arrived at the club moments later, his brow was indeed adorned with an unaccustomed furrow.

'Ah, there you are, Malik, A.B., Patel. Good.' He took from his briefcase a single sheet of paper. 'I'll cut straight to the chase, gentlemen. This morning I received by courier this letter from the office of the Minister for the Interior. It is short and to the point, simply calling my attention, as President of the Asadi Club, to Statute 232 of the 1901 British East Africa Protectorate Regulations, later passed into law *sine legislatio* at Kenyan independence in 1963.'

'Ministry?' said Mr Malik.

'Statute?' said Mr Patel.

'Sorry, old boy,' said Mr Gopez, shaking his head. 'I don't get it.'

The Tiger put the letter down on the table in front of him.

'The statute in question relates to a regulation that all non-governmental, non-religious organizations are required to register with the proper authority at or within three calendar months of establishment. Those that fail to do so will be deemed non-lawful and liable to have their assets seized.'

'Register?' said Mr Malik.

'Proper authority?' said Mr Patel.

'Assets seized? Sorry, Tiger,' said Mr Gopez, 'I still don't get it.'

'It is quite simple, gentlemen,' said Tiger Singh. 'They are trying to get their hands on the Asadi Club.'

Mr Gopez groaned. 'Not a-bloody-gain.'

'But they can't,' said Mr Patel. 'I mean, it's ours, the members'.'

'They are saying we have to prove it.'

'Of course we can prove it,' said Mr Gopez. 'Good God, it's been here a hundred years.'

'A hundred and seven, to be precise,' said Mr Malik. He turned to Tiger Singh. 'It's something to do with that certificate, isn't it? The registration certificate, the one that isn't there any more.'

'I suspect that the two events – the disappearance of the certificate and the receipt of the letter – are not unconnected.'

'And the lion too, of course,' said Mr Malik.

'Never mind the lion,' said Mr Patel, 'if it's just a registration certificate we need, there must be a copy of it somewhere, in some government office or something.'

'One might reasonably suppose that to be the case,' said the Tiger, 'and I spent most of the morning making enquiries. I have been assured by my contacts in the Interior Ministry, the Land Registry and the City Council that no such copy exists.'

'Of course,' said Mr Malik. 'The fire.'

'Fire? What are you talking about, Malik?'

'The fire, A.B. – the one in Erroll's office.'

The Tiger nodded.

'Exactly. On Tuesday the eleventh of September 1940, a fire started in the office of the then Military Secretary Lord Erroll, destroying most of the records of the Kenyan Secretariat.'

'Yes, I was reading a book about it again only this morning.'

'The one by the woman who thought he was knocked off by the British Secret Service?' said Mr Gopez.

'That's right,' said Mr Malik. 'Her theory was that Erroll lit it himself – to destroy incriminating evidence.'

'Sounds like poppycock to me.'

'Like the theory that he was murdered by Juanita Carberry?' said Mr Patel, smiling.

Tiger Singh held up a hand.

'I think we need to focus all our attention on the current problem, gentlemen. But it does seem almost certain that among the documents destroyed in that fire were the original records pertaining to Statute 232. This means that the only existing proof of registration is the certificate that, until last Friday, hung on the walls of this very club. The only way we can prove we are registered is to produce the certificate. This afternoon I talked to the minister's office, to his private secretary Mr Jonah Litumana. He most kindly informed me that rules are rules. We have fourteen – no, thirteen days to find it.'

25

A snake may shed its skin but not its soul

I think it was the great seventeenth-century Dutch philosopher Baruch Spinoza who said that searching for the meaning of life is like looking for the purpose of the human earlobe – or it may have been my friend Kennedy. Sitting upstairs in front of her computer on that cloudy Nairobi afternoon, Rose Mbikwa was thinking of her past, her present and her future. She could see that caring for an ancient parent had a purpose. She could see that raising a child had a purpose. But what of her life now? What about life in general? She thought back to Saturday night. She'd had so much fun with Harry Khan – she hadn't laughed so much since she couldn't remember when. There was nothing wrong with having fun, was there? There was nothing wrong with laughter? And yet . . . and yet. Her thoughts were interrupted by the sound of laughter from outside her window. Rose smiled – the sound of children's laughter always made her smile. Elizabeth and Reuben's youngest grandchildren had come to stay for a few days. Now that both their parents were dead they often came up to Nairobi. It gave them a break from the heat and dust of the plains where they had grown up and now went to school. And it gave their great-aunt,

Elizabeth's sister, a break from looking after three such boisterous and active young things.

Rose Mbikwa's house was smaller than most in Serengeti Gardens but its garden was large and contained spacious staff quarters – home to Elizabeth and Reuben Mahugu. They had joined the family just after Rose and Joshua were married. At first Rose had refused to have servants. This was the twentieth century – she was a modern woman used and quite able to look after herself, thank you very much. Did her husband think they were still living in the days of the British Empire? It had taken Joshua several weeks – weeks during which the servants' quarters lay empty and unused – to persuade her that it might be a good idea to give at least two of the tens of thousands of unemployed people in Nairobi a job and a decent place to live. There had been times after Joshua's death when money was tight and Rose had thought of letting Elizabeth and Reuben go. But where would they go? And what would they do? Even with Elizabeth's skills as a cook and housekeeper and Reuben's magical ability to make plants grow (and the old lawnmower perform its weekly duty long after it should have been replaced), employment prospects were never good in a Nairobi that was still sucking in hundreds of people a day from all over the country. But she had no real need for household help now. Perhaps they could retire. With the money invested from the sale of her father's house Rose would be able to afford them both a decent pension.

And perhaps it was time that she herself moved – somewhere smaller and easier to manage. It seemed wrong, somehow, that just one person should have so large a house and garden to enjoy. Well, not quite one. Rose looked out of the window. The older two children were helping the youngest climb on to the lowest branch of the jacaranda. Some of Angus's toys were probably still around somewhere. She should try and find them.

There was a soft knock on the door.

Elizabeth wanted to know whether she'd mind if the children stayed two more days.

'No, no, not at all. I was just thinking how lovely it is to hear the sound of children's voices in the garden again.' She stood up; there were things to be done. 'And would you ask Reuben to come in when he's got a minute – and bring the short ladder. I want to look up into the attic.'

'Come on, Tiger,' said Mr Gopez as he put the tray of drinks down on their usual table by the window. 'Surely it can't be as bad as all that?'

'I'm very much afraid it is,' said the Tiger. 'They've wanted this land for years – and now they think they've found a way to get it.'

He helped himself to one of the glasses. He didn't have to explain who *they* were.

'Then,' said Mr Gopez, 'they've got another think coming.'

'While your optimistic spirit does you proud, A.B., the fact remains that without the certificate – and according to the law – this club cannot be shown to be legally registered. It is therefore illegal – as the minister's private secretary Mr Jonah Litumana seemed rather too pleased to tell me.'

'How long did you say we've got?'

'Until Monday week, just as it says in the letter.'

'But why us? Why not the Nairobi Club or the Muthaiga?'

'I phoned Pongo Hepplewhite this morning. He said he wasn't surprised – they've been trying to get hold of the Muthaiga Club for years too. When I told him about the registration certificate he whipped theirs straight off the wall of his office and into a bank vault.'

'But we've been here even longer than they have,' said Mr Gopez. 'Surely that means something? Law of primogeniture – or whatever you legal chaps call it.'

Tiger Singh shook his head.

'While the principle of primogeniture, A.B. – whether it be agnatic, cognatic, uterine or absolute – has done sterling work in ensuring the succession and inheritance of innumerable royal houses both within Europe and without, I fear it is inapplicable to the present situation. We have to prove to the ministry that we are registered. Without the original document we cannot do so. Ergo we are illegal, ergo they can close us down.'

'Well,' said Mr Patel, 'we'll just have to pay them off.'

'As a lawyer, my dear Patel, I did not hear that. Besides, it would take millions of shillings – tens of millions. Have you looked at the accounts recently?'

'Couldn't we all, well, chip in a bit?' said Mr Malik.

'A noble thought, Malik. There are currently two hundred and forty-three full members of the Asadi Club, with another thirty or so country members. Some of us might be able to scrape together a lakh or two, but I know most couldn't.'

'But hang on a minute, Tiger,' said Mr Gopez. 'Is it not a basic principle of law that a party is assumed innocent until proven guilty? We may not be able to prove that the club was registered, but under the law would we not be given the benefit of the doubt, so to speak?'

'An excellent point, A.B., but I fear the principle in question relates to matters of criminal law,' said Tiger Singh. 'Our case, unfortunately, falls within the civil jurisdiction.'

'But if this damned burglary wasn't criminal, what is?'

'I suppose you could have something there,' said the Tiger. 'What you're saying is that in this case, although by law proof of registration is incumbent on the respondent, if said proof can be shown to have been destroyed, removed or otherwise made inaccessible by criminal act then, under the civil code, such proof must be assumed. Is that about it?'

'In a coconut shell, yes.'

'I will certainly give the matter some thought. Does anyone else have any ideas?'

'It seems to me,' said Mr Malik, 'that we should consider fighting this on two fronts, as it were. First, the legal one. A.B.'s idea is a good one, and perhaps we can prove registration some other way, or question the regulation, or –'

'Or tie them up in so much pink ribbon that they won't be able to lift a legal finger.' For the first time that evening the Tiger smiled. 'I'll certainly see what I can do. And the second front?'

'We need to make an all-out effort to find the missing certificate.'

'If it still exists,' said Mr Patel. 'After all, the powers of darkness might have already destroyed it.'

'You have a good point, old chap,' said Mr Gopez. 'If they have taken the certificate it would make sense to destroy it asap. But still, trying to get the damned thing back has to be a priority. Perhaps we can ginger up the police, get them to launch a proper investigation.'

The Tiger shook his head.

'As far as the police are concerned, all that was stolen is a stuffed lion and a framed certificate – neither of which are of great monetary value.'

'What about if we offer a reward?'

Again the Tiger shook his head.

'Under present circumstances, A.B., I fear that would be of little use. There are complicating factors, you see. I happen to know that the Minister for Police is a close friend of the Minister for the Interior. They play golf together – I've seen them at the Sandringham. Whatever we do, we cannot count on much help from official quarters.'

'One thing I'd like to do is have another word with our club manager,' said Mr Malik. 'We might have missed something.'

When the manager was called to the table, he confirmed the story that on Friday night the Tiger and Harry Khan had been the last to leave the club. He told them again about the incident with the front door being accidentally locked.

'But Mr Khan brought the spare back-door key straight back from Mr Singh's house.'

'And when you locked up, you are absolutely sure the lion was still there – and, as far as you know, the certificate?'

'As far as I can remember, Mr Malik. I locked up as

usual. It is a routine. I had already checked all the windows were closed while Mr Singh and Mr Khan were in the billiard room – what with so many members being on safari, it was a quiet night. After Mr Khan brought me the key I went back inside, emptied the till and put the money in the safe in my office. I checked that all the keys were on the board there and switched on the alarm. Then I went out again through the back door. The alarm gives you thirty seconds to get out.'

'What about the front door – did you lock that?'

'It was already locked, sir. Mr Khan –'

'Ah yes, of course, Mr Khan had closed it behind him. So you didn't need to check that it was closed.'

'No, sir. And there is the alarm board too – all the door and window locks show up on the board. It is easy to see if anywhere is unlocked.'

'Do you lock the door to your office?'

'No, sir, it is not necessary. The internal doors are not alarmed – but, as I say, I always check the key board in my office before I leave. No keys were missing, and all the keys were certainly there the following morning.'

'Then it's quite clear what must have happened,' said Mr Gopez.

'It is?'

'Someone must have hidden in the building – stayed on after everyone else had gone.'

'Or snuck in through the back door,' said Mr Patel, 'while everyone was out the front.'

'Yes,' said Tiger Singh, 'I suppose either is possible. Then after our meticulous manager locks up, he – or they – have the run of the place.'

'That's all very well,' said Mr Patel, 'but why take the lion? And how did they get out? All the doors and windows are alarmed. And why take the certificate?'

'Well, I don't think it's difficult to work out,' said Mr Gopez. 'Let's not forget that two days later that letter arrives. As the Tiger says, they must be connected.'

Since rereading all the accounts of the Erroll murder, Mr Malik had been thinking a lot about connections. Everyone assumed that everything about the case – the position of the car and the body, the bloodstains and the marks on the seat, even the inconsistencies in Juanita Carberry's accounts of what had happened – were all somehow linked. But what if they weren't related at all?

'Of course,' he said, 'they might *not* be connected. I mean, the person or persons responsible for taking the lion are not necessarily the same persons who removed the certificate.'

'While logic is on your side, Malik,' said the Tiger, 'I fear circumstances are not.'

'The Tiger's right, Malik,' said Mr Patel. 'That would be stretching coincidence a little too far.'

'Well, it's no use sitting around,' said Mr Gopez. 'I'm going to jolly well do something. First thing – house-to-house enquiries. Someone might have seen something.'

'And I'll talk to the staff again,' said Mr Patel. 'One of them might have remembered something.'

'And I,' said the Tiger, 'will call an extraordinary general meeting, for tomorrow.'

'Excellent idea,' said Mr Patel.

'By the way, sir,' said the manager. 'I have had two

quotes for repainting the clubhouse. What would you like me to do about them?'

'Nothing,' said Tiger Singh. 'I rather fear that the way things are looking at the moment, the club may never need repainting again.'

26

Worm is to frog as frog is to snake as snake is to
pig as pig is to man as man is to worm

What with the threat to his beloved Asadi Club, the closing of the *Evening News* and the imminent celebration of
his only daughter's nuptials, you might think that Mr
Malik had enough to think about. But as he sat on the
veranda peeling a meditative banana, his mind was on
other things. It was Tuesday. In half an hour's time he
would leave the house and drive the mile to the museum.
He would meet his friends – perhaps Rose Mbikwa
would be there. He would give a lift to Thomas Nyambe,
and as many others as could fit into the back seat of his
old Mercedes, to wherever that day's bird walk would be.
After the bird walk he would come home and write his
'Birds of a Feather' column. He would seal it in its customary plain brown envelope and drop it in the postbox
at the corner of Garden Lane and Parklands Drive. He
would then drive over to the Aga Khan Hospital – as he
did so often these days. In a separate building at the back
of the main complex is a large ward whose patients see
few visitors. It is the Aids ward, and it was where – eight
years ago, and unknown to Mr Malik at the time – his
own son Raj had died.

When Raj had told him three years earlier that he was gay, Mr Malik had stormed and Mr Malik had fumed. 'Go from my house,' he said, 'and take your unnatural perversion with you.' How strong was Mr Malik's anger, how righteous his indignation. And so Raj had gone away, and had died unloved and unacknowledged by his father. Only when he learned that Raj was dead did Mr Malik's love for his only son come flooding back into his heart, but no one and nothing could make up for the mistake he had made and the sin he knew he had committed. It was too late to repair the damage. There was one small thing he could do, though. He could make sure that other people's sons and daughters did not die alone and unloved. For some years now Mr Malik had been a familiar figure in the building at the back of the hospital, where he would sit beside the sick and dying. He would talk or not talk, and much was the comfort he brought.

A small sound behind him interrupted his thoughts.

'Oh, hello, darling.'

'Good morning, Daddy dear. What were you thinking about – the wedding?'

'In a way. I was just thinking about Raj, actually. How he would have liked to be there on Saturday. He was so fond of his little sister, so proud.'

Petula came over to his chair and put a hand on his shoulder.

'And I was proud of him. I still am.'

'You know . . .' said Mr Malik.

'Yes,' she said, 'I know.'

Together they looked out into the garden. The bougainvillea was a riot of yellows and pinks and mauves, the canna lilies were bright orange splashes against the green of the camellias and hibiscus.

A full minute passed before he spoke again.

'So, everything's really all right?'

'Yes, Daddy. Salman's coming tomorrow. I'm picking him up at the airport. We still have quite a lot to talk about.'

'I suppose you have,' said Mr Malik.

There was a knock at the door.

'I'll get it, Daddy.'

Petula returned to the veranda, wearing a large smile and carrying a bunch of red roses wrapped in a fat red ribbon. Mr Malik watched as she put the roses into a vase, humming a tune. Salman, it seemed, was learning.

'I might be a bit late home tonight, darling. There's a special meeting at the club.'

Petula took a banana from the table, kissed the top of her father's head and picked up her car keys.

'That's all right, I'll be late too. CI meeting.'

Mr Malik looked at his watch. Time for a second banana before he had to leave for the bird walk.

It had felt strange getting behind the wheel of her old Peugeot 504, strange being back in the hectic Nairobi traffic, strange pulling up outside the museum to be greeted by a buzzing crowd of old friends. Rose had not been prepared for such a large gathering – most of whom, it was soon clear, had come especially to welcome her back. Though there was a new pack of YOs, she saw many familiar faces. Hilary was there, of course, and old Tom Turnbull. Though he had not changed a bit, he had swapped his old Morris Minor for a smart new Hyundai. She could also see

Patsy King and Jonathan Evans. Were they still having their Tuesday morning affair? Standing a little apart from the others she noticed Mr Malik talking to his old friend – what was his name? Mr Nyambe, that's right. Thomas Nyambe.

Perhaps because news had spread that Rose was back, more people had turned up than could be accommodated in the various cars. It was decided they would go to the arboretum. This shady few acres of trees and grass was only a twenty-minute walk from the museum. Mr Malik, leaving his old green Mercedes in the museum car park, set off in the company of his good friend Thomas Nyambe.

Not all of the morning was spent listening to the stories Thomas Nyambe told. The arboretum contains trees from all around the world, and it was Australia's day to flower. Down by the river the grove of lemon-scented gum trees was in full bloom. Bees buzzed, sunbirds flitted, and sixty feet above them a male vervet monkey – easily recognizable even at that distance – sat plucking and sucking the honey-filled blossoms.

'But have you heard, Mr Malik, about the *Evening News*?'

'That it will be closing down? Yes, I'd heard rumours but wasn't sure whether to believe them.'

'I think it is true. What the government couldn't do with threats it is doing with red tape and regulations. The paper has just one more week to find some piece of paper they have lost.'

'Then tomorrow's could be the last "Birds of a Feather" column, Mr Nyambe.' Mr Malik put away his notebook and pen. 'I will try to make it a good one.'

When the time came for the group to disband, Mr Malik had recorded three more species of mammals and thirty-one species of birds – as well as enough government gossip to fill several pages. He never did talk to Rose Mbikwa. She had seemed so busy with all her other friends that he had thought it best not to intrude.

At six o'clock that evening the Asadi Club car park was already packed. There had been no time to send a mailout to members about the extraordinary general meeting, but in spreading the word Tiger Singh had left no communicatory stone unturned. Telephone calls, emails and word of mouth had ensured a larger turnout than at any club meeting Mr Malik could remember – even three or four country members had managed to make the trip into town. It might well be, he realized, even larger than the legendary meeting of October 1936 called to discuss the 'Ranamurka Affair', which had eventually led to the banning of women from the club – a ban which had lasted more than forty years. Realizing that there would not be enough room in the bar, the manager had opened up the folding doors into the dining room – even so, it was standing room only when Tiger Singh got up to speak.

'Members, gentlemen.' Tiger Singh surveyed the crowd. 'You will all have heard that this meeting has been called to discuss a threat to the very future of the Asadi Club as we know it. As many of you will know, last week a burglary was committed here at the club. Two items were taken – the club mascot and our certificate of registration.'

A murmur arose from the crowd, in which Mr Malik thought he could hear mentioned the names of two members, both absent. The Tiger continued to explain to the increasingly indignant audience the events so far.

'They've got us over the proverbial barrel. We have twelve days to find that certificate. If we do not, the Asadi Club will cease to exist.'

After some more discussion, during which little was resolved, the meeting broke up. The four friends retired to the bar, where Mr Gopez reported that his own enquiries had so far drawn a blank. Nor had Mr Patel's further questioning of the staff revealed anything new.

'None of them saw a thing – well, those of them who were actually here. We had most of the kitchen and dining-room staff on safari with us, of course. It seems that Friday was an unusually quiet night. The barmen went home early, so that just left the manager, the undergardener and the askari. The Tiger and Harry Khan were the last to leave. At the probable time of the theft the undergardener was asleep in his room. The askari was probably sleeping too, but anyway swears he didn't see anything. And as the manager said, the first he knew of it was when he opened up in the morning.'

Tiger Singh looked glum.

'I've looked at every law book, every case history I could think of. If you will excuse my mixing sporting metaphors, gentlemen, the ball is in our court and they have all the trumps.'

'Tiger,' said Mr Malik, 'I think you have done a magnificent job. All of you are to be congratulated. I'm sure something will turn up.'

'I wish I could agree with you,' said Mr Patel. 'But I can't.'

Mr Gopez gave a long sigh.

'If it's any consolation,' said Mr Malik, 'it seems that

we're not the only ones. I heard this morning from a friend on the bird walk that they're pulling the same trick with the *Evening News* – though it's not the premises they want, just to close down the paper.'

'You mean their registration certificate has disappeared too?'

Mr Malik nodded. But even if what he'd heard from Thomas Nyambe that morning was correct, and the 'Birds of a Feather' column that he'd written that very afternoon would indeed be his last, at least he had the satisfaction of knowing that it would go out with a bang. Not only would his readers learn that the car being driven by the wife of the chairman of the parliamentary anti-corruption committee had been paid for by the owner of the civil engineering company who had just got the contract for the new airport terminal, but also that the CEO of the Mombasa Port Authority had, in all the years he had been drawing his considerable salary, never been to Mombasa. It was a pity, thought Mr Malik, that Thomas Nyambe hadn't been able to come up with anything to pin on the new Minister for the Interior. He might have been able to use it to save the Asadi Club. He stood up.

'Come on, chaps. Sitting around feeling sorry for ourselves isn't going to help things. Who'd like a game of billiards?'

'Hey,' said a voice behind him. 'If anyone's going to be playing billiards with Jack here, it's me.'

27

The worm will reach the water

Of all the sayings in the English language, two in particular have long puzzled me. The first is 'The exception proves the rule', and last year I thought I'd finally got a handle on this one. If something is seen as an exception it must be an exception *to* something – that something being what we usually expect to happen. So, in a sense, any exception by its very nature gives support to the rule to which it is an exception – if you see what I mean (and I don't blame you at all if you don't). But then I was talking to my friend Kennedy and he said that the meaning of this phrase is quite clear when you realize that two words are missing – it should be read as 'the exception proves *to be* the rule' – and I was pretty much back where I started. Another phrase that has always flummoxed me is 'The more things change, the more they stay the same.' Kennedy said he couldn't help me with that one – though that wasn't surprising as he was almost certain it was originally French. As Mr Malik sat on the veranda of his house at Number 12 Garden Lane the morning after the meeting at the club – the morning after his second billiards defeat in a week by Harry Khan – his thoughts were of things changing and *not* staying the same.

What if, he thought, as he put down one of the books he had been perusing and picked up his cup of Nescafé, what if the club really did close down? Change was inevitable – it should not be resisted, but accommodated. Certainly some changes are more under our control than others. Mr Malik was aware, for instance, that he could have done little about Chinese producers undercutting his business in cigars. But he had been able to react by changing (with Petula's help) the direction of the Jolly Man Manufacturing Company from cigars to confectionery. Petula herself would soon be leaving him. Though he would miss her sorely, her marriage was surely a good thing, a change to be welcomed. And as Petula had herself said to him just the other day, so what if the *Evening News* was forced to close? No government could close the internet. He gazed out into the garden. Benjamin would not be back from his family visit until tomorrow. Fallen leaves littered the lawn. Change, everywhere. In the grand scheme of the universe, was the continuing existence of the Asadi Club really that important?

His thoughts were interrupted by the sound of a truck and a knock on the door. Of course, the marquee was going up today. He had no sooner shown the men into the garden than he heard another knock and opened the door to see a taxi driving away and a thin, dark-suited man standing in front of him with a suitcase in his hand.

'My dear Salman, how very good to see you. Welcome. Come in, come in. But I thought Petula was going to meet you at the airport?'

'I was expecting her, but then she sent me a text to say that she had to go into work. Do you think it is just possible that I am being paid back for last week?'

Mr Malik laughed.

'It is indeed just possible, Salman. But I think that perhaps you have been forgiven.' He gestured to the bunch of roses now in a glass vase beside the door. 'I didn't see her last night, I'm afraid. She was at a meeting and I was in bed before she came home.'

'Clarity International, I suppose.' Salman put down his bag. 'Tell me, Mr Malik, do you think there's much point in it?'

'Point? Yes, I think so. But I'm surprised she wasn't at the airport.'

'It was no problem to take a taxi. Between ourselves, Mr Malik, I always feel a little uncomfortable with a woman behind the wheel – even your daughter.'

Mr Malik smiled.

'So – this is it, I hope. The wedding is on? No more going back to Dubai?'

'Yes, this is it – though I might have to drop into the office next week. It will be no problem. We have to go through Dubai on our way to Paris.'

Mr Malik already knew that the newly-weds were planning a honeymoon in Paris – he had insisted on paying for the hotel – but Petula had done all the travel plans. He took Salman through the house and on to the veranda, where they watched five men unroll the large white sausage of a marquee and begin fitting together the poles.

'Did Petula say when she will be home, Salman? Perhaps I should give her a ring at the office.'

'I have already done so, Mr Malik. I'm sure she will be home very soon.'

It occurred to Mr Malik that right now two might be company, three a crowd.

'If you don't mind, I won't wait for her. I should really get along.'

Leaving Salman with instructions to make himself at home, Mr Malik picked up the keys to his old green Mercedes. He wouldn't go straight to the club, though. He would spend the morning at the hospital. By the time he got to the club after lunch, it was just possible someone might have heard something about the certificate.

'Any more luck with the house-to-house enquiries, A.B.?'

Mr Gopez looked up at Mr Malik and shook a weary head.

'Not a sausage. Wait – I lie. Mrs Mohutu two doors down over the road said she hadn't seen anything but she thought it could have been monkeys. Only last month she swears they stole two handkerchiefs and an item of ladies' clothing – she didn't say what exactly – from her washing line.'

'Perhaps,' said Mr Malik, 'the Tiger will have some news.'

They did not have long to wait for his arrival.

'Well, gentlemen, it's not the best news but it's not the worst. I've managed to arrange a hearing. Wednesday next at ten sharp, before Judge Kafari. *Dum spiro spero*. At the very least we should be able to delay them and pray that something else turns up soon.'

'Speaking of news, I don't suppose you chaps have had a chance to look at this?' Mr Patel was holding open a copy of the evening paper. 'That fellow Dadukwa has done it again. Looks like the anti-corruption committee is going to need a new chairman.' He dropped the paper on to the table. 'Do you think Harry Khan's right? Do you think they'll really shut it down?'

'The *Evening News*? They've been trying for a long time,' said Mr Malik, 'but I think this time they might do it.'

Yes, his last 'Birds of a Feather' column. Perhaps, thought Mr Malik, it was finally time to reveal that he was Dadukwa. To reveal how for the past seven years it had been he who weekly penned the words that had kept Kenya informed of the real goings-on behind the scenes of government and business. Over those years only two people knew his secret. Thomas Nyambe was one of them. The other was Rose Mbikwa.

Rose had made the discovery only by accident. Four years ago she had found a notebook near where she lived, scorched from a bonfire and wet from the rain. From the crude sketch of an eagle on the cover she thought she recognized it. Sure enough, when she opened it she knew it must belong to Mr Malik – there were the records of the bird walks she had noticed him taking every week. But she couldn't help also noticing the other notes – notes which she knew from her regular reading of the 'Birds of a Feather' column in the *Evening News* could only mean one thing. So Mr Malik – quiet, diffident, kind Mr Malik – was Dadukwa. She couldn't help herself, she had to tell someone. On the night of the Nairobi Hunt Club Ball she revealed her discovery – to wise, brave, wonderful Mr Malik himself. So then he knew that she knew, and she knew that he knew that she would never, ever tell another soul. But even if the paper was to be closed, Mr Malik knew he might still be in danger. Many a businessman and government minister, present and past, still had a score to settle with Dadukwa. No, it was probably better that the secret be kept.

The next evening, no better news.

'Ten days to go.'

'Yes, A.B., I know.' Mr Malik gave a small shake of his head. 'Nothing new, I suppose?'

'Not a sausage.'

'By the way,' said Mr Patel, 'how's the wedding going?'

'Wedding,' said Mr Malik. 'What wedding?'

When Petula had told him on his return from the club the previous evening that the wedding was off again, he had at first thought she was teasing him. It wasn't as if she looked angry this time, or even sad. She seemed calm, almost happy.

'Yes, Daddy dear . . . I'm very sorry, but it's off. Definitely. I've just taken Salman back to the airport.'

'But . . .'

'But why?' She picked a single red rose from the vase on the table beside the door. 'Here we are, Daddy. First witness for the prosecution.'

'I don't understand. What have the roses he sent you got to do with it?'

'This, Daddy dear, is not a rose that Salman sent me. This is a rose Salman didn't send me.'

'I'm sorry, darling. I still don't understand.'

'It's true, Daddy dear. You and I were wrong. How do I know? Because when I thanked dear Salman this morning for these lovely roses, and told him how pleased I was to get them and how much they meant to me, do you know what he said?'

Mr Malik did not know. He was not sure that he wanted to know.

'He said that there seemed to be some confusion. Why did I think the roses were from him? Why would he send me roses? Why would he send me roses, he said, when we both knew that the garden was full of roses? And then he said . . .' Petula's smile was looking a little forced now. 'And then he said that he didn't like roses anyway – all those nasty thorns.'

'Doesn't like roses?'

'No.'

'I see.'

'Yes.'

'Anything else?'

'There is, actually. He said that while we were on the subject of things he didn't like there *was* something else. He said that he didn't like my work with Clarity International. He thought it unwise and unsuitable.'

'Unwise?'

'Unwise.'

'And unsuitable?'

'His very words. Then, reverting to the previous subject, he said that even though he didn't like roses, he didn't like the idea of someone else sending roses to his fiancée. And he said he certainly hoped no one would ever send roses to his wife.'

'Hmm,' said Mr Malik.

'He said his father never sent his mother roses, and she

always said that the kind of woman to whom other people sent roses was probably the kind who couldn't cook a decent dhal and gave women drivers a bad name.'

'Ah,' said Mr Malik. He thought for a moment. 'Petula dear,' he said.

'Yes, Daddy?'

'I think I understand, but . . . we won't be going through all this again, will we?'

She came round behind him and gave him a hug.

'No, Daddy.'

28

As the hyena loves the vulture, the vulture loves
the worm

Sitting on the veranda watching the workmen roll up the
marquee, Mr Malik felt suddenly tired. It had been a hectic weekend. After cancelling mosque, flowers and cars, he
had spent most of Thursday and all of Friday on the
phone trying to contact all the guests. It was too late to
cancel the food, but Ally Dass would be happy to deliver
what had already been bought and prepared to various
hospitals around Nairobi. Mr Malik was able to supply
him with addresses and ward numbers.

Oh well, perhaps Petula was just not the marrying type.
He looked back into the house. She should be back soon.
She'd left on Friday afternoon for a weekend away with
Sunita Depawala. Ever since schooldays the two of them
had relied on each other for advice and support in times
of trouble. Ah, that sounded like her Suzuki now.

'Good morning, Daddy dear.'

For a woman who had just cancelled a marriage Petula
sounded remarkably chirpy, thought Mr Malik, as he tilted
his cheek for the customary kiss.

'Hello, darling. How was Lake Naivasha?'

'Great fun. The old hotel, it never changes.'

Which is not quite true. At the Hotel Naivasha today you will not find the bar packed on a Friday night with passengers and crew from the Imperial Airways flying boat service from England to South Africa that has just landed on the lake – as you might have in the 1930s. You will not see Lord Delamere pull up outside the front door in a buggy harnessed to a pair of zebras – as you might have in the 1940s. No longer can you spend a long week-end at the hotel for four pounds nineteen shillings and eleven pence full board including champagne on arrival and a complimentary ticket for a trip on the pleasure steamer *Pride of Africa* – as you might have in the 1950s. But even today you *feel* as if you might, and the Hotel Naivasha is just the place to go to get away from it all – whether it be the pressure of city living, the demands of a hectic working life, or a broken romance.

'You're not too upset then – about the wedding, and everything?'

'Sunita and I agreed that marriage is an outmoded institution, and that anyway few men deserve us – one, in particular. As far as I am concerned, it was a lucky escape. And guess who we saw at the hotel? Angus Mbikwa – you know, you met him on the safari. His mother was there too. She's been away, in Scotland. Just got back.'

'Ah yes, I saw her last Tuesday.'

'Yes, she mentioned she'd seen you. She and Angus were staying at the Khans' place. We had quite a chat. I like Rose.'

Mr Malik remembered that Harry Khan's uncle had built a house beside the lake in the 1950s and that it was still in the family.

'The Khans – really? Was Harry Khan there by any chance?'

'Yes. He's such fun, isn't he? He asked us all round for lunch on Sunday. Lovely place they've got there, right next to Oserian.'

'Oh yes, Lord Erroll's old place – the "Djinn Palace" they used to call it.'

'That's right. Anyway, he said to tell you he was looking forward to another game of billiards. And Rose said she was looking forward to seeing you at the next bird walk – that must be tomorrow. I must say, Sunita seemed pretty keen on Angus. She even offered to help him set up his new office.'

Mr Malik had already half made up his mind that he would not be going on the next bird walk. What with the *Evening News* shutting down and the Asadi Club about to follow, incentive seemed distinctly lacking. But if Rose Mbikwa was going to be there again . . . well, perhaps. On the other hand, if Harry Khan was going to be there, perhaps not.

'And speaking of Rose, I found out such a funny thing. You know the red roses that arrived last week, the ones we thought were from Salman. They were from Angus. To thank me for giving him a lift home from the safari. Wasn't that sweet?'

'Very sweet.'

'I know what you're thinking,' said Petula. 'You're probably thinking that perhaps a note with them might have prevented all this confusion.'

'Something along those lines.'

'Yes, Sunita and I talked about that. But if Angus *had*

sent a note, just think – I might be married to Salman by now.'

'So, Mr Malik, it is true that they have shut down the *Evening News*.'

Mr Malik had decided that on balance it would be a good idea to keep up his regular attendance at the Tuesday bird walk. After all, he had started going for his health, not to meet Rose Mbikwa or chat to Thomas Nyambe. It turned out that Harry Khan's Mercedes had not been among the cars lined up that morning in front of the museum, but there were enough seats to take everyone out to River Road. The juxtaposition of thorn scrub and suburban development could usually be relied upon to attract a variety of birdlife.

'Yes, my dear friend, today is the last day of publication. No "Birds of a Feather" tomorrow, I'm afraid.'

'I think this is sad. All people should know what their government is doing, not just we drivers.'

'Yes, Mr Nyambe, it is sad. But I have been thinking perhaps not so bad. My daughter is involved in an organization that does this same thing – shows people what their governments are doing – all over the world. But now it is not so much with newspapers, it is with the internet. I think that this will be the new way.'

'This is true, and the truth will always find its way to the light. Do you not think so, Mr Malik?'

'I do – well, perhaps not everything.'

Mr Malik had not wanted to give any more thought to the Erroll case, it was just that his mind still refused to let it rest. Every day it kept bringing up the inconsistencies between the different accounts. And what if each apparent clue – the white marks on the car seat, the gym shoes on the bonfire, the lipstick-stained cigarette on the floor of the car – was just a red herring?

'I have been thinking a lot recently about a strange story from long ago,' said Mr Malik to his friend. 'It is more than fifty years now – and I think that for this the truth will never be known. Perhaps you have heard of the murder of Lord Erroll?'

'I know the story well – my father told it to me. But the truth, it is there for people to see if they so wish.'

The two men continued to walk slowly together down the road, and if Mr Malik was less than usually interested in the glossy starlings and red-eyed doves – even the rare sight in Nairobi of three wood hoopoes in a pine tree – he was more than usually interested in listening to what his friend had to say. He was indeed so engrossed in their conversation that when they all found themselves back where they had left their cars, he was surprised when he felt a soft touch on his arm and heard a soft voice speak his name.

'Mr Malik.'

'Mrs Mbikwa. It is a great pleasure to see you.'

Rose Mbikwa gave him a most friendly smile.

'And for me to see you. I'm so sorry we didn't have time to talk last week. Did your daughter tell you that I met her at the weekend, down at the lake?'

'Yes, and no doubt your son has told you that I met him the weekend before, at your friend Mr Johnson's. Tell me, Mrs Mbikwa, is it true that you are back in Nairobi now for good?'

'Yes, for good. So I hope we shall be seeing more of each other. Tell me, are you still doing your Aids work?'

How did she know about that? Then he recalled the Hunt Club Ball, and dancing with her. Yes, they had talked about a lot of things then. Yet how remarkable that she'd remembered.

'As long as there are people dying alone, Mrs Mbikwa, I will do my best,' he said. 'I think that maybe now things are getting just a little bit better.'

'Yes, I hear more and more people are being treated. But I can't help thinking about the ones left behind – the children, you know. I've been doing a little bit of research on the internet – there may be a million Aids orphans in Kenya alone.'

'Then they will be needing a lot of love and looking after, Mrs Mbikwa. How fortunate we are that we have been spared to love our own children.'

'Yes, Mr Malik, a lot of love . . .' she paused for a moment. 'I was very disappointed to see that the *Evening News* has been closed down. I used to so enjoy reading it – especially on Wednesdays. And Harry Khan's been telling me that your club's in a bit of a pickle.'

'We have been having a few problems, it is true, though I am hopeful that everything will be resolved at the court hearing tomorrow.' Surely the Tiger – good old Tiger – would sort it all out? 'Tell me, Mrs Mbikwa, did he – Harry – say anything about a lion?'

'Yes, the club mascot mysteriously vanished, I hear. You must tell me all about it – but not now, I'm afraid. I must rush. I've got someone coming for lunch.'

'Perhaps we will have time to talk more next Tuesday.'

'I'm sure we will, dear Mr Malik – if not sooner.'

As Rose Mbikwa drove away in her battered old Peugeot 504, Mr Malik could not help wondering what she meant by that – nor could he help wondering with whom she would be having lunch.

29

A hyena stung by a wasp is scared of a gnat

From the kitchen came the sound of a woman's laughter. Rose turned down the stereo. Angus must be home. He always came in the back door, just as he had when he was a child, and he almost always said something that would make Elizabeth laugh out loud.

'Hello, darling. I wasn't expecting you. How was your day?'

'Good, thanks.' Angus flung his bag and jacket on to one of the armchairs and leaned over his mother to kiss her. 'We seem to be making some headway at last. I don't know if I told you that Sunita said she'd drop in this afternoon. She was great. Used her mobile to get on to Telkom – wouldn't take no for an answer. They sent a couple of men round straight away, and at last the landline's working.'

'Good . . .' Rose paused, as if unsure whether to continue. 'I had lunch with her today, as a matter of fact.'

'Really? Sunita? She didn't mention it.'

'Oh, it was nothing important – just an opportunity for a bit of girls' talk.'

Angus Mbikwa flopped into an armchair.

'Anyway, Mother, how are you today? Feeling at home yet?'

'Oh yes. It was such fun to be down at the lake again – just what I needed. I really felt back in Africa at last.'

'Me too. Bit of a coincidence, meeting Petula Malik – and you knowing her father. What's he like? I met him at Uncle Dickie's, but I didn't get much chance to talk to him.'

'Mr Malik?' Rose thought hard for a moment, then gave a small smile. 'Mr Malik is a most remarkable man. He's been going on the bird walk for years. I saw him there this morning.'

'And tell me about Harry Khan? I didn't think he really seemed like your type, but you seem to get on well.'

Rose laughed.

'Yes, he's a bit of a wheeler-dealer is Harry. Into property development at the moment, apparently – shopping malls. He's been telling me lots of stories about meeting all these government ministers – he can be very funny. He's really the most terrible tease, but there's a lot of good in Harry. I'm having dinner with him again tonight as a matter of fact.' She got up. 'We thought we might try Tusks – haven't been there for ages. But Mr Malik . . .' again, she paused. 'Yes, Mr Malik is a most remarkable man. Now, I suppose I should go and get changed. Are you going out tonight?'

'Yes, I'm meeting someone in town.'

'Anyone special?'

'Oh,' said Angus Mbikwa, 'you could say that.'

Petula was surprised to find her father still up when she got home. Her meeting had taken much longer than expected.

'Hello, Daddy dear. How did it go?'

'Hmm?'

'The bird walk this morning. How did it go? Did you see Rose?'

'Oh yes. Yes, I did see Mrs Mbikwa, but only briefly.'

Petula looked at him and gave a small frown.

'Is there something on your mind, Daddy? You're not still worried about the wedding, are you?'

'No, no, not the wedding.'

What with her forthcoming marriage, Mr Malik hadn't wanted to bother Petula about the difficulties they'd been going through at the Asadi Club, but now . . . He began telling her all about what had happened.

'Not that we've really got anything to worry about with Tiger Singh on the job.' He smiled. 'Never lost a game of billiards, never lost a case in court. They don't know what's coming to them. Still, I can't help thinking a lot of bother could have been avoided if only I'd done something.'

'But it all happened while you were away on the club safari. What could you have done?'

'Oh, I don't know – something.' He looked up. 'I promised your grandfather, you see.'

Mr Malik reminded Petula about his father's last words. For a minute, neither of them spoke.

'You know, don't you, Daddy, that this is just the kind of thing that Clarity International is fighting against? Crime and corruption. But I'm sure you're right. Mr Singh will work it all out tomorrow.'

It was with optimism tinged with just a hint of apprehension that the following day Messrs Malik, Gopez and Patel awaited the arrival of Tiger Singh at their usual table in the bar of the Asadi Club. If anyone could persuade the court that the business with the missing registration certificate was a legal nonsense, or that the theft of the certificate gave a sure and unquestionable extenuation of circumstances, it was Tiger Singh.

'Well, Tiger?'

His face told them all they wanted to know.

'Ah well, you know what they say,' said Mr Gopez. 'You can't fight Tammany Hall.'

Though the others had only the vaguest knowledge of nineteenth-century New York politics, they were pretty sure they got A.B.'s drift.

Mr Patel shook his head.

'I suppose we should have guessed.'

Tiger Singh picked up the glass of Tusker in front of him and took a long swallow. He gave an equally long sigh.

'So what exactly happened, Tiger?' said Mr Malik.

'The ministry – or, to be more precise, the minister's representative Mr Jonah Litumana – was able to persuade the judge that according to the letter of the law the government is perfectly within its rights to seek confirmation of registration. The judge ruled that notwithstanding the fact that the government itself may have once held such records, the statutory onus is on us to provide such evidence within the time limit set by the minister. *Diem perdidi*, I'm afraid. I have failed you.'

'If I may say so, my dear Tiger,' said Mr Malik, 'you have in no sense failed us. All of us here know that you did your very best for the Asadi Club. I for one would like to thank you again for the tremendous work you have done.'

'Hear, hear,' said Mr Patel.

'That's right, Tiger,' said Mr Gopez. 'The Asadi Club thanks you and salutes you.'

'Thank you, gentlemen. Friends.' Tiger Singh sat down beside them. 'There is just one tiny ray of hope. On my way out of the court I bumped into Harry Khan. He told me that he himself was about to see the minister.'

'The minister?' said Mr Malik. 'Oh, something to do with that shopping centre thing he mentioned?'

'I suppose so. I told him what had just happened in court and he said he'd see what he could do.'

'Do?' said Mr Gopez. 'What do you mean, do?'

'I'm not exactly sure,' said Tiger Singh, 'but here he is. Why don't you ask him yourself?'

Harry Khan swept into the bar.

'Hey, guys, I heard the news about the club. Too bad.'

'Yes,' said Mr Malik. 'But the Tiger says you've been to see the minister.'

'That's right. And according to my good friend the Honourable Brian Kukuya it looks like it's all systems go – right here, right now.'

'I'm not sure I understand you, Harry.'

Harry Khan clapped Mr Malik on the shoulder.

'The megamall, Jack. The minister has offered me a site – subject to the usual . . . er . . . final negotiations. I thought I'd come right over and tell you.'

'Well,' said Mr Malik, 'I'm sure we're all delighted for you. Very good news for you and for Khan Enterprises, I'm sure – though, as I'm sure you'll understand, we're feeling a bit glum at the moment.'

'Then be glum no more, guys. Don't you get it?'

'Get what?'

'Yes, get what?' said Mr Gopez.

'The site. The new site.'

Mr Malik's jaw dropped.

'You don't mean . . .?'

'Damned right I do. Yep, we're sitting right on it. And you know what? This club, it's been here how long – a hundred years? It's like part of history, right? And I'm a member, right?'

'You mean . . .?'

'You got it, Jack. I mean Khan Enterprises puts aside a bit of space – maybe even on the fourth floor. I haven't put it to my fellow directors back home yet, but I can usually swing things my way. What Harry wants, Harry gets – right?'

'I don't think I quite understand you either, Harry,' said Mr Gopez. 'Space for what?'

'Space for you guys.'

'For us? You mean, for the Asadi Club?'

'Sure, in the new mall. Well, maybe not a swimming pool or tennis courts – but there'll be a fully equipped fitness gym and sauna in the basement, and we should be able to arrange special rates for club members. And what with the Fooderama on the fifth floor, it's not like you'll be needing your own dining room – right? But a bar, sure. Hell, maybe even a pool table somewhere – why not? And how about a big room for video games – get the young folk in, right? Anyway, think it over. Now, if you'll excuse me, guys, I can't stay. Hot date.' He turned to Mr Malik. 'Wouldn't want to keep a lady waiting – right, Jack?'

30

The gnat that does not see the swallow's beak will
see its stomach

The first to break the silence that followed Harry Khan's
exit from the bar of the Asadi Club was Mr Patel.

'Video games!'

Mr A. B. Gopez was not far behind him.

'*Pool* table!'

Mr Malik came in a close third with a somewhat more
muted, 'Fooderama?'

Tiger Singh just shook his head.

'Do you think he could really do it?' said Mr Patel.
'Build a shopping mall on the site of his own club?'

'In my experience,' said Tiger Singh, 'the mind of the
property developer is a thing apart from the minds of
other men. You may remember he was telling us a few
days ago we should modernize. He might actually think
he is helping us – as well as himself, of course. Win-win,
as I think they say these days.'

Mr Gopez gave a snort. 'Heads he wins, tails we lose,
more like.'

'I'm so sorry,' said Mr Malik, 'all this is really my fault.'

'Your fault?' Mr Gopez and Mr Patel spoke as one.

'Yes, Malik,' said Tiger Singh. 'Please explain how the

theft of the certificate of registration of the Asadi Club is your fault?'

'How can the criminal actions of a conniving, corrupt, contemptible . . . *politician*,' continued Mr Gopez, 'be your fault?'

'I should have seen it coming. I knew about the fire in Erroll's office, and that all the government records had been destroyed. I should have seen it coming. I should have done something before it was too late.'

'My dear Malik,' said Tiger Singh. 'If you are to blame, then I am to blame – we are all of us to blame. No, there are some events which simply defy prediction.'

For a long time no one could find anything else to say.

'On another subject,' said Mr Patel at last, 'more bad news, I'm afraid. You know how I lined up that chap at the safari for the talk this week?'

'Angus Mbikwa, you mean?'

'Yes, you may remember he said he'd give us a talk on the organization he works for – Clarity International. He can't make it. Terribly apologetic, of course. Some last-minute thing or other. I think there was going to be quite a good crowd.'

'Can we postpone it to next Thursday?' said Mr Gopez.

Mr Patel looked at him.

'My dear A.B., again you seem to be forgetting that the way things are looking there won't be an Asadi Club next Thursday. That's why there was going to be such a good crowd. Seems a pity to let them down. It would have been good to keep up the old traditions to the last, as it were.'

'I know what you mean,' said Mr Gopez. 'The band

playing on as the ship goes down. Don't suppose you've got any bright ideas for a talk, have you, Malik?'

'Not really,' said Mr Malik. 'Although . . .' he paused. 'Well, there's always the Erroll case.'

'The Erroll case?' Mr Gopez stared up at the ceiling as if trying to recall something. 'Didn't we once have something about the Erroll case here at the club – a debate or something? Patel, you remember it, don't you?'

'I was reading those books again,' said Mr Malik, 'especially Juanita Carberry's autobiography. There are still a few points that don't quite add up. Then I was talking to a friend of mine yesterday.'

Tiger Singh shook his head.

'What else is there to say?'

'Oh, a couple of things.'

'Such as?'

Mr Malik put down his glass.

'Well, now you ask, Tiger, I am sure you spotted that in the last debate one very important piece of evidence was – how shall I put it? – overlooked.'

'Go on.'

'The position of the body when it was found. You will remember that the body was not in the driver's seat but was crouched on the floor, hands over head. The police report was adamant that the body could not have slipped down into that position after death. It must have been put there deliberately, and it would almost certainly have taken more than one person to do so. How, and why?'

Seeing he had now gained his friends' attention, Mr Malik continued.

'And then there was the dairy farmer.'

'He gave evidence at the trial, didn't he? Saw the body soon after the police arrived.'

'That's right, Tiger. He happened to be driving around Karen at 2.40 a.m. and said he'd seen nothing unusual. But nobody asked *why* the dairy farmer was driving around then, and again driving past at 4 a.m., just after the body was found.'

'I don't really see –'

'And nobody asked whether a dairy farmer driving around in Karen might have any connection with a milk truck being driven around at the same time and place.'

'Now you come to mention it,' said Mr Gopez, 'I think there was something about it in that conspiracy book. Didn't they work for the same dairy company?'

'Yes, A.B. – the Grange Park Dairy in Karen. Leslie Condon was the manager. He lived in the house at the dairy.' Mr Malik looked at each of his friends seated round the table. He sat back in his chair. 'And it so happens that one of the delivery drivers was the father of the friend I was talking to yesterday.'

'Do you mean,' said the Tiger, 'that this chap – your friend's father – was one of the men who found the car, who found the body?'

'Yes.'

'This driver, though – he gave a statement to the police, didn't he?'

'He answered their questions.'

'Hmm,' said Tiger Singh. 'But did he, I am now wondering, tell the truth, the whole truth and nothing but the truth?'

Over the last day or two Mr Malik had been giving

some thought to that very question. Is there such a thing, he wondered, as the truth? If so, where did it lie? Was the truth about what happened to Lord Erroll in the written word – in the policemen's notebooks and court reports, in all those books and articles about the case? Was it in mind and memory? Or was it somewhere else – hidden away in plain view perhaps?

'Did my friend's father tell the truth, Tiger?' said Mr Malik. 'That was the very question I asked him.'

'And he gave you the answer?'

'Yes. So I was wondering if tomorrow the members of the Asadi Club might be interested to discover who really killed Lord Erroll.'

The barman of the Jockey Bar at the Hilton Hotel gave a broad smile of recognition.

'The usual, sir?'

After receiving a nod from his customer he dropped three ice cubes into a highball glass and added two shots of Jack Daniel's.

'And will you be dining at the hotel tonight?'

'Not tonight,' said Harry Khan, taking the glass. 'I'm meeting a . . . a friend.'

'Would that be a lady friend, sir?'

Harry Khan grinned.

'How did you guess?'

He looked at his watch. There was plenty of time before he was due to pick up Rose at her place. Drink in hand, he wandered over to the jukebox at the back of the Jockey Bar. The discs hadn't changed since the last time he was here. Put a ten-shilling coin in the slot, press button A then button 6 and Bill Haley would be only too pleased to rock you around the clock. Press G9 to hear Little Richard express high-pitched surprise at exactly what Miss Molly has lately been up to, or press C4 for three minutes and forty-two seconds of Chantilly lace and a pretty face that might make you forget that the Big Bopper ever passed on to that great rock-and-roll heaven in the sky.

Harry Khan went to the window and looked out over the darkening city. Nairobi sure wasn't New York. But still, he kind of liked the place. Now the new mall was going ahead it looked like he might be spending more time here. Maybe he should think about renting an apartment. He could talk it over with Rose tonight. Yeah. If he reminded her about the jukebox, maybe she'd even come back to the hotel for a dance. Rose liked dancing. He smiled. Yeah, maybe she would. As he turned back towards the room he noticed a man and a woman at a table in the corner of the bar. Wasn't that Rose Mbikwa's son, the guy he'd met at the weekend down at the lake? He was about to go over and say hi, but something about the way Angus Mbikwa was leaning over the table towards the woman he was sitting with, and the way she was leaning towards him, made him change his mind. He thought he recognized the woman too. They were talking in low voices but even so, as he left the bar, he couldn't help but overhear their words.

'Are you sure, Sunita?' said Angus Mbikwa.

'Yes, Angus, I'm sure.' Her eyes were bright. 'I've never been so sure of anything in my life.'

31

The swallow does not line its nest with its own
feathers

'Ladies and gentlemen,' said Tiger Singh.

Again the dining room of the Asadi Club was crowded
with members and an almost equal number of their wives.
Mr Malik had been rather hoping that Petula would be
able to make it, but she was busy again. Clarity International seemed to be taking up an awful lot of her time
these days.

'Before we begin our talk, several members have asked
me if there is any news on the future of the club. I fear I
have nothing new to tell you. But tonight we will try and
forget about the problems facing us and conduct business
as usual. Two weeks ago you will remember that instead
of our usual lecture we staged a debate between two of
our members, Mr Patel and Mr Gopez. The subject of the
debate was a crime committed here in Kenya nearly sev-
enty years ago – the murder of Josslyn Hay, the
twenty-second Earl of Erroll. Mr Patel suggested that,
despite the fact he had been acquitted of the crime in a
court of law, the man who shot Lord Erroll in his car that
dark night in January 1941 was Sir Jock Delves Broughton,
whose wife was having an affair with Erroll. As evidence,

he pointed to the fact that an English journalist later revealed that Broughton had confessed his guilt to no fewer than three independent witnesses – including, just two days after the murder, to a fifteen-year-old girl, Juanita Carberry. Mr Gopez then drew your attention to certain inconsistencies in this claim. Firstly that Broughton's confessions each differed in several key respects, and secondly that Juanita Carberry's evidence also appeared unreliable. He suggested instead that the murderer was in fact the young girl Juanita Carberry herself. By a narrow vote you, the audience, found Mr Gopez's claim the more convincing. But since then more facts have emerged.'

The Tiger now turned towards the two chairs beside him, where a short, round, balding man was seated beside another man, black-skinned with white hair.

'Mr Malik,' he said. 'Do we understand you to say that you have new evidence pointing to the true identity of the murderer of Lord Erroll?'

Mr Malik stood.

'Evidence would probably be too strong a word, Tiger. But thanks to my friend Mr Thomas Nyambe I think I can shed some interesting light on the case.'

The Tiger looked around the room. All eyes were on Mr Malik.

'And are you willing to share with us your discoveries?'

'With my friend's permission, I would be pleased to.'

A nod and a smile from Thomas Nyambe gave him the answer he needed.

'Mr Malik, the floor – the stage – is yours.'

Mr Malik turned to his audience.

'Ladies and gentlemen, you may remember from our last debate that Lord Erroll's car was first discovered just outside Karen by two milk delivery drivers, on their regular early morning run to Nairobi. So far, neither of these drivers has figured much in the stories that have been written about the case, nor in the debate. But as one of these men is going to play an important part in the story I am about to relate, allow me to tell you a little more about him. After the war, one of these delivery drivers decided to give up driving lorries. In 1946 he applied to join the public service, where his skills eventually led to him being appointed personal driver to a senior government administrator – a post he held for many years. When he retired, his son – also a skilled driver – took over the job. It is this man, my good friend Mr Thomas Nyambe, who is now sitting beside me. I will now disclose what his father told him of the events of that night.'

From his seat beside Mr Malik, Thomas Nyambe made a small bow of acknowledgement.

'Let us go back to that dark damp night in January 1941. Two delivery drivers see a black car pulled up on the side of the road with its lights on. They stop to investigate. At first they can't see anyone inside, but when they open the front passenger door they see a man lying on the front seat.'

'They opened the door, Mr Malik?' said Tiger Singh. 'But in their evidence I seem to remember them saying that they did not open the door.'

'I will shortly come to that point.'

'I see. The man, was he dead?'

'At first they didn't think so. Remember that Erroll had

been shot from the left side. He was now slumped on to the passenger seat. The two drivers couldn't see the wound – as far as they were concerned it was probably just another *mzungu* on his way home from the Karen Club who had pulled over to sleep off a few too many drinks. But then they notice that in the back seat is another person – a young woman.'

There were gasps from the audience.

'At first they think she must be sleeping too, but then she speaks to them – in fluent Swahili. As I'm sure you know, this was unusual at the time. Most of the white settlers, especially the so-called Happy Valley crowd, knew only enough words of Swahili to shout orders to their servants.'

Mr Gopez spoke.

'You mean it was Juanita?'

'Yes, A.B., it was Juanita Carberry.'

'Ha! What did I tell you? *Cherchez la* jolly *femme*, every time.'

Mr Malik held up a hand.

'But perhaps things are not quite that simple, A.B. The girl was shaking like a leaf but managed to tell them who she was and something of what happened. She had been hiding in the back of the car. She felt the car slow down and stop. She heard Erroll greet someone and ask what was wrong, heard the door being opened, heard another man's voice. Then two shots. She was terrified both by the shots and lest whoever had fired them saw her. She stayed hidden in the back seat not moving a muscle, scarcely daring to breathe. After a minute or two she heard a door slam shut and a car drive off. She peeped over the back of the driver's seat. Erroll was already slumped over on to the front passenger seat. He was clearly dead.'

'She didn't see who did it?'

'That's right, Tiger. She saw neither the murderer nor his – or her – car. As soon as she thought the coast was clear, she tried to get out of the back seat but found the doors wouldn't open – Erroll always drove with his car doors locked, apparently, since someone had taken a potshot at him a few months before. She tried to force one of the doors open – hanging on to an armstrap and pushing with her legs – only to find the strap come away in her hands. When she tried the other side, the same thing happened. Then she saw the lights of another vehicle coming down the road. Fearing it must be the murderer coming back to the scene of the crime, she once more tried to hide.'

'But what was she doing there in the first place, Mr Malik?'

'I'll get to that in a minute, if I may, Tiger. The vehicle she hears, though, is not the murderer's car. It is the milk truck, on its way to Nairobi. When the two drivers discover Juanita in the back seat of the car she pleads with them not to tell anyone they have seen her. She isn't meant to be there – and if her father finds out, she's bound to get a thrashing. Both men know all about *Msharisha* Carberry and his rhino-hide whip. They respond as African gentlemen. They promise her they will say nothing. The last they see of Juanita is her white gym shoes disappearing into the night.'

'Well,' said the Tiger. 'The broken straps, the shoe whitening on the seats – it certainly explains them. But the mysterious murderer? She hadn't seen him. Are you saying it was Broughton all along?'

'No, it was not Broughton. Broughton was, as he always claimed, at home – as was Diana his wife. I must say that this was the part of the case that always puzzled me the most. Both Broughton and Diana had alibis – not strong alibis, but alibis nonetheless. It wasn't until I talked to my friend Mr Nyambe that I realized where I had been going wrong.' Mr Malik surveyed the now silent room. 'As you may know, Lord Erroll never seemed satisfied with having just one woman on the go. It was well known that at the time of his murder he had another mistress who was away in South Africa. What was not so well known was that he had also been having an affair with the attractive wife of the manager of the Grange Park Dairy.'

'Good God,' said Mr Gopez under his breath. 'Makes Casanova look like bally Bertie Wooster.'

'And may I ask how you know this, Mr Malik?'

Mr Malik looked again at his friend Thomas Nyambe, who was still sitting quietly beside him.

'All the men who worked at the dairy knew who drove the black Buick that would often be parked outside the Condon house soon after Leslie Condon had left early in the morning for Nairobi.'

'I see. But Condon, what's he got to do with the murder?'

'It was hard to keep secrets in such a close-knit community. Condon had found out about his wife's affair – most probably told about it by a fellow member of the Muthaiga Club. That night at the club, he was there. He overheard the conversation at Broughton's table – half the club did. He heard Broughton tell Erroll to bring Diana home by three. This was his chance. After Erroll and Diana had gone off dancing he left the club. He knew from overhearing their conversation when Erroll would be taking Diana home to Karen. Erroll was almost sure to then return to his own house in Nairobi along the same road – this time, alone. Condon's plan was to ambush Erroll in a deserted spot somewhere along that road. He drove back to the dairy to get his revolver, then hid his car near the turn-off. At about 2.15 a.m. he saw Erroll and Diana drive past towards Broughton's house. As soon as they were out of sight he pulled on to the road, got out of his car and lifted up the bonnet. He didn't have to wait long for Erroll to come back. He waved him down. Erroll stopped and wound down the passenger window to ask what was the matter. Condon pointed the gun through the open window and fired two shots. He then got back into his car, turned round and went home again to his house at the dairy.'

'If I may interrupt you, Mr Malik,' said the Tiger, 'by my calculations he would have got back at about 2.45 a.m. Why did he tell the police he had been past the junction at 2.40 a.m., but had seen nothing? Why tell them he had been there at all?'

'The delivery drivers. As usual, they were loading the truck at the dairy at that very time, ready to take the milk to Nairobi. They had seen him return. Condon knew that if the police began asking questions they would be bound to say something. By telling the police himself that he had indeed driven past the place where the car was found, he pre-empted this possibility.'

'But the car, Mr Malik. How did it get into the ditch, and how did the body get on to the floor?'

Mr Malik looked once more towards the white-haired man sitting beside him, then back to the hushed crowd before him.

'Yes, ladies and gentlemen, I haven't quite finished the story. You will all remember that the two delivery drivers are already implicated in Juanita's deception. They now decide to try to dispose of the evidence – at least, for long enough to buy time for the little memsahib. In the light of their lorry's headlights they see the reflection of what looks like a ditch on the opposite side of the road. If they can push the car into the water, it might be a while until it is found. First they have to move Erroll's body out of the way of the steering wheel and the pedals. They manage to manoeuvre it on to the floor. With one of them pushing the car from behind, and the other pushing and steering through the open window, they eventually heave it across the road and towards the water. The reflection is deceptive. The water is just a shallow pit where some murram has been removed for surfacing the road. The car comes to a halt with one front wheel in this pit. It is stuck. They drive the truck closer to get more light and try again, but no – after the rain the road is too slippery.'

'So that explains the tyre tracks,' said Tiger Singh.

'Exactly. But what should they do now? If they leave the car as it is, it will soon be found – they know that their boss Leslie Condon will be driving into Nairobi soon, as he does every morning. With a dead man in the car they also know the police will be involved. They can hardly pretend they hadn't noticed the big black Buick in a ditch when they had driven by. There was only one thing to do. *They* will have to call the police. They will have to say that they discovered the car just as it is now. They will have to say that they thought they had seen a body in it but they hadn't touched anything. Whatever happens, though, they both agree to say nothing about the other person in the car, the person who has just run back to the house at Karen, hidden her mud-stained white gym shoes beneath the ivy, climbed up the drainpipe, and is already safely back in her bed.'

32

The swallow does not ask the weaver bird to build
its nest, nor the weaver bird the swallow

'A most intriguing story,' said Tiger Singh, joining the others at the bar. 'Well done, Malik. It certainly explains the missing pieces of the puzzle. And thank you, Mr Nyambe. You have been most generous in sharing your tale with all of us here at the Asadi Club. But, Malik, I still don't understand what she was doing there. Why was Juanita Carberry hiding in the car? Was A.B. right? Had she and Erroll been having an affair or something?'

'No – as she says in her autobiography, she had never met the man. It is quite simple. She was running away. You may remember that ever since the previous November, when her father had found a soldier climbing out of her window at the house in Nyeri, she had been locked in her room every night. This was the first time since then that Juanita had been away from there. This was her first chance of escape. And a few months later she really did run away to her uncle's house in Nairobi – never to live with her father and stepmother again.'

'So she really had nothing to do with Erroll? Well, I have to say that makes sense too. He always seemed to go for married women. But where does all this leave

Broughton? Are you saying she made up all that stuff about him confessing?'

'I have to admit,' said Mr Malik, 'that was indeed a puzzle. Neither my friend Mr Nyambe here nor I could work it out – until I remembered that though Juanita had been in the car when Erroll was shot, she didn't see who did it.'

'I still don't understand.'

'Well,' said Mr Malik, 'let us suppose that Broughton did indeed confess to Juanita. Why should she not believe him?'

'Just a minute. Are you saying that Mr Gopez was right, that it was all bravado?'

'Possibly. Or perhaps . . .' Mr Malik paused. 'Or perhaps Broughton believed that Juanita Carberry was actually the murderer.'

'*He* thought *she'd* done it? Why?'

'Think about what happened later that night. Through his bedroom window Broughton sees Juanita returning to the house. He sees her hiding the gym shoes. The next morning he hears that Lord Erroll has been found dead in his car just down the road.'

'He thinks there's a connection?'

'Quite so, A.B. But if the girl did have something to do with it, Broughton wouldn't want to expose her – he'd want to protect her. At lunch he's introduced to Juanita – remember, they'd never actually met before. He takes her to see his horses, just the two of them together. He can't just come straight out with it – I saw you sneak home last night and hide the gym shoes, and I know you killed Lord Erroll, but I won't say anything.'

'Because he isn't absolutely sure she'd done it.'

'Exactly, A.B. He takes her past the bonfire. When she sees her shoes burning she will surely realize that he is destroying the evidence linking her with Erroll, that he is on her side.'

'But hang on a minute, Malik. A few minutes ago you said that she hadn't done it.'

'Yes, but Broughton still thinks she did.'

'Wait,' said Tiger Singh slowly. 'Are you now suggesting that Juanita Carberry thinks that Broughton did it, that his was the voice she heard while she was hiding in the back of the car?'

'Not at this stage. She is surprised that her shoes have been found – and perhaps still worried that she'll get into trouble. And no doubt she's puzzled as to why he's burning them.'

'But the next day he took the police investigator right past the bonfire too,' said Mr Gopez. 'What was that all about?'

'It was quite deliberate, to ensure that he is the number one suspect and so protect the girl – though, of course, at the same time he denies any knowledge and is confident the police don't have enough evidence to arrest him.'

'Which they didn't.'

'That's right, Tiger. At the inquest he hears about the white marks on the car seat. He's seen her hide the shoes, so now he's even more sure that Juanita Carberry must have had something to do with it. He drives to Nyeri to find that June Carberry and his wife Diana are out. By this time he's thought up another plan to let Juanita know that he knows. "I killed Lord Erroll," he says.'

'Now you've completely lost me,' said Mr Gopez. 'How

does him saying to her that *he* did it, tell her that he knows that *she* did it?'

'It was meant to be a sort of code. Broughton had now convinced himself that Juanita was the murderer. By telling her that *he* shot Erroll, he thought she would realize that even though he knew the truth, he wasn't going to say anything.'

'So he still thought *she'd* done it, and now she was convinced *he'd* done it.'

'That's right, A.B. And all the time it was neither of them.'

Tiger Singh smacked both hands to his head.

'Brilliant, Malik, absolutely brilliant. Malik, my dear chap, your sleuthing skills are as impressive as your friend Benjamin's. Yes, of course – I should have seen it. *Tempus veritas revelit*. I do believe you've solved the case.'

'No, no, Tiger, not solved it. It's just a story – based like all the others on no more than circumstantial evidence and hearsay. The witnesses are dead, the suspects are dead. But perhaps now so is the crime.'

'Excuse me, gentlemen,' said the barman. 'Mr Malik, your daughter is on the line. She says she has something important to tell you.'

Mr Malik took the phone.

'Hello, darling – can't it wait? I'll be home very soon . . .' he paused. 'Oh, I see.'

Mr Malik put down the phone and turned to his friends.

'Excuse me please, gentlemen, I'd better get back home. My daughter tells me she has thought of a way to save the Asadi Club.'

33

It is by coming and going that the weaver bird
builds its nest

It had been, thought Mr Malik, as he watched Benjamin
cut some twigs to bind on the broom handle for his morning leaf sweeping, a very good idea. Petula had been so
excited. The time for defence was over, she told him when
he'd hurried back from the club last night. Now it was
time to attack.

'Publicity, that's what you need. I was talking to Angus
– Angus Mbikwa, you know – just a few days ago and this
evening it came to me. Let the people see exactly what is
going on. Shine the light of truth on the murky doings of
this *honourable* minister.'

'This seems like an excellent idea,' said Mr Malik. 'But
how exactly do you propose we do it?'

'I've thought of that too.' Petula slammed down a copy
of the *Evening News*. 'We haven't got the whistle-blower
website going yet, but you know about that Dadukwa chap,
the one that writes the "Birds of a Feather" column? Get
in contact with him, let him know what's going on. The
Evening News prints the story, and bingo! Problem solved.'

Mr Malik picked up the paper. How much should he
tell her?

'I don't know if you looked at the date on this paper?' he said.

She took it from him.

'Tuesday the twenty-first. The column comes out on a Wednesday. There's plenty of time.'

'Then I suppose you haven't heard.'

And Mr Malik explained to Petula how there would be no paper next Wednesday. That as from yesterday there was no more *Evening News*.

'They used the same trick to close down the paper as they're using to close down the club. The paper's certificate of registration mysteriously disappeared. No certificate, no newspaper.'

He wished he hadn't had to tell her even this much. When she came to kiss him goodnight, she had looked so sad. In the morning she left the house before he was up.

Benjamin had finished making the broom and was already sweeping up the leaves at the bottom of the garden into neat piles. If only his life was as simple as Benjamin's. Mr Malik thought back to his revelations of the previous night at the club. He should be feeling just a little triumphant, but he wasn't. Though the Tiger had been most flattering about his deductive skills, it was his friend Thomas Nyambe who had really solved the mystery. And really, it was not important. What mattered was not the past but the present. In three days the Asadi Club would be no more. Never mind solving the mystery of who killed Lord Erroll – what about the mystery of the vanishing lion and the missing certificate? Mr Malik reached for his cup of Nescafé and took a troubled sip.

For the umpteenth time he went over the sequence of events that Friday night at the club. It might be best to treat the lion and the certificate separately. So . . . when had the lion last been seen? It was when the Tiger and Harry Khan went to leave. There had been that business with the keys and the briefcase. Could Harry Khan have had anything to do with it? He had come out of the club with the Tiger, gone back inside, then come out and closed the door behind him. Had he seen the lion again on his way out? As far as Mr Malik could remember, no one had asked him. Harry had taken the Tiger home, returned to give the manager the spare key to the back door, then driven back to his hotel. The manager had gone into the club through the back door, locked up and left – again through the back door. He had only noticed the lion missing the next day when he opened up. The lion could have gone missing any time between the three men walking out of the front door and the following morning – but how?

Now for the certificate. This was more difficult. Even though he had himself noticed its absence quite soon after getting back to the club after the safari on Sunday night, he couldn't swear that it had definitely been there on Friday – or Thursday or any other day, for that matter. Nor could anyone else. And were the two disappearances linked or weren't they? Removing a small framed certificate was certainly a different matter from stealing a stuffed lion. There could be little doubt that the theft of the certificate was linked to the letter from the minister – but as for the lion . . . If only that could be tracked down as easily as Benjamin had tracked those leopards on the safari.

Benjamin was now sweeping up the last of the leaves near the veranda. Wait. It had been two weeks now, but perhaps there was still just a chance.

'Benjamin,' he said out loud. 'Benjamin, I have had an idea.'

Benjamin had no time to object or even speak before he found himself being bundled into the front seat of Mr Malik's car. On the way to the Asadi Club Mr Malik told him all about the recent goings-on.

'I know it has been two weeks since the robbery – or robberies – but there is just the chance that some trace remains. I have seen you track a leopard and I have seen you track an ocelot. Benjamin, would you be able to use those clever young eyes of yours to track down a lion?'

As soon as they arrived at the Asadi Club, Mr Malik hurried Benjamin into the lobby.

'This is where it was,' he said. He showed Benjamin to the oh-so-empty space inside the front door.

'The lion, Mr Malik, was it very heavy?'

Mr Malik thought for a moment.

'No, not heavy – but it would be very awkward to carry. It would really need two men to lift it.'

Benjamin looked at the place where the lion had been. He looked at the walls, he looked at the ceiling. He got down on his hands and knees and examined the floor.

'And all these doors, Mr Malik, what are they for?'

Five doors led off the lobby. There was the front door through which they had just come. Just to the left of that was the manager's office – which you could also enter from the dining room – and then the double glass doors that led through to the dining room and bar. On the right-hand side of the lobby were two smaller doors.

'That one is the cleaner's cupboard, where he keeps all his buckets and things, and the other one is the club dark-room – for making photographs, you know – though nobody uses it much these days. We've been thinking of turning it into a computer room.'

Benjamin went round the lobby examining each door and door frame.

'People do not bring other animals here?'

While the club rule forbidding women to enter the club had, after much heated debate (and even the threat of murder and/or suicide by Jumbo Wickramasinghe), been rescinded as long ago as 1977, Rule 11 forbidding pets was still in force – a fact which Mr Malik was able to confirm to his friend.

'Then this, I think,' said Benjamin, taking something from one of the door frames and holding it up between finger and thumb, 'must be the hair of a lion.'

Mr Malik went over to where Benjamin was standing beside the door to the darkroom.

'But this door is always kept locked. No one goes in there. Only the manager has the key, in his office.'

He tried the door handle and, sure enough, it was firmly locked.

'But look, Mr Malik.' Benjamin pointed to the floor. 'Tracks.'

Mr Malik looked down at the polished wood, almost expecting to see the wide round footprints of a big cat. What he saw were not prints, but scratches. With the light coming in through the front door he could see a definite line of faint scratch marks leading to where he stood. It took only a minute for him to find the manager, who quickly found the key to the darkroom hanging on the board in his office.

He unlocked the door, pushed it open and turned on the light.

34

The weaver bird does not build its nest over the
crocodile

Rose Mbikwa looked up at the black shapes scything the
blue – swifts on the wing. Circling high above them were
a pair of augur buzzards. Were the ancients right? she
wondered. Was the future to be read in the flight of birds?
If so, what were they telling her? She turned towards the
house. Angus would be home soon. He didn't usually
come to see her at lunchtime, but he'd phoned that morning to say he had something important to tell her. Elizabeth
had been in the kitchen all morning steaming the plan-
tains and grinding the peanuts for matoke – one of his
favourites. But if what Harry Khan had told her last night
was true, soon Angus wouldn't be eating at home with her
quite so often. She caught a sweet scent on the air – ah
yes, the jasmine. Before she came to Africa Rose had
never smelled jasmine. She looked up again at the black
birds. Were they European swifts? Had they been born
under Edinburgh roofs, perhaps, and ridden the North
winds to Kenya? A smaller bird was hopping and pecking
among the buds of a Cape chestnut tree. A warbler of
some kind, she supposed. Bracken warbler? Woodland
warbler? It could even be a willow warbler. She should get

her binoculars. She had just stepped on to the veranda when she heard a scream and saw Angus race out.

'Don't worry, Mother, don't worry. It was just Elizabeth.'

'What is it? What's happened? Tell me.'

'I've just told her some news. I'm sorry, I had no idea she'd react like this.'

'News? What news?'

His face broke into a broad grin.

'The news, dear Mother, that your son is getting married.'

When Mr Malik had opened the door of the darkroom and seen the Kima Killer, his reaction was not a loud scream of joy, nor even a small whoopee. There was the lion all right, safe and undamaged, but a quick glance followed by a thorough search of every shelf and cupboard in the darkroom revealed not the slightest trace of the missing certificate. But was it too much to hope that the reappearance of its mascot might at least augur a little good luck for the Asadi Club?

'My friend,' he said, turning to Benjamin, 'once again I find myself in your debt.'

'Mr Malik, I am very happy to do this for you.'

'It is not just for me, Benjamin, it is for all of us. For the Asadi Club.'

With the help of the manager it took no time at all for them to lift the lion into its old position by the front door and only slightly longer for the word to spread that the Kima Killer was back.

Benjamin had never seen so much Coca-Cola. It seemed every member arriving at the club insisted on buying him a glass. It would have been impolite to refuse it, and by the time Mr Patel and Mr Gopez arrived seven empty glasses and five full ones were lined up along the bar.

'And the reward,' said Mr Gopez. 'What about the reward?'

'You're right, A.B.,' said Mr Patel. 'We did talk about offering a reward. What do you say, Malik?'

Mr Malik cleared his throat.

'Benjamin, will you please allow me, on behalf of my fellow members, to express our thanks in more tangible form? Is there anything – anything at all – that you would like as a token of my – *our* – appreciation?'

Benjamin thought.

'I would very much like an umbrella, Mr Malik. I have an umbrella, but it is a very small umbrella.'

'A new umbrella you shall have, Benjamin – a large one. But is there anything else you want, perhaps something that you have always wanted?'

It so happened that there was another thing Benjamin wanted. Something he had wanted ever since he had first seen one in the schoolmaster's house outside the village where he grew up. Benjamin loved words – not only the words of his native language, but the Swahili and English words that he learned at school. How wonderful that every object, every thought and feeling, could be described in these magical sounds. How doubly wonderful that each of them could be transformed into squiggles on paper, which could then be read out and turned back into sounds. He remembered the first time the schoolmaster had shown the class a dictionary. To think that every word in the language was in just that one book. That was what he would like, he told Mr Malik, his very own dictionary. So out of the club they went and into Mr Malik's old green Mercedes.

Amin and Sons General Emporium was sure to have just the thing.

Finding a place to park your car in a big city is always a problem. In Nairobi the problem is compounded by the fact that when you have found your parking space you have only to leave your vehicle out of sight for a moment to find that mysterious things will happen. First its wheels disappear. Give it a few more seconds and the rubber mounting around its rear window will part, as if cut through with a sharp blade, and the glass will be gone. Another minute and the entire portable contents of the car will vanish. Just a few more minutes and doors, seats, interior fittings, muffler – even the complete engine – just won't be there any more. The solution to this problem is to employ the services of one of the young men to whom has been passed down the dark knowledge of how to protect motor vehicles against these disappearances. Fortunately for motorists, representatives of this brotherhood are to be found on every Nairobi street, only too willing to offer their services for what is, all things considered, a most reasonable fee.

Mr Malik parked right outside the shop and, after negotiating the provision of vehicle security, the two friends entered. Mr Malik introduced Benjamin to Godfrey Amin himself.

'And what did the young gentleman have in mind? A concise dictionary – or a pocket version, perhaps? It all

248

depends on how and where you intend to use it, you see.'

He took them up to the second floor and showed them a shelf containing several of the volumes he had just described. Lying on its side on the bottom shelf, and still wrapped in plastic, Benjamin spotted a large blue box.

'Is that a dictionary?'

'Ah, the Compact Oxford. A lovely volume – well, two volumes actually. What with computers and the internet and everything, though, I'm afraid there's not much call for a book like this these days.'

As his assistant lifted the box on to the table and began unwrapping it Godfrey Amin explained that the two-volume set contained all the information in the twelve-volume Complete Oxford ('And, I think, the five later supplements – though I'm not sure about that'), but that it had simply been printed in smaller type on finer paper.

'And as you can see,' he said, sliding open a little card-board drawer at the top of the box, 'it comes with its own magnifying glass.'

Mr Malik took one look at the expression on Benjamin's face.

'Thank you, Godfrey, we'll take it. And an umbrella, if you please. Your very largest.'

With the purchases locked in the boot, the guardians of the car paid and thanked and Benjamin strapped in the passenger seat, they headed for home. At the intersection of Kenyatta Avenue and Uhuru Highway the traffic was, as usual, locked almost solid and several policemen were, as usual, attempting to unlock it. While he waited, Mr Malik found his mind turning once more to the case of Lord Erroll.

When the police (and every investigator since) had investigated the murder, they had naturally assumed that it had been somehow linked to all those other clues – the position of the car, the tyre tracks, the broken armstraps. If Mr Malik's theory was correct, they had turned out to be not really linked at all. Could the disappearance of the lion and the disappearance of the certificate also be separate events – their only connection being the approximate time at which they happened? And the more he thought about it, the clearer it became. By the time the police had sorted out the snarl and he was heading north up Uhuru Highway, he knew how the lion came to be in the darkroom and why. By the time he reached the Westlands turn-off, he was sure he knew what had happened to the certificate. And, of course, the Asadi Club would be safe – just as he had promised his father. But there was only one person who could save it.

Had you been standing on the corner of Mama Ngina Street and Taifa Road at two o'clock that Friday afternoon, you might have noticed two figures emerge from the law chambers opposite. One is a tall man in dark suit and dastar to match. He puts a small envelope in his pocket before shaking the hand of a shorter, fatter man, hailing a taxi and climbing inside. The other man crosses the road in the direction of an old green Mercedes. After handing some money to the young person who has been protecting his car from unforeseen eventualities he sets off for the Aga Khan Hospital, where he will spend the rest of the day and much of the evening sitting beside the patients in the large ward at the back of the hospital, talking or not talking. Perhaps on the way home he will be thinking that the cell in which he will soon be incarcerated cannot be much worse than that room.

The tall man asks his taxi driver to take him straight to the Ministry for the Interior. They turn out of Taifa Road into Freedom Street. He takes the envelope from his pocket and reads the single sheet of paper it contains. As they pass Amin and Sons, he taps the taxi driver on the shoulder.

'Stop here a moment, would you?' says Tiger Singh. 'There's something I need.'

As he leaves the store, carrying a very small parcel, he recognizes Mr Malik's daughter's friend Sunita also coming out.

'Hello, Mr Singh,' she says, smiling. She is looking very pretty. She looks down at the larger parcel in her own hands. 'A new sari,' she tells him, 'for the wedding. Amin's is still the best place for that something special.'

The Tiger smiles.

'You know?' he says. 'I couldn't agree more.'

35

The crocodile does not heed the rain, nor the
dying butterfly

In his bed that night at Number 12 Garden Lane, Mr
Malik tossed and Mr Malik turned. He had stayed late at
the hospital, then gone straight home and straight to bed.
But while his body felt exhausted, his mind refused to let
go of the day. When at last sleep came it was filled with
dreams of lions – not stuffed and smiling lions, but living,
snarling lions with long sharp teeth and claws to match.

He awoke late but unrefreshed, donned dressing gown
and slippers and headed for the kitchen to prepare his
morning cup of Nescafé. Petula, it seemed, had already
left the house. There was no sign of Benjamin either,
though he noticed that the night's leaves had already been
swept into neat piles on the lawn ready for the afternoon
bonfire. The phone rang. It was Tiger Singh – yes, everything had gone according to plan. The certificate of
registration had been returned, the Asadi Club was saved.
How long now, wondered Mr Malik as he put down the
phone, before they came for him? Though tired, he felt
perfectly calm. It had all been quite straightforward. He
had known what he must do and he'd done it.

From the croton tree at the bottom of the garden a

hadada called out its three-note cry. A troop of speckled mousebirds were chasing each other in and out of the bougainvillea. Mr Malik shuffled over to the hall table and picked up his binoculars from beside the bowl of fading roses. With his Bausch & Lomb 7 x 50 binoculars in one hand and a cup of Nescafé in the other, he sat down in his favourite chair on the veranda. A small dusky-pink bird flew into the climbing fig nearer the house, trailing a long piece of grass in its beak. So the red-billed firefinches were nesting again. High overhead two black kites – which are not really black but brown – made lazy circles on four broad wings.

He heard a knock at the door. So soon?

'Malik,' he heard a voice shout. 'Malik old chap, open up.'

Strange – that sounded like the Tiger. Of course, the Tiger would want to be present when they came. Always best to have a lawyer on hand. Good old Tiger. He went to the front door and opened it.

Tiger Singh rushed in.

'Come on, Malik, we haven't got much time. Are you ready?'

'Yes,' said Mr Malik, 'I'm ready.'

'Well, you don't look ready. You can't go like that, you know. Aren't you going to put on a suit and tie?'

So they were going to court, eh? – some sort of mock trial before they locked him up and threw away the key. Well, so be it. Never let it be said that a Malik was seen to cower before a bully. You can break many a Malik bone, you may even break his heart – you will never break his spirit.

'That's better,' said Tiger Singh as Mr Malik emerged from his bedroom dressed in best blazer and club tie. In one hand he was clutching a small overnight bag with a few things he'd thrown in – toothbrush, pyjamas, razor (did they allow razors?).

Tiger Singh looked at the bag.

'I don't think you'll need that, old chap, but never mind. Oh, and as I expect you've noticed, Petula and Benjamin have already gone.'

'Gone?' Mr Malik's heart sank into his socks. 'Gone where?'

'To the club, of course.'

'The club?'

Tiger Singh gave him a puzzled look.

'To the club, for the celebration. Come on, we'll be late.'

'Celebration? Oh, of course, the certificate. Well done, Tiger. I knew you could do it. But the minister –'

'My dear Malik, don't worry about the minister. Just hop in the car – I'll explain it all on the way.'

And so it was that on the drive from Garden Lane to the Asadi Club, Mr Malik learned how Tiger Singh had indeed been to see the minister the previous afternoon and had indeed persuaded him to exchange the registration certificate of the Asadi Club for the one thing he wanted more than the land it stood on. That was to know the identity of the man who had so regularly raised his blood pressure and robbed him of his sleep – the real name and identity of Dadukwa.

'They'll be coming for me then?'

Tiger Singh pulled an envelope from his pocket and

handed it to his passenger. Mr Malik recognized it as the one he had given his friend the afternoon before, the one containing the single sheet of paper with his name on it.

'It's been opened.'

'Yes,' said the Tiger. 'I thought I'd better have a look – lawyer's privilege, you know.'

'But he read it – the minister, I mean?'

'No. No need.'

'So you didn't give him the letter, you just told him it was me?'

'Well, not exactly.'

'But you just said you went and saw him yesterday afternoon.'

'Oh yes – I went, all right. I don't suppose you've ever been in the office of the Minister for the Interior, have you? Quite grand. There's even a lion-skin rug on the floor, stuffed head and everything. Elsa's mother, apparently – or so Harry Khan told me. Said the minister was rather fond of it.'

'But you said you were going to give him the letter. We agreed.'

'I know that, Malik my dear chap, but before I could hand it over I happened to put my hand in its mouth.'

'In its mouth?'

'Yes, that's right, the lion – in its mouth. I was just admiring it when I thought I noticed something there. A little wire or something. The minister said he couldn't see it himself, but when I reached in what do you think I pulled out? A miniature transmitting device. The minister was most surprised. He'd never seen one, but I recognized it immediately – they sell them in Amin's, you know. I happen to know these things don't have a very big range, so we went into his secretary's office – he'd just been called out on urgent business, something to do with shopping malls, I believe – and what do you think I discovered in one of the drawers? The receiver – tiny little thing. This secretary chap, Jonah Litumana, had obviously been bugging the minister – and his predecessor, no doubt, and who knows who else – all the time. Explains everything, wouldn't you say?'

Mr Malik stared at Tiger Singh with open mouth.

'You can imagine how grateful he was,' continued the Tiger, 'the Honourable Brian Kukuya, I mean. Handed the certificate over without another word. He even accepted my offer of a lift to the Sandringham Club, and who should we meet at the nineteenth hole but Judge Kafari. So – everything sorted out. On Monday morning I've arranged to see the judge in chambers, just to dot the legal i's and cross the administrative t's, so to speak.'

Mr Malik's mouth remained open but no words came out.

'Just one more thing. The minister assured me that that secretary of his would be ... er ... castigated, I think he said – and I said we'd be quite happy to leave it at that.'

Even when Tiger Singh suddenly swore and swerved round a cyclist on a blind corner, Mr Malik said not a word.

'Did you see that? Shouldn't be allowed on the roads. Anyway, as far as your part in the thing goes, Malik old chap – and, of course, none of this would have happened without you – I wonder if you'd mind keeping it under the old turban. Not the Kima Killer business, of course –

damned fine work – but the certificate. Might be best. And perhaps you could mention it to that Dadukwa chap too, if you see him.'

At last Mr Malik found himself able to speak.

'But . . .'

'Of course – the *Evening News*, I'm glad you reminded me. Yes, before I agreed to anything I raised that subject, and I'm delighted to say that the minister seemed to think that in view of recent developments, as it were, he wouldn't be at all surprised if the *Evening News* certificate were to turn up too. What a piece of luck, eh?'

'So . . .'

'Mm, I know what you're going to say. I've been wondering about that too. I know you told me yesterday that it must have been those painting contractors who stole the certificate in the first place – the ones who came to the club to give the quote just as you were leaving for the safari – and presumably the same fellows who swiped the one at the *Evening News*. But I still can't see why they would have wanted to hide the lion. Had any more thoughts?'

At which point Mr Malik found that though he could speak, on reflection it might be better if he didn't. Lions in darkrooms, petroleum-jelly sandwiches, pythons in pyjamas – perhaps some truths were better left in the past. In the present, it truly seemed that everything was all right.

36

Happiness is a butterfly

He was surprised to see so many cars at the club. The car park was chocker, and dozens more cars were lined up all down the street. Some of them were even decorated with ribbons, which Mr Malik thought was a nice touch – though perhaps overdoing it a bit. Tiger Singh seemed confident that they would find somewhere to park nearer the clubhouse, and sure enough they were in luck – there was a space right outside the front door. Mr Malik was also surprised to see Benjamin coming down the steps to open the car door for him, until he remembered that the Tiger had said he'd gone on ahead. The Tiger hadn't told him that Benjamin would be wearing a collar and tie, though. Mr Malik had never seen Benjamin in a collar and tie.

'Benjamin, how lovely to see you. This celebration is as much for you as for anyone, you know. If you hadn't tracked down that lion, I'm sure none of the rest of this would have happened.'

'Come, Mr Malik, come inside. Miss Petula, she is wait-ing.'

And there, just inside the door beside the Kima Killer – back in its rightful place and also decked with ribbons

– stood his daughter. She was wearing a crimson sari with gold threads and seemed to have done something to her hair. But more surprises. Standing on one side of her was Sunita, dressed in a sari almost as magnificent as Petula's. On her other side was Angus Mbikwa, and standing beside him his mother Rose. Rose was wearing a hat. Mr Malik hardly had time to register all this before an enormous cheer went up from the crowd behind them.

The Tiger appeared at his side.

'Three cheers for Malik,' he boomed, 'elucidator of crimes and conundrums.'

'Three cheers for Malik,' echoed Mr Patel, 'king of the club safari.'

'Three cheers for Malik,' repeated Mr A. B. Gopez, 'saviour of the Asadi Club.'

At the first cheer, chandeliers shook on the ceilings; at the second, bottles rattled in the bar; at the third cheer, two cues in the billiard room and a six-foot spider rest clattered from the rack on to the floor. Never in the 107 years of the club was heard such vociferous jubilation.

Rose Mbikwa stepped forward.

'Dear Mr Malik, may I too salute you? You are a truly remarkable man.' With a fond look, she turned towards her son. 'And now, I believe Angus has something to say.'

'Mr Malik, my mother has told me something of your talents and achievements. I can only echo her statement – you are a man among men. And – if I may say so – your daughter Petula Malik is a woman among women.' He exchanged a glance with Petula. 'This is indeed a most happy day – not only for the Asadi Club and all its members, but for Kenya. It is a day of triumph and a day of hope. Above all, it is a day of happiness.' Again he looked towards Petula. 'And on this special day I have a request. May I have the great honour of asking you for your daughter's hand in marriage?'

Mr Malik stared at him, then at the radiant face of his mother beside him – there seemed little doubt about Rose Mbikwa's thoughts on the matter. He looked at his beautiful daughter Petula, who he loved with all his heart. In her crimson sari, and with the emerald bindi on her forehead, she looked just as her mother had looked when she had accepted his proposal of marriage under the mango tree. It was some time before he could speak.

'With my daughter's permission,' he said, 'you may –'

At which Petula flung her arms round him.

'Oh, Daddy . . . oh, Daddy . . . oh, Daddy,' was all she could say.

Once more the room erupted into cheering – if anything, even louder than before. Mr Malik had almost to shout to Petula to make himself heard.

'And when, dear daughter, were you thinking of having the wedding?'

'Well,' she said, taking him aside, 'I know how you feel about long engagements. So I said to Angus – he only plucked up the courage to ask me yesterday, you know, I'm afraid that's why he couldn't give the talk at the club on Thursday – I said that if he wanted to marry me it would have to be soon.'

'How soon?'

'Today, actually. You know, before I change my mind?'

'Today? Get married today? But the priests, the reception . . .?'

Rose Mbikwa appeared beside him and slipped her arm into his.

'I hope you don't mind, dear Mr Malik, but I've been busy too. At rather short notice I've managed to persuade my old friend Bishop Hodgkinson to come out of retirement and preside – he married my husband Joshua and me.'

'And,' said Petula, 'Mr Kalia will be coming from the temple.'

It had been Pundit Kalia who, more than forty years ago, had blessed the marriage of Mr Malik and his dear wife.

Mr Malik felt a sudden panic.

'But the food, what about the food?'

'Don't worry, Malik old chap,' said Mr Patel. 'Ally Dass has been working all night. I've just seen the birianis – not just silver leaf this time, but gold too.'

'And he let me try one of the samosas – not a single pea,' said Mr Gopez.

'But the loos, what about the loos?'

'I think I saw the Portaloo people just leaving,' said Tiger Singh. 'And I think that I can see someone else arriving.'

Above the hubbub inside the club could be heard the hoot of a car horn and a screech of brakes. From the red Mercedes convertible that had pulled up beside the Tiger's Range Rover they heard a familiar voice.

'Hey, Rose baby!' Harry Khan leapt from the driver's seat and raced up the steps. 'They're right behind me.'

'Hello, Harry. Who is right behind you?'

'The police?' said Mr Patel.

'The men from the ministry?' said Mr Gopez.

'No – don't worry, guys. All taken care of.'

'Then who?' said Mr Malik.

'The band. Rose told me you might need some music later, right?'

Rose Mbikwa laughed.

'Don't tell me . . .'

'Sure. Like I said yesterday, Rose baby, leave it to me. What Harry wants, Harry gets.'

A bus turned into the car park and pulled up behind the Mercedes. Harry Khan turned to Mr Malik.

'I bring you Milton Kapriadis and his Safari Swingers – courtesy of Khan Enterprises. OK with you, Jack?'

And so as the Nairobi sky turns from blue to black, as the stars come out and lanterns are lit around the lawns and rose beds of the Asadi Club, after Petula and Angus have exchanged their vows and circled the holy fire seven times, after the champagne has been drunk, the samosas swallowed, the countless dishes of curry consumed and the cake cut, we find the bride and her groom on the dance floor close in each other's arms. The band is playing the 'Blue Danube Waltz'. Also dancing to the music are their many relatives and friends, while on the edge of the floor, keeping slightly apart from the others, a short brown man is dancing with a graceful white woman. Perhaps Rose Mbikwa has been telling Mr Malik about the orphanage she is planning to start at her home in Serengeti Gardens. Perhaps he has offered to supply as many Jolly Man bonbons as the children will ever need. They both look very happy.

At a table beside the dance floor Mr and Mrs Patel are in earnest conversation with Mr A. B. Gopez and his wife. No doubt they are discussing the significance of the small ripe mango that Benjamin had brought with him from Mr Malik's garden that morning and presented to him at the end of his daughter's marriage ceremony. It must have been a very special mango. Mrs Gopez says she was certain she saw a tear in Mr Malik's eye as he took it.

Harry Khan has been getting on very well with Sunita, radiant in her special new bridesmaid's sari from Amin and Sons. He has been showing her a few new moves on the dance floor but now they are both sitting at a table, chatting with Dickie Johnson and Tiger Singh and his wife. Sunita has just finished explaining to everyone that the whole wedding was entirely her doing. Was it not she who told Angus Mbikwa at the Hilton only three nights ago that she was sure Petula would say yes? The Tiger has already told everyone that, after much reflection, he has changed his mind about helping Harry Khan with his shopping mall development. On Monday they will both be meeting the Minister of Transport – the old railway goods yard, right in the centre of town, could be just the place they're looking for. With them at the table are Sanjay and Bobby Bashu, looking fit and trim after their three-week spiritual retreat down at the coast.

Now everyone is laughing. I expect Harry has told them one of his stories about the American franchisees' wives. He may even have admitted that it was he who hid the Kima Killer in the darkroom that night he played billiards with Tiger Singh. He still could never resist a tease.

I hope Harry hasn't said anything about who really won that game of billiards at the Asadi Club the night that the lion disappeared. When the Tiger agreed to help him, Harry promised that he wouldn't. And as for me, I never shall.

NICHOLAS DRAYSON

A GUIDE TO THE BIRDS OF EAST AFRICA

Reserved, honourable Mr Malik. You wouldn't notice him in a Nairobi street – except, perhaps, to comment on his carefully sculpted comb-over – but beneath his unprepossessing exterior lie a warm heart and a secret passion. Not even his closest friends know it, but Mr Malik is head over heels in love with the leader of the local Tuesday-morning bird walk, Rose Mbikwa.

Little can he imagine the hurdles that lie before him. Even as he plucks up the courage to ask for Rose's hand, thieves, potential kidnappers and corrupt officials, not to mention one particularly determined love rival, seem destined to thwart Mr Malik's chances.

Will an Indian gentleman in the heart of Africa be defeated by the many obstacles that stand between him and his heart's desire? Or will honour and decency prevail?

'A funny, ingenious and touching love story' Joanne Harris, *The Times*

'A delightful comedy . . . It invites comparison to The No.1 Ladies' Detective Agency books, but it's original and, if anything, has more depth' *Daily Mail*

'Sweet, charming and utterly wonderful on the subject of birds' *Metro*

He just wanted a decent book to read ...

Not too much to ask, is it? It was in 1935 when Allen Lane, Managing Director of Bodley Head Publishers, stood on a platform at Exeter railway station looking for something good to read on his journey back to London. His choice was limited to popular magazines and poor-quality paperbacks – the same choice faced every day by the vast majority of readers, few of whom could afford hardbacks. Lane's disappointment and subsequent anger at the range of books generally available led him to found a company – and change the world.

'We believed in the existence in this country of a vast reading public for intelligent books at a low price, and staked everything on it'
Sir Allen Lane, 1902–1970, founder of Penguin Books

The quality paperback had arrived – and not just in bookshops. Lane was adamant that his Penguins should appear in chain stores and tobacconists, and should cost no more than a packet of cigarettes.

Reading habits (and cigarette prices) have changed since 1935, but Penguin still believes in publishing the best books for everybody to enjoy. We still believe that good design costs no more than bad design, and we still believe that quality books published passionately and responsibly make the world a better place.

So wherever you see the little bird – whether it's on a piece of prize-winning literary fiction or a celebrity autobiography, political tour de force or historical masterpiece, a serial-killer thriller, reference book, world classic or a piece of pure escapism – you can bet that it represents the very best that the genre has to offer.

Whatever you like to read – trust Penguin.